WATCHING YOU

LYNDA RENHAM

ALSO BY LYNDA RENHAM

Remember Me

Secrets and Lies

PROLOGUE

Her bare feet pounded the gravel, the sharp stones cutting mercilessly into her skin. The wind whipped cruelly at her hair and played with her new chiffon dress until her legs became entangled within it. She pulled herself free from the material without once slowing her pace, her heart drumming in her chest. She could hear the blood pulsating in her ears like a wild war dance. Her scalp tingled. Something had touched her. She fought back a scream. It was a branch, just a tree in the blackness of the night. Keep going. She couldn't stop. A firework boomed and lit up the night sky. She tripped, scattering the detestable gravel. A small sob escaped her lips before she dragged herself up and continued on. Keep running. Don't look back. An orchestra of colours exploded in the sky and lit up the tall iron gates of Manstead Manor ahead of her. She thought back to the house and nausea rose up in her gut. Soon she would smell the pungent odour of seaweed. Her heart beat a steady rhythm now. She knew the beach wasn't far away. Excited voices and the sound of drunken laughter broke through her pulsating eardrums. People were partying on the beach. It was

1

the beginning of something new, something exciting, a new start.

'Happy Millennium,' someone shouted.

She tripped in her haste to reach them. Her mouth connected with cold sand, it scratched her skin.

'Help me,' she choked. 'Please.'

'Had too much?' said a voice.

There was laughter from a small group huddled around a camp fire.

'Hold on,' said another. The voice concerned.

She felt someone touch her.

'Fuck, she's bleeding.'

'Call the police,' yelled another.

There was scuffling, and someone wrapped a coat around her. It was warm and comforting.

'Christ, what happened?' he said.

'Someone shot my aunt and uncle,' she moaned, 'I think they're dead.'

CHAPTER ONE

PRESENT DAY

E wan Galbreith sauntered into the room. He took his time before sitting down. Lionel waited and then drew a folder from his briefcase, laying it on the table between them. It was a déjà vu moment for both of them. Lionel glanced up. He thought Galbreith looked weary. There was a faint blue mark around his right eye.

'What's that?' Lionel asked.

Ewan sat down and touched the bruise.

'It's nothing,' he said in his soft Scottish accent. 'I walked into a door.'

'Sure you did,' said Lionel. 'Had a hefty punch did it, that door?'

Ewan looked out of the window. It was blowing a gale outside.

'You could have brought better weather.'

'Hurricane Lavinia,' said Lionel. 'I don't know where they get the bloody names from.'

Ewan turned from the window, his hard brown eyes falling on the folder.

'Well?' he said dully.

He had no expectations these days.

'They took longer to deliberate,' said Lionel. 'That's why I haven't come sooner.'

Ewan's expression didn't change.

'They turned me down, right?'

'Not exactly.'

Ewan's head snapped up. 'What does that mean?'

'They want you to apply in six months.'

Ewan's lips curled into a smile.

'Six months?' he questioned.

It was February. He could be out by the summer. It was no time at all. He'd done fourteen years and six months. He could do a bit more.

'You'll need to agree to see the psychiatrist again.'

Ewan nodded.

'I'm not guaranteeing anything, Ewan, but I feel things may go in your favour at the next hearing.'

Ewan cracked his knuckles and Lionel winced.

'You can't put a foot wrong the next six months. You know that?'

Ewan smiled.

'You've got to keep out of trouble.'

'I always keep out of trouble.'

Lionel pushed the papers back into his briefcase, zipped it up and said, 'Good, because there won't be another chance after this one.'

Ewan walked to the door and then stopped with his hand on the handle.

'Will she be told?'

'She's asked to be made aware, yes. If you do get out, Ewan, you must not go anywhere near her, do you understand? Don't even think her name. One wrong move and you'll be back in here.'

'Yeah sure,' said Ewan, popping gum into his mouth.

'Don't mess this up, Galbreith, you're not out yet.'

Ewan smiled. Six months wasn't that long. He was well prepared.

CHAPTER TWO

Fifteen years earlier

She opened her eyes. Fran leaned in closer. Libby began to panic at the unfamiliar surroundings. Her body stiffened in fear while her hands grappled at the bedsheets.

'Libby,' Fran said gently.

Libby turned her eyes to the woman who sat at her side. She was young, maybe early twenties. A neat pageboy haircut framed her face. It was a kind face and Libby relaxed slightly.

'Where am I?' she asked.

'You're in Padley Hospital, Libby. You collapsed on the beach. I'm Sergeant Fran Marshall. My colleague, Inspector Mike Magregor and I have been assigned your case.'

Libby sat up and gripped Fran's arm. Fran winced as her fingers pinched the flesh.

'My aunt and uncle...'

'Yes, we know,' Fran said softly, carefully removing Libby's fingers.

Libby's body fell back onto the bed, limp and exhausted.

'Is there someone we can call? A family member?'

Libby shook her head.

'Aunty Rose and Uncle Edward were my family.'

'There must be someone?'

'My parents died when I was seven. I'm an only child. Aunty Rose and...'

She broke off with a sob. Fran handed her a tissue.

'They are my parents,' Libby finished.

'I need to know what you saw, Libby,' Fran said gently.

Don't push it, Mike had warned her. She'd be in shock. Take it slowly, he'd said. This was Fran's first big case. She was eager. There'd been other cases but nothing like this. This was going to be big. Fran could feel it in her bones.

'I saw... I saw...' began Libby. She squeezed her eyes shut.

'Take your time,' Fran said.

'Are they dead?' Libby asked, her eyes widening.

Fran hesitated. The doctor had said if she asked it was better to tell her the truth, but still Fran hesitated. Libby stared at her.

'I'm afraid so,' Fran said finally.

Libby's clenched fists released the bedcovers and she stared up at the ceiling.

'I came home,' she recalled, her voice strained. 'I'd been to a friend's party...'

'Laura's party.' Fran nodded.

'We'd been celebrating. I walked back along the beach. There were lots of people. I could have phoned for a cab, but it was so exhilarating with everyone celebrating that I wanted to walk.'

'What time did you arrive back at your aunt and uncle's house?'

'I don't know.'

'Was it before midnight?'

'No, it was after. We'd celebrated the New Year.'

'So it was gone midnight when you arrived at Manstead Manor?'

Libby nodded. She rubbed her eyes. They were gritty and sore. Fran waited impatiently.

'So, you reached the house. Did you see anyone?'

'No.' Libby's voice faltered.

'Don't be scared, Libby. No one can hurt you.'

Libby was silent.

Fran swallowed, took a deep breath, and said, 'You entered the house. Can you describe what you saw?'

Libby closed her eyes.

'There was music playing... I remember my shoes were covered in sand, so I took them off before going in.'

She hesitated. Fran waited. Best not to push it, she thought. But she was eager, desperate to hear.

'I went into the hall,' Libby said slowly. 'I heard voices from the morning room. I started walking towards it and...'

'Take your time,' said Fran while desperately wanting to hurry her.

Libby squeezed her eyes shut.

'Aunty Rose started screaming and then I heard a shot. It deafened me. I was scared. I pushed the door open and saw a man shoot my uncle in the back and...'

Libby broke off and opened her eyes. She was struggling to breathe.

Fran clasped her hand.

'It's all right, Libby.'

'I slipped on the floor. There was blood everywhere.'

Her hands shook and the bed quivered under her trembling body. Fran wondered if she should call a nurse. She was reluctant. She'd wait just a few more minutes.

'The man that shot your uncle, Libby, did you see his face?'

Libby bit her lip until it bled.

'I'm afraid,' she said.

Fran fought back a sigh. Libby was just a kid, best not to push it. There was time.

'So you ran. You ran to the beach?'

Libby nodded and clenched her fists.

'Did the man with the shotgun follow you?'

'I don't know, I can't remember,' Libby said, getting agitated. 'I couldn't think clearly. All I could see were their bodies and I kept thinking I should go back, to try and save them, but I couldn't.'

'What happened then?'

'I ran to the beach.'

'You saw no one else?'

Libby shook her head.

'Where do I go now?' she asked.

Fran hesitated. Jesus, this was a tough one.

'I think your uncle's lawyer is coming to see you later today. William Stephens, you know him, right?'

Libby nodded.

'Yes.'

The nurse swished back the curtain and strapped a blood pressure monitor on Libby's arm. Fran excused herself, promising to return the next day. Once outside she pulled her mobile from her bag and called Mike.

'How did it go?' he asked.

He seemed distant, disinterested. It didn't bother Fran. She'd come to know Mike well over the past ten months. He was most likely going over a report at the same time. She couldn't remember Mike ever doing just one thing at a time.

'Poor cow,' said Fran. The chill of the January air stung her face, but it made her feel alive and she was grateful for that.

'Yeah, we know that much,' said Mike.

'She saw the killer,' Fran said, unlocking the door of her

Mini. Her fingers felt like icicles. 'She won't say who it was, but I feel sure she recognised the murderer. I could tell by her body language. I'm sure once she feels safe she'll say who it was.'

Mike seemed to perk up.

'Yeah, I don't suppose she described him, did she?'

'I never said it was a man,' said Fran, pulling the car door shut and blowing on her hands. How did Mike manage to be one up on her all the time?

'Apparently, Ewan Galbreith was overheard threatening to take a shotgun to Edward Owen just a few hours before. It wouldn't surprise me if it was him she saw.'

'Ewan Galbreith?' questioned Fran. 'But wasn't he the one...?'

'Yup, the gamekeeper. It's like those thriller novels you devour. It's always the gamekeeper isn't it?'

CHAPTER THREE

PRESENT DAY

Six months later

He looked at the wallet and pushed it into his pocket. Any minute they would open the door, any minute now. The seconds felt like hours before the iron door's hinges shrieked and finally, shielding his eyes against the sunlight, he stepped outside. There was no one to meet him. Why would there be? His sister, Dianne, had the kids. It was difficult to get away, she'd said. A taxi driver waved. He probably did this all the time.

'Ewan?' questioned the driver.

Ewan nodded.

'14 New Road is the address I've been given. Is that right?'

Ewan nodded again and threw his suitcase into the boot. He looked back, expecting someone to bark at him, telling him not to go any further.

'You getting in then?' asked the driver.

'Yeah,' mumbled Ewan.

'All different,' muttered the cabbie.

'What?'

'Some of you can't stop talking while some of you look dazed. How long did you do?'

It was his whole life. His whole miserable fucking life, that's how long.

'Fifteen years,' he said.

'A long stretch then,' said the driver, starting the engine. 'You've got a lot to catch up on. Made any plans?'

Oh yes, he thought. He'd been making plans for the past five thousand four hundred and seventy-five days. He'd thought of nothing else apart from what he would do when he got out. It had kept him going, got him through the darkest days.

'Got a job lined up?' asked the cabbie.

Ewan didn't answer. What business was it of his? Dianne had got him sorted.

'For a short time,' she'd said. 'Greg needs someone to help out at the garage. It won't pay a fortune but still it's...' She'd trailed off.

'I don't know much about mechanics' he'd admitted. He knew he'd sounded ungrateful. They'd gone to a lot of trouble to make a job for him. It couldn't have been easy for them.

'You won't get a gamekeeper job, Ewan. Not after what happened,' Dianne had said. 'Just give it a go,' she'd pleaded.

It would tide him over. But he had plans. He hadn't spent fifteen years doing nothing. He just needed time to adjust and then he'd be ready.

He pushed his hand into his jacket pocket. It felt rough and unfamiliar. He had to pull it tight to zip it up. He was heavier now. He had worked out daily. They passed a retail park, but he didn't recognise it. Everything was different. He looked at his hands. They were shaking. Had they told her? Was she thinking about him now? He clenched his fists tightly to steady the shaking.

'Can you stop at a pharmacy?' he said.

'You all right, mate?' the cabbie asked, looking at him through the rear-view mirror.

Ewan unclenched his fists.

'Fine,' he said, looking out of the window.

They drove through the town of Padley. It was mid-morning. There was no one around. Later it would be packed with holidaymakers. They'd be queuing outside the fish and chip shop, except he realised the fish and chip shop was no longer there, it was a McDonald's.

'Look different?' said the cabbie.

'Yes,' said Ewan.

'Nothing stays the same does it?'

'Do you know what happened at Manstead Manor?' asked Ewan, meeting the cabbie's eyes in the mirror.

'Everyone around here knows what happened at Manstead.'

Ewan continued to stare at him. The cabbie fidgeted under Ewan's piercing look. Ewan didn't have to tell him who he was. His hollow brown eyes told the cabbie everything.

CHAPTER FOUR

PRESENT DAY

Libby

'Can't I see a photo of him?' I ask.

Merlin claws the couch and I make a hissing sound at him.

'What was that?' asks Fran.

'I'm trying to train the cat.'

Fran laughs. It breaks the tension.

'Look Libby, I'm not allowed to show you a photo of him. I do understand how you're feeling...'

'Do you?' I interrupt.

How can anyone know what I'm feeling? Every night I close my eyes and I see his. I hear him calling my name.

'Libby, you knew this day would come.'

'I know,' I say resignedly.

I jump as a motorbike backfires outside the flat. My hands tremble. I check the locks on the door for the tenth time.

'If there is anything that worries you, anything at all, you know you can phone me. It doesn't matter what the time is. Will you promise to do that?'

'Yes,' I say, glancing out of the window.

'He knows not to come near you.'

'You think that will stop him?'

'He won't want to go back inside, Libby.'

'Yeah,' I say.

'Just get on with your life and don't think about him.'

I never stop thinking about him.

'Right,' I say, picking up Merlin.

'Try and sound convincing.'

I smile.

'Thanks Fran.'

'If you're even slightly concerned just call me. You have my mobile number. It's there for you, day or night. That's what I'm here for.'

'I promise.'

She hangs up and I look out of the window at the busy London street below. It's a perfect summer's day. People are out enjoying the sunshine. He'll come looking for me. I know I will. I turn from the window and with Merlin at my heels walk into the bedroom. Will it be soon, or will he wait? I hold my hands out in front of me. They're trembling. Damn it. I'd taken all the precautions I could. It is impossible to find me on the internet. The front door has two triple locks. The main entrance has a concierge. I'm well protected. I should take Fran's advice. Forget about him. He can't touch me now.

I put on my Jaeger suit and look at my reflection with pleasure. I slip into my heels and then everything is perfect. I'm different now. The gawky seventeen-year-old girl has gone. The thick auburn hair is now blonde. My freckles have been bleached away. I'd changed my surname by deed poll. There is nothing left of the old Libby Owen. Perhaps he won't find me. I take one final look in the mirror and then unlock the front door. I step into the plush lift. A fragrance lingers. It's a man's aftershave. It won't be his. He's too rough and earthy for aftershave. The concierge greets me with a nod. I walk from the air-conditioned building and onto the pavement, the hot sticky air hitting me. Two women pass me. I recognise them but we don't speak. I'm anonymous, nobody in the block knows me. I talk to no one. I could be a ghost flitting in and out for how much people notice me. I've deliberately kept it this way. It suits me. I look up and down the street. Would I recognise him? Would I know his voice? I sometimes hear his Scottish lilt in my dreams, but do I really remember it?

The cab I'd booked is waiting by the kerb.

'Ladbroke Grove,' I say. 'Walton Street.'

I study my phone and check my appointments. I've two meetings and a presentation for a prospective client. There'll be time to look at the project Donna had told me about before I meet her for lunch at The Ivy.

'Busy day?' asks the cab driver.

'Every day is busy,' I reply.

'It's the only way.' He smiles through the rear-view mirror.

It's as though he knows that keeping busy is the only way I can keep sane.

CHAPTER FIVE

FIFTEEN YEARS EARLIER

'Come on, Ewan, you can do it.'

Ewan laughed, exposing his pearly white teeth. He twirled the darts in his hand and waited for the noise to die down. He didn't want any distractions. His eyes feasted on the trophy sitting on the bar.

'Ewan,' someone shouted impatiently.

Ewan ignored him and took a long drink of his bitter while eyeing the dartboard. He was so close. He flexed his fingers, enjoying the tension around him. With a half-smile he lifted the dart and threw it. The crowd cheered as the dart hit triple twenty.

'Come on,' someone yelled. 'Get on with it.'

Anticipation rippled all around him. Ewan studied the board and slid his finger along the dart. It was all on him. He didn't want to rush things. This was a moment to savour. Dianne nodded at him, her face proud. He took a deep breath, pulled his arm back, hesitated for the briefest of moments and then threw the dart. He watched it glide through the air. The pub was silent. You could hear a pin drop. Then there was the thud as the dart hit the board and the pub suddenly erupted.

He'd done it. He struggled to stay upright from all the pats on his back. There were grunts from the opposing team. Before he knew what was happening, Ewan was lifted from the floor and held aloft. Luke, the landlord, thrust the shiny trophy into Ewan's hands.

'Drinks on the house,' shouted Luke over the raucous cheers.

Ewan was lowered, and everyone crowded to the bar.

'Well done,' said Dianne, hugging him. 'You'll be Padley's hero for some time to come.'

He laughed. It was only a stupid darts match, but he felt good. Patti grinned at him from across the room. He looked for Ben but couldn't see him in the throng. He took two pints from the bar and strolled over to her.

'You're going to be popular for a while,' she drawled, taking a beer.

Several men slapped him on the back.

'You clever bastard,' roared one.

'Where's Ben tonight?' Ewan asked.

'They're out night-fishing,' she said, tossing back her hair.

Ewan glanced down at the swell of her breasts in the tight-fitting top.

'I hope you brought a coat. It's cold out there.'

'Of course, do I look daft?' She smiled.

Ewan licked his lips and said, 'Someone better see you home. No woman's safe with this drunken rabble.'

'Ben will be grateful,' she said.

Dianne brushed against him, her eyes flashing a warning.

'Some of us are going for a curry. Are you coming, Ewan?'

'Nah, I need to get back to the manor. Cover the horses. It's going to be a cold one.'

Dianne glanced warily at Patti and said, 'Well, if you change your mind that's where Greg and I will be.'

Ewan glanced at Greg and waved. Greg was a good bloke. Steady and reliable.

'Have a good night.' Ewan smiled.

'You're mad playing around with her, Ewan?' Dianne whispered.

Patti was pulling on her fake fur coat.

'If Ben ever finds out you won't stand a chance against him and his fisherman mates,' Dianne warned.

Ewan kissed her on the cheek.

'Don't worry about me. I can handle myself.'

Dianne shook her head and followed Greg from the pub. Patti gave her a half-smile as she passed.

'Your sister is pissed at me,' she said, sidling up to Ewan.

'Not in here,' Ewan said, pushing her away.

She gave a sulky look.

'I'll meet you round the corner, behind the fish and chip shop,' he said, turning his back on her.

Patti shrugged.

'Okay, lover boy,' she whispered before turning to the men at the bar.

'See you, Luke,' she called to the landlord.

'You take care of yourself now, Patti,' said one of the men. 'Don't get waylaid on the way home now.'

The other men laughed. Ewan grabbed his jacket and said, 'I'm getting some air. You lot going to be here when I get back?'

'*Air,* he calls it,' said one with a laugh.

Ewan grinned and wandered outside. The cold sea breeze stung his cheeks. He looked down the road for Patti but there was no sign of her. He pushed his hands into his pockets and sauntered to the fish and chip shop. The sound of the waves breaking against the rocks reached his ears and he thought of Ben. Stupid bastard fishing in this weather, he thought. A hand grabbed his sleeve and he was pulled into the alley behind the chip shop.

'Where have you been?' said Patti hoarsely.

He was pulled into the warmth of her open fur coat.

'Here you are, big boy,' she said, placing his hand onto her swollen breast.

His breathing quickened.

'Not here,' he muttered but he couldn't think clearly where else they could go.

'It's as good as anywhere,' she groaned into his ear, her hand expertly undoing his flies.

Her cold lips met his and he buried his hands deep in the coolness of her hair.

'Fuck me now,' she whispered.

He turned her roughly so she was facing the wall. She slid her hand down her panties and felt the wetness.

'Jesus, Ewan, you make me so horny.'

It was quick. It was always quick with Patti and he liked it that way.

He pushed himself into her and sank as deep as he could. She groaned and leaned back to grasp his hips, pulling him deeper into her wetness.

'Oh Jesus,' she groaned, the mountain of pleasure overwhelming her.

'Fuck me hard, baby.'

He gripped her breasts and quickened his pace. There were footsteps and laughter. People were leaving the pub. It heightened their excitement, the thought of being discovered.

'Make me come, Ewan,' Patti begged.

He slid one hand down the front of her panties and touched her. Within seconds she jerked and thrashed beneath him. He pounded her roughly and then groaned into her hair as his own orgasm shook his body.

Within seconds Patti had pulled her panties up and wrapped her fur coat around her. She pecked Ewan on the cheek and said, 'See you, baby.'

Ewan exhaled and zipped up his jacket. He listened to Patti's footsteps and waited until they became faint before heading out of the alley and into the fish and chip shop.

CHAPTER SIX

PRESENT DAY

Ewan walked along the pier and past McDonald's. What happened to the chippy, he wondered. He turned the corner and smiled. There it was, The Crown. That hadn't changed, at least not from the outside. The doors were open. It was lunchtime and it was busy. He hesitated. It had been fifteen years since he'd been inside. He had no idea what reception he would get. The mood before the court case had been supportive. No one thought he'd get banged up, least of all him. Molly and Kevin had visited. He'd been grateful for that.

'Everyone's behind you,' they'd said.

Now he would find out if that was the truth. He walked slowly towards the doors. A few heads turned to glance his way, but they were strangers and didn't recognise him. He walked through the throng outside the pub and entered. It was several minutes before heads began to turn. The room was buzzing but slowly it quietened down and it seemed like everyone was looking at Ewan Galbreith.

Kevin on his lunchbreak left his table and hurried over.

'All right, Ewan,' he said, ignoring the stares and shaking Ewan by the hand.

'Yeah.' Ewan nodded, looking around.

Luke waved from the bar.

'What are you having, Ewan? I've got a nice malt whisky.'

'Sounds good.' Ewan smiled. 'Glad to see you're still here.'

'They'll take me out in a wooden box, mate.' Luke laughed.

'Sit at our table,' said Kevin.

A young man sitting there looked curiously at Ewan and it took a few seconds for Ewan to realise it was Peter.

'Hey Peter.' He smiled.

'Ewan.' Peter nodded.

'You're no longer a lad,' Ewan said with a smile.

Luke brought over a bottle of whisky and placed it on the table.

'On the house. Look at it as a welcome home present. Good to see you, Ewan.'

'Thanks,' said Ewan, 'that'll go down well.'

'Have you got a job?' asked Peter shyly.

'Yeah, at Greg's garage. It's not my thing. Where do you work?'

'With Kevin at Hard Acre Farm. It's okay work.'

They drank in silence, speaking only when someone came over to acknowledge Ewan. Finally, Peter leant forward and said, 'Have you been back to Manstead?'

Ewan threw back his whisky.

'No reason to.'

'It's like a mausoleum isn't it, Kev?'

Kev nodded.

'No one has been there since... Well... they just shut the place up. Furniture is still there. Everything is the same, just no people.'

Ewan's ears pricked up.

'Everything is the same?'

Kevin nodded.

'She hasn't been back?'

'No.'

'Where's Molly working these days?'

'She works in the café on the beach front, Sally Anne's.' It doesn't pay as well as Manstead. I don't think we appreciated that place.'

A group of men approached the table and Peter stiffened.

'Ewan,' said one.

Ewan turned in his seat.

'Good to see you back here,' said another.

They patted him on the back and offered to buy him a drink.

'I've got a bottle.' Ewan grinned.

'Next time then, mate.'

Peter relaxed.

'What are you stressed about?' asked Kevin. 'Ewan can take care of himself, always could. Isn't that right, Ewan?'

Ewan poured whisky into their glasses.

'But I'm not looking for trouble.'

'Trouble may come looking for you,' said Kevin.

Peter felt sure that Kevin was right. A lot of the blokes in Padley said Ewan was innocent, but Peter wasn't so sure. He remembered how Ewan used to blow hot and cold. Peter had liked Libby. Not many employers mixed with the staff like she used to. If Libby said she saw Ewan shoot her uncle then he believed her.

CHAPTER SEVEN

PRESENT DAY (SIX WEEKS LATER)

Libby

Donna opens the door and looks at me, her nostrils flaring and her eyes flashing with anger.

'Oh you're here. I was just about to text you again. Where the fuck have you been? Jesus Libby, you're nearly an hour late.'

'Sorry,' I say meekly.

I should have texted.

'I got cold feet and...'

'Christ,' groans Donna pulling me in. 'It's a good job I didn't do a hot meal.'

'Sorry,' I mumble.

'It's only a few friends,' she says with a sigh.

'I know.'

'I just thought you might hit it off with Simon that's all,' she says nodding to the kitchen.

I see him through a gap in the doorway and my heart starts to race. He looks up and my mouth turns dry.

'Come on in,' says Donna.

I'm thrust into the bustling kitchen where Joel is uncorking a bottle of champagne and several people I recognise as Donna's work colleagues are laughing by the buffet table.

'Finally,' says Joel, thrusting a flute of champagne into my hand. 'We'd given you up.'

'Sorry,' I say again.

I feel the man's eyes on me. I'm afraid to look at him.

'Come and meet Simon,' Donna says. 'And stop being so paranoid. He's a nice guy.'

I turn and he's there in front of me. His blond hair is gelled back from his forehead. He seems very studious with his black-rimmed glasses. He isn't anything like Ewan Galbreith. He's looking at me uncertainly. There's nothing of the Ewan confidence about him. Donna's right, I'm becoming paranoid. Ewan's been out six weeks now and I haven't heard a thing. Everything is going to be fine after all. He's most likely forgotten about me and is getting on with his life.

'Libby finally made it,' says Donna. 'This is Simon Wane. Simon's a property surveyor. I told Simon you were in graphic design. Libby designed the Plaslow promotional posters.'

He's holding a cheese and pineapple stick in one hand and a flute of champagne in the other.

'Erm,' he says, looking at each in turn.

He shrugs and pops the cheese and pineapple into his mouth and then puts his warm, soft hand into mine.

'Hi Libby, nice to meet you,' he says. 'Plaslow is a beautiful complex.'

He sounds nice. I feel myself relax. He has a slight north-country accent, at least I think it is north-country, and beneath his black-rimmed glasses I can see his eyes are a deep blue.

'Thank you,' I say.

'Help yourself to food,' says Donna. 'Now you're finally here, Libby, we can all bloody eat.'

'I'm in trouble,' I say.

He smiles, revealing slightly crooked teeth. He's good-looking in a clean-cut kind of way. He loosens his tie and nods to the buffet.

'After you,' he says.

I'd been so anxious about coming that my hands are still trembling. I'm sure he can tell.

'So, how long have you been in graphic design?' he says, handing me a plate.

'About twelve years.'

He seems to be waiting for me to say more. I don't.

'How long have you been a surveyor?' I ask.

I try to remember what Donna had told me about him. 'He's lovely. He's single, I'm not sure why. A bad relationship, Joel said. He's still a bit tender, apparently.' I glance at him as he studies the buffet. I'd guess him to be late thirties. I picture his blond hair falling over his forehead. He would look younger without it gelled back. He's just your type, Donna had said. She has no idea what my type is.

'How do you know Joel and Donna?' he asks.

I'm so hot. I fan myself with a serviette. My cheeks feel flushed from the champagne. I need to eat something.

'I did the graphics for her marketing brochure three years ago,' I say, helping myself to some quiche. 'How do you know them?'

He grins self-consciously.

'I rescued their dog.'

'Sammy?'

'Yes. It was in Regent's Park. By chance I'd been chatting to them about what a beautiful dog he was when his lead broke and he ran off. About ten minutes later I saw him running towards the park entrance. I remembered his name and luckily caught him before he went into the road.'

He seems embarrassed by the story.

'Donna adores Sammy. She would be heartbroken if anything happened to him.'

'So why were you late today?' he asks. A half-smile plays on his lips. Does he know I was apprehensive about meeting him? What has Donna told him? Donna is one of the few people I've trusted with my story. I learnt early on that 'so-called' friends will quickly betray you, if there is money involved. The press are always hungry for stories like mine. The public feasts on the horror like vultures. It's easy for them to read it from a distance and pull apart my life for entertainment. I still get offers to appear on chat shows. The fascination for my story seems endless. William said it would have died a natural death if only I had agreed to do them.

'Now there's a sense of mystery surrounding you,' he'd explained.

'I'm not a celebrity,' I'd snapped.

'That's just it, in the eyes of the public that's what you are. You're an heiress whose only family were butchered by an insane gamekeeper. You're good entertainment, face the fact.'

I'd received hundreds of letters. William passed them on. Most were in plain white envelopes with scribbled notes inside. Others came written in bold red ink calling me all kinds of names.

'Some of them are no doubt fucking weird,' William had warned.

I never told him what was in the letters; how some were scrawled with what looked like a bloody nail.

I read each and every one, even those that referred to Ewan as the innocent victim of the bourgeois. Then there were the female devotees of Galbreith. It seems there is something sexy and romantic in a murderer's eyes. I remember those eyes as they'd bored into mine when I gave my evidence. He should have served twenty years. I should have had five more years knowing I was safe from him.

A movement at my side makes me start. It's Simon pouring champagne into my glass. It spills down the front of my dress.

'Jesus, I'm sorry,' he says reaching for a serviette. 'I can be so clumsy at times.'

'It was my fault,' I say, taking the serviette and dabbing at my dress. 'I'm not good at social occasions.'

'We've got something in common then. You still haven't told me what made you late.'

I sigh.

'I felt sure Donna was going to try and set me up. I don't need setting up, you see.'

Donna squeezes between us.

'There's food fresh off the barbecue,' she says. 'God, it is muggy isn't it? I don't envy Joel slaving over the thing. We've got loads, so stuff your faces.'

Simon glances at the barbecue and I take the opportunity to study his profile. The laughter lines around his eyes and the tiny wrinkle around his mouth indicate he may be older than I had first thought.

'I'm starving,' he says. He knows I'm looking at him. 'Can I get you something?'

I shake my head. Donna catches my eye and rushes over as soon as Simon has left.

'What do you think of him?' she asks excitedly. 'He's nice isn't he?'

'Donna, what have you told him about me?'

'Nothing,' she groans. 'I just said you were a good friend and that I felt you would get on well together.'

'You didn't tell him about...'

'Don't be ridiculous. Of course I didn't. I'm not a fool.'

'He'll pity me if you did.'

'I don't think that's true. You should perhaps be more open. People might surprise you.'

'I can't risk it,' I say, throwing back the champagne.

I don't want the attention. I don't want it to flare up again, the strangers staring at me, pitying me, the comments whispered behind my back. That's her, they'd say. She found her family slaughtered on the night of the millennium. A madman out for revenge shot them both with their own shotgun. Can you imagine what it must have been like, finding them? The poor thing.

'He's a nice guy,' Donna says, breaking into my thoughts.

I shake my empty glass.

'Wine or champers?' She grins.

'Either,' I say.

People smile at me. No doubt they remember me from Donna and Joel's previous do. They're probably wondering why Donna invites me. They don't try to approach me. I didn't communicate very well the last time they met me. Simon is laughing with a brunette by the barbecue. She's relaxed and carefree, unlike me. Even the alcohol isn't loosening me up. I down the wine from the glass Donna hands me and say, 'I may have to go. I've got stuff to catch up on.'

'What stuff?' Donna asks, her tone disbelieving.

'Just stuff,' I say.

'I'm worried about you, Libby.'

'Don't be silly,' I say.

'Have another drink and let yourself go,' she orders.

I nod but she's unconvinced.

'He can't get to you, Libby,' she says, lowering her voice.

'Of course he can. He could be anywhere.'

'You only have to phone the police and they'll put him back inside.'

'Yeah, I know,' I say.

'He can't get to you,' she repeats.

I feel sure she is wrong.

CHAPTER EIGHT

FIFTEEN YEARS EARLIER

Libby brushed Georgie's coat until it shone. It was freezing in the stables, but she never felt the cold when she was with Georgie. Besides, she was still hot and sweaty from their long ride.

'All right?' said Ewan, acknowledging her as he entered the barn, his arms full of hay. He carried it to the corner of the stables and without waiting for Libby to reply, walked out again. He returned a few moments later with more. His brown hair had fallen over his forehead and she couldn't see his eyes. Ewan grabbed a pitchfork and began mucking out, talking softly to Princess as he did so. The white mare shook her mane in pleasure. The portable CD player was playing The Police. It was Ewan's favourite band and Libby thought how nice it would be if Aunty Rose and Uncle Edward bought him one of their albums for Christmas. She'd mention it to them.

'You're cold, girl,' he said to Princess. His soft Scottish accent seemed to soothe the horse. 'Your Aunty Rose said to tell you they are putting the Christmas tree up.'

'Oh,' said Libby pulling a face.

'Don't you want to help?' He smiled.

'I'd rather be with Georgie,' she said, brushing his coat lovingly.

'Yeah, I know what you mean.' Ewan smiled.

Libby liked Ewan's smile. She knew the women liked Ewan. He was handsome in a rugged way. There was an air of certainty about him and a confidence that made a woman feel safe when with him. Ewan Galbreith was always sure of himself and his warm brown eyes, when they looked at you, somehow made you feel special. Like in that moment he had eyes only for you.

Libby pulled off her hat and allowed her long curly auburn locks to fall around her face. Her scalp felt sweaty. Cold air blew into the barn, sending a whisper of snow with it. She breathed in its freshness. It was three weeks before Christmas. Libby and Aunty Rose had been shopping the day before for staff presents ready for the party.

'What do you want for Christmas?' Ewan asked.

'I haven't thought about it.'

That wasn't true. She had thought about it. In fact, she'd done nothing but think about it. But she wasn't going to share her thoughts with Ewan.

The early whisper of snow had now turned into heavy flakes. Ewan lifted a thick blanket and draped it over Princess.

'There you go, darling,' he said.

'What do you want for Christmas?' she asked.

He shrugged. 'Me?' he said, as if surprised she would ask. 'I don't want anything.'

Libby was used to Ewan's short responses. He didn't say much to those who employed him, but she'd heard tell he always had plenty to say when he was down the pub.

Ewan's phone trilled and he looked at it. He glanced back up at Libby before clicking into it.

'Patti, it's difficult to talk...' he said.

Libby turned back to Georgie, her cheeks turning red. She considered going back to the house and leaving him to his call. She knew he had women. The kitchen staff gossiped about it. She reckoned Ewan had had more women than she could count on all her fingers and toes.

'He's a fool,' Molly the housekeeper had said. 'Playing with fire like he does, I'm telling you, he'll come unstuck one day.'

It was as she was about to leave the barn that everything happened.

'Patti, slow down...' Ewan said into the phone.

Libby went to walk past him when the barn door swung open. She gasped as three men wearing balaclavas burst in. She saw something swinging in the hand of one of them and opened her mouth to scream but nothing came from her lips. She ran to the barn doors, but strong arms stopped her before she could get through them. They held her so tightly that her ribs ached. She struggled against them, but it was useless and the screams that now wanted free rein were locked inside her by the gloved hand that covered her mouth.

'Let her go,' growled Ewan. 'This has nothing to do with her.'

Libby looked at him pleadingly.

'Thought you could put your filthy hands on anything didn't you, Galbreith?' said one of the men, his voice deep and hard. His evil eyes stared through the slits of the balaclava. Libby watched horrified as he lifted a cricket bat and brought it down with a sickening crack on Ewan's arm.

Libby fought against the strong grip that held her tight and squeezed her eyes shut. She wanted to block out the sound of the thuds as the punches hit Ewan's body. Georgie stamped her hooves in fear and neighed loudly. Libby prayed the men wouldn't hurt the horses. She couldn't bear that. Blood spattered onto her face. She felt the wetness of it. Her heart was pounding so hard in her chest that she felt sure she would faint. Even the buzzing in her ears didn't block out the sound of Ewan's groans. She kicked out, but it was useless. Ewan struggled to protect himself but one of the men was holding him while the other pummelled mercilessly into his body. Ewan's face was now dripping in blood from a gash over his eye. Libby bit angrily at the hand that was clamped across her mouth and tasted rancid fish before biting hard into it again. The man cursed and released her. She screamed, louder than she had ever screamed in her life. The man whacked her around the head making her ears ring but still she continued to scream. It was the loud crack of a gunshot that finally silenced her.

Edward Owen stood in the doorway, a shotgun aimed at the back of the man standing over Ewan.

'Get off him,' he roared. 'Or so help me God the next shot will be in your back and don't think I won't do it.'

The men stepped back and Edward snatched the balaclavas from their heads.

'Well, if it isn't Ben Mitchell,' Edward said, jabbing the rifle into Ben's ribs. He turned to the man that had been holding Libby. 'If you touch my niece ever again so help me God I'll blow your head off. Now get the hell off my property.'

The men sauntered past Edward.

'Keep your hands to yourself in future, Galbreith,' said Ben.

Edward threw a phone to Libby before bending down to Ewan.

'Call for an ambulance,' he ordered.

'Shall I call the police?'

'Just an ambulance, Ewan won't want the police involved, will you, lad?'

Ewan gurgled something and then spat blood.

'You bloody fool,' said Edward.

'I'll get them,' muttered Ewan.

Libby flushed and stumbled out of the barn, her legs were like jelly and her hands trembling so much she could barely punch the numbers into the phone. She shakily asked for an ambulance and then threw up.

CHAPTER NINE

PRESENT DAY

Libby

I wake with a start. Did I hear something? I look at the bedside clock. It says 6.50am. The alarm will go off in ten minutes. My heart pounds in my ears. I'm wet with perspiration. I'm afraid to leave the window open at night. It's madness. I'm four flights up. Unless he has Superman powers he isn't likely to come through the window. I hear something beneath the beating of my heart. My body jerks up in fear. There's a scratching sound coming from the bedroom door. I reach for my phone, my finger poised over the speed-dial button for Fran. Then I hear it. Merlin meowing. I exhale and flop back onto the pillows. My throat feels dry and raw. I'm desperate for a drink. I force my shaking body from the bed and pad barefoot to the door where Merlin darts in as it is opened. The sun is already filtering into the room.

'Hello gorgeous,' I say. patting Merlin.

After pouring myself a glass of water I feed Merlin and check my phone. There's a text from Donna.

Great night last night. A shame you had to play Cinderella. Simon asked for your number. I said it was more than my life was worth to give it to him. He asked if you would call him. Make sure you do!

My head thumps from the champagne. I try to picture Simon in my head. I say his name out loud. It wouldn't hurt to phone. My fingers hover over the number Donna had texted. Instead, I switch on the TV that sits on the kitchen counter and watch the news for a few minutes, and then I text Donna.

Thanks. I'll think about it.

Instead, I phone William. He answers immediately.

'Libby?' he says. 'Did you not get our invitation?'

Shit. I thought I'd answered that.

'I can't make it,' I say.

'Couldn't make it,' he corrects. 'It was last night.'

'God, I'm sorry.'

'It's Caroline you should be apologising to. I didn't imagine you would come for one minute. She had a better opinion of you, however.'

I curse inwardly.

'I'll phone her straight after.'

He grunts.

'We've had an offer for Manstead. It's a good one. I think you should take it. You'll need to come and clear the place.'

'Have you seen Ewan?' I ask.

'No and I don't want to. I think you should come and clear out the house. Sell it and you'll never have to come to Padley again.'

I clench my fists tightly.

'I'm not going to let him stop me coming back.'

'I presumed that was why you didn't come last night?' he says surprised.

'I... I forgot. I've had Galbreith on my mind,' I admit.

'He's not worth it,' he says tiredly and then in a resigned tone, 'We've had an influx of letters. I suppose it's connected to his release. Do you want me to forward them?'

I take a deep breath.

'Yes.'

Why do I torture myself? You know why, replies a voice in my head.

'Thanks William,' I say. 'I promise to come down soon. I'll phone Caroline.'

'Sure,' he says.

I hang up and make some coffee. I wonder what Ewan Galbreith is doing. Is he sitting at a kitchen table somewhere, eating breakfast, nursing a coffee? Is he thinking about me? Is he in Cornwall or is he somewhere else? I jump up, throwing Merlin off my lap.

I type *Ewan Galbreith prison release* into Google Search on my laptop and am hit by a picture of Uncle Edward and Aunty Rose. It's a wedding photo. They're smiling. They're happy. I clench my jaw before scrolling down. I ignore the pictures of the girl I no longer recognise.

Ewan Galbreith was sentenced today to twenty years for the murder of his employers Edward and Rose Owen. There was outcry at the Old

Bailey from the deceased's family. It was thought that Galbreith would be sentenced to life. The judge advised that due to Galbreith having no previous convictions, that twenty years was a fair sentence. Galbreith, aged 24, from Padley, Cornwall, was impassive when the verdict was given but yelled out threats as he was taken down to the cells. The deceased's only living relative, Libby Owen, had to be helped from the courtroom.

The web pages are so familiar to me that I could recite the articles backwards. There is nothing new, nothing about his prison release. There are no new photos. I sigh and click into my Facebook page. Merlin jumps onto the table and tries to lick the milk bottle. I pour some into a saucer before scanning my Facebook profile. I rarely look at Facebook. I don't have many friends. It's a tool to promote my business so when I see a new friend request, I'm surprised. Could it be Simon Wane? I click on it curiously. Did Donna tell him my surname? I struggle to remember. The page opens, and I reel back in shock. It feels like someone has just punched me in the chest. I can't breathe. My hands tremble so much that I have to lower my coffee mug. I try to swallow the bile down, but it rises up so fast that I barely make it to the bathroom sink. I vomit viciously while Merlin meows behind me. I stay with my head over the bowl, my temples throbbing with the beating of my heart. Finally, I go back to the kitchen and force myself to look at the screen, I then grab my phone and hit button two.

'It's me,' I say as Fran picks up.

'Libby?'

'He's made contact,' I say.

'When?' she asks, there's disbelief in her voice.

'I've had a friend request on Facebook.'

My voice is calm. It's happened. The anxiety and apprehension were far worse. He's finally made contact.

'From Ewan Galbreith?' she asks.

'No,' I say looking back at the screen. 'From Uncle Edward.'

CHAPTER TEN

FIFTEEN YEARS EARLIER

Ben cursed. His hair was soaked with sweat and it ran down his face.

'Fucking Edward Owen,' he growled.

'You gave Galbreith a good seeing to though,' said one of the men.

Ben crunched the truck into gear and sped out of Manstead Manor. After all, he couldn't be sure that Owen wouldn't still take a shotgun to them. He drove fast into Padley, the adrenaline rushing through his veins. Everyone in the truck was silent. They knew better than to speak when Ben was in this kind of mood. He was jittery. There was unspent anger in him.

'If it weren't for bloody Owen, Galbreith would be on life support,' growled Ben.

The men were silent. None of them had anticipated Ben going that far.

'See you on the boat tomorrow,' said Matt when they arrived back in the town. 'Weather's going to be calmer.'

'It will still be fucking freezing though,' retorted Ben.

His body felt like a coiled spring. He climbed the stairs to the flat, slamming the door behind him.

'Ben,' Patti called. Her voice was anxious. She came to the kitchen door.

'Where have you been?' she asked nervously.

She stopped at the expression on Ben's face and took a step back. Her eyes took in his bruised knuckles.

'I didn't know if you'd be back for dinner, so I haven't made anything. I can do cheese on toast though,' she said.

She was wearing a skimpy dress and the heating was on high. Ben's jaw twitched.

'Put something decent on,' he snapped, his voice hard and even.

'I thought you would...'

He rushed towards her. She tried to hurry past him, but he grabbed her by the arm. The skimpy dress had enraged him even more. He dragged her crying into the bedroom.

'Put something decent on, you disgusting little whore. Did you really think I wouldn't find out what you'd been up to?'

'Ben,' she pleaded.

Her whiney voice irritated him and he sprung towards her again, slapping her hard across the face. The blow left a red swelling. Ben slapped her three more times, splitting her upper lip and bruising her eye. Patti's body trembled with shock.

'Ben...' she begged, grabbing at his arm.

He pulled his arm back and slapped her again, her screams resounding in his ears. Patti sobbed and curled herself into a ball on the bed. He'd hit her harder than he'd thought for he could see her eyelid had ballooned out of proportion and her nose looked misshapen. He threw a tissue at her and walked from the room.

'Fucking whore,' he shouted.

CHAPTER ELEVEN

PRESENT DAY

Fran stood at the entrance to Greg's Garage and wrinkled her nose at the smell of engine oil and diesel fumes. It was hot, too hot. Fran hated the hot weather. Give her below zero temperatures any time.

'He's there,' Greg said in a gruff voice.

She followed his finger to a pair of tatty trainers that poked out from under a Peugeot.

'Ewan, someone to see you,' he yelled over the noise of a radio. 'Brown Eyed Girl' was playing. Fran bloody hated that song.

'Can you turn that down?' she said, pointing to the radio.

Greg sighed and switched it off.

'He's done his time. Why can't you leave him in peace?'

Fran ignored him and focused her attention on the tatty trainers. It was Ewan Galbreith she'd come to see. She'd never imagined she would ever come face to face with him again. Her mind strayed back to fifteen years earlier. She'd been young and eager in those days. Not like now. She felt tired and weary. Weary of the crimes that never get solved. Weary of being alone. She never pictured this being her life fifteen years ago. Stupid, that's what she'd been. Fantasising about Mike in that ridiculous fashion and living in hope that he would notice her when all he ever noticed was his whisky bottle. The Owen murders had been her first big case. She still thought about it. Still tried to find that missing piece of the jigsaw, but she knew she wouldn't. Not now. Mike said it didn't exist outside of her head and maybe he was right. Ewan Galbreith had threatened all of them. 'I'll make you all sorry,' he'd screamed as he was taken down. Libby had never forgotten those words or the other threats he'd made. They would have haunted her every day for the past fifteen years, and now here he was, ready to carry out those threats. Fran couldn't let that happen. Not on her watch. She remembered his twisted features the last time she had seen him, his eyes fierce with rage and his lips tight. Libby had clutched Fran's arm. She'd had no one else.

The clatter of tools brought Fran back to the present. The tatty trainers pushed forward, and a lean muscular body slid out from beneath the Peugeot. He'd jumped up before she had time to prepare herself. He wasn't what she was expecting. Time had stupidly stood still in her head. He wasn't the same Ewan Galbreith of fifteen years earlier, any more than she was the same Fran Marshall. Fifteen years inside had changed him. All the same, he still looked good at thirty-nine which was more than could be said for her. He looked stronger and heavier than when she last saw him. He'd been a young man then. His eyes met hers and didn't leave them. She fought to hold his gaze. She let her eyes linger on the small scar over his left eye.

'Well, look who it is,' he said. 'Sergeant Fran Marshall.'

She remembered that deep and melodic accent. If it had belonged to anyone else, it might have been charming.

'*Inspector* Fran Marshall,' she corrected. 'It's been a long time.'

'Fifteen years, that's how long it's been.'

She was painfully aware of the spanner that hung from his hand. Don't rile him, she told herself. People don't change.

'You got out early?' she said coldly.

'Good behaviour.' He smiled but his eyes remained cold and hard.

'Staying on the coast?' she asked.

'What's it to you?'

He turned to wipe his hands on a rag and she took the opportunity to relax her tense body slightly.

'Not thinking of leaving Padley any time soon are you?' she asked.

'I might and I might not,' he said, meeting her gaze again. 'Any reason I shouldn't?'

'Are you on Facebook, Ewan?'

'Why, do you want to be my friend?'

'Don't play smart with me, Galbreith.'

He laughed. 'Sure I'm on Facebook. A guy like me who's been banged up for fifteen years is going to have loads of friends. What do you think?'

'I think you'd better keep away from Libby Owen is what I think. You know the rules. You come within one hundred yards of her and I'll have you thrown back into the nick quicker than you can say *friend request*.'

'Why would I be interested in Libby Owen?' he asked with a sneer.

Fran smiles for the first time. She doesn't need her notes. Ewan's words are printed on her brain.

'"I'll get you, all of you. Don't think you're safe because I'm going down. I'll be out one day and then you'll all be sorry". Remember those words, Ewan?'

'Can't say I do. I was twenty-four. It was a long time ago.'

'One hundred yards, Ewan. You understand?'

'Sure,' he said, popping a strip of gum into his mouth.

She turned and started to walk from the garage.

'Inspector. It sounds good. Did you get your man too?'

She felt herself blush.

'Stay out of trouble, Ewan,' she said, turning to face him.

'Yes ma'am,' he said with a mock salute.

She left the garage and headed back to her car. She didn't relish the thought of getting into its hot interior. She felt Ewan's eyes on her back and shivered. Maybe she'd drive over to Mike's place and see what he makes of this Facebook business. If only Libby had stayed in bloody Cornwall. It would have been so much easier to monitor things. She detested her contact with Scotland Yard. They'd assigned some young eager sergeant to the case.

'Leave it with me,' he'd said cockily. 'If that murdering little bastard tries to get near her then he'll have me to contend with.'

Fran had just sighed wearily. He reminded her of the young Fran of fifteen years earlier. Would he be world weary fifteen years on, she wondered?

'I'd prefer it if you liaise with me before doing anything,' she'd said. But she doubted he'd even heard her.

She started the engine and drove from the garage without looking back.

CHAPTER TWELVE

FIFTEEN YEARS EARLIER

Ewan grimaced as pain shot through his arm.

'I can get the stable lad to move it,' Molly said, seeing him wince.

'I've got one good hand,' said Ewan.

'You're stubborn, you are.'

Molly stood the other side of the Christmas tree and helped Ewan pull it forward.

'That's better,' she said.

She began to place the stack of Christmas presents that sat on the dining-room table around the tree. Ewan walked to an ornate sideboard and opened it, pulling a bottle of whisky from inside.

'What are you doing?' asked Molly, wide-eyed.

'Getting something to kill this pain.' He grimaced.

'You can't just help yourself.'

Ewan ignored her and poured a large measure into a glass and downed it in one.

'If Edward Owen saw you...' she began.

Ewan put the bottle back and exhaled. The bastard had fractured his arm. He'd like to think Patti was worth it, but he knew she wasn't. He'd bloody deserved it. They'd never have done this much damage if he'd been ready for them. Faceless cowards, but he'd known who they were long before Edward had ripped off their balaclavas. His jaw throbbed and the stitches above his eye felt tight. He knew if Owen hadn't come to the barn that night he would surely be dead now. He'd let it lie. No point stirring it up more. Besides, he was in no fit state to do anything. His ribs were bruised and his arm was in a plaster cast. He'd never let on just how much he hurt.

He walked into the kitchen with the glass, topped it up with water and swallowed two painkillers from the bottle in his pocket.

'You shouldn't mix those with whisky. Don't you ever learn?'

He turned to see Edward Owen standing in the doorway. Molly hurried from the dining room.

'Oh, he didn't take any whisky,' she said.

'They work well together,' said Ewan.

Molly sighed. Ewan walked a tightrope. It was as though he enjoyed the excitement of getting caught.

'Just be sober for the shoot this afternoon,' said Edward, leaving the kitchen.

'I don't know how you keep this job. You want to watch yourself. There's a lot of people would like that gamekeeper's cottage of yours,' said Molly.

Ewan didn't answer but went through the door that led to the gunroom. He'd clean and check the guns, that shouldn't cause him too much pain and then he'd go to the pub for lunch. The shoot wasn't until two. He'd got plenty of time. A few more glasses of whisky and he'd feel fine.

———

The pub was quiet when he walked in. He looked around and then made his way to the bar.

'A whisky, Luke,' he said to the landlord.

The darts trophy stood proudly on the bar.

'You all right, Ewan?' asked Luke.

'Oh yeah, I'm just great.'

'You've got a shoot at Manstead later, haven't you?'

The door opened and Dianne hurried to him.

'I just heard. You stupid idiot, are you okay?' she said tearfully. 'Why didn't you let us know you were at the hospital?'

He lifted the arm that was in the sling.

'It's nothing. Three cowardly bastards who didn't even have the balls to show their faces.'

'I warned you,' she hissed.

He smiled but it was difficult, and she saw the strain on his face and tears sprang to her eyes.

'Please promise me you won't get involved with any of that lot. No revenge, Ewan, okay?'

'Yeah.' He smiled, throwing back the whisky.

'You want lunch?' asked Luke.

Ewan nodded.

'On the house.' Luke smiled. 'You're Padley's star don't forget.'

'All right, Ewan,' shouted someone from across the room.

Ewan lifted his hand.

'Bastards,' said someone else. 'You get them, Ewan.'

Ewan didn't respond. He wanted a quiet lunch, another whisky and then he'd be fortified enough for the shoot. He promised Dianne he'd go to hers for dinner the next night and after she'd left he paid for his drink and went outside. He hovered at the entrance to the little supermarket where Patti worked. He stood there for a while, shrugged and then began the walk back to Manstead. Patti saw him first. She was on her way to work to do the afternoon shift. She stopped, lowered her head and turned back. Ewan saw her. She began to run, and he had trouble catching her. He reached for her arm, spun her around and fought back a gasp. He put his knuckles to his mouth and bit hard on them. Her face was a mass of bruises. He couldn't see her eye for the dark red swelling. Her beautiful sultry lips were puffy and huge. Tears ran down her cheeks. She hadn't wanted Ewan to see her face like this.

'Let me go, Ewan,' she begged.

He couldn't stop looking at her.

'Jesus,' he whispered. 'He did this to you?'

'I made a fool of him.'

Ewan wanted to clench his fists but he couldn't. He bit hard on his lip, making his jaw ache and punched a nearby door with his good fist.

'Ewan,' Patti pleaded.

'I'll kill him,' he vowed.

'It was my fault.'

'He took it out on me, that was enough. A man doesn't hit a woman.'

'I've got to go,' she said anxiously.

He nodded.

Ewan looked over at Ben's boat as it bobbed in the bay. Ewan's father was a fisherman. Ewan knew when they went out and what time they came back. He pulled the collar up on his jacket and began whistling.

CHAPTER THIRTEEN

PRESENT DAY

Libby

The café in Chelsea was Fran's choice. I would never have chosen it. It smelt of greasy fry-ups and cheap coffee. Students lounged on sofas and sipped cappuccinos. It's the 'in place' if you're young, but neither Fran nor I are young anymore. There were other places we could have met. I'd suggested them, but she'd been firm about coming here. I look around at the faceless people sitting at the tables eating cholesterol-laden all-day breakfasts. I search for Fran's face and find it at a table by the window. She'd been watching the street, waiting for me to arrive. It's been twelve years since we last saw each other. It was natural she would be curious. She looks tired. The years haven't been kind to her. Her skin is sallow. She looks hot and uncomfortable and fans herself with a menu. Her pale-grey eyes widen at the sight of me. I no doubt look very different from when she last saw me. She stands up, revealing black cotton slacks and a long-sleeved checked shirt.

'It's too damn hot,' she grumbles, wiping perspiration from her forehead.

'Thirty degrees,' I say.

'You look well,' she says, pointing to the chair opposite her.

I see she's been nursing a mug of iced tea.

'Am I late?' I ask.

'I got an earlier train. Don't worry. The tea here is good.'

'You should have phoned me. After all, you've come all this way. I could have come sooner.'

'It's not that far.' She smiles and for a brief moment she looks younger.

'What can I get you?' she asks.

I try not to show my distaste, but she sees it.

'I couldn't have met you in the restaurants you suggested,' she says. 'You understand that.'

I nod.

'I'll have a latte,' I say.

She gets up to order it and I quickly clean the table with a wet wipe from my bag. She returns with the latte and two slices of cake. She places one in front of me.

'You don't have to eat it,' she says.

'Did you see him?' I ask. There seems little point in niceties. She's travelled all the way from Cornwall to tell me. There's no point wasting any more of her time.

'Yes I did.'

I realise I'm holding my breath.

'Did you recognise him? Does he look very different?'

She frowns.

'I can't discuss his appearance with you, Libby. I did tell you that on the phone.'

I clench my fists in irritation. The bastard has threatened me, and is still threatening me, and I'm supposed to understand that no one can tell me what he looks like?

'Did you confront him with the Facebook friend request?'

Fran looks me in the eye.

'I didn't accuse him, Libby.'

I sigh.

'Whose side are you on, Fran?'

'It's not a matter of sides, Libby.'

'I beg to differ,' I say, raising my voice. 'You're supposed to be protecting me, not him.'

'So far he hasn't done anything,' she says, her voice even.

I lean across the table.

'But you know it was him,' I persist.

'We don't know anything.'

'Well, it wasn't Uncle Edward was it?' I say, fighting to keep the sarcasm from my voice and failing miserably.

Fran sips her tea, her face impassive.

'I'm sorry,' I say.

Her expression softens.

'I understand your anxiety, Libby, but there's a limit to what we can do. So far, Ewan Galbreith hasn't done anything. It could be anyone.'

'He murdered my aunt and uncle,' I say bitterly.

'He's done time for that. I can't arrest him just because you had a friend request on Facebook.'

'You know it's him.'

'I don't know anything.'

'He knows my new name.'

I push the latte away from me. The smell of it is making me nauseous. Surely we could have gone somewhere decent to discuss this? The frustration is overpowering. I want to scream to release it.

'Are you telling me that I've got to wait until he does something, and only then you'd take action? What about all that crap you feed me on the phone? *I'm only a phone call away, Libby.*'

The words seem to pain her and I look away. It's not her fault. It's the whole stupid fucking system. Wait until he kills you and then we can do something.

'You need to get it into perspective, Libby. He's served fifteen years. He doesn't want to go back. Why would he risk that?'

'I'm not in his head,' I say, standing up. 'He's a maniac. Who knows what he's capable of?'

'All the psychiatric reports say quite clearly that Ewan Galbreith doesn't have mental issues.'

'Then he's just plain evil. I'm a woman who lives alone. I shouldn't have to live in fear. I should...'

'You could get private security,' says Fran and I sense a tinge of hostility in her tone. She thinks I'm overprivileged, that I'm making too much of a fuss.

'If you're afraid isn't it worth it?'

'What advice do you give those women who can't afford it?' I shoot back.

I don't know why I am defending myself. He's the criminal. He's the one hot out of prison, not me. Fran lowers her eyes.

'My hands are tied, Libby. I'm sorry. If you think you see him or anything strange happens you should let me know.'

I pull a twenty-pound note from my bag and place it on the table. I'm disappointed. This wasn't how I'd expected our meeting to go. I had hoped for more.

'You don't need to pay...' she begins.

'He's in Padley, isn't he?'

She nods. 'There's no reason to think he'll leave,' she says. 'He knows that if he comes within one hundred yards of you he'll be in court.'

'No one seems to leave Padley,' I say.

'You did.'

I walk to the door.

'Libby,' says Fran.

I turn.

'Don't be too independent. We're here to help you whether you believe it or not.'

I nod and leave the café.

CHAPTER FOURTEEN

Fran watched Libby get into a taxi and then ordered herself another tea. It hadn't gone well. She knew that.

'Don't you have air conditioning?' she asked the owner.

'It's on,' he said.

She took the tea back to the table and glanced out of the window. Libby was scared. Fran would be if she was in her shoes. Libby had received bulging boxes of post over the years. At the beginning she had forwarded them to Fran. They'd been obscene, written by repulsive little shits with warped evil minds. Fran had been unable to do anything about them. Libby had become immune to the obscenity and had stopped forwarding them. Her contact with Fran ceased, apart from the odd letter sent from Fran via Libby's lawyer to advise her on Galbreith's appeals. Fran learnt that Libby had left Padley. Manstead was boarded up and never sold. Fran pictured Ewan Galbreith as he had looked fifteen years ago. He hadn't looked like a killer with that handsome face of his. But then most killers didn't look like one. She'd learnt that. He'd had his women devotees during the trial which Fran had found sickening. He was too innocent-looking to have committed such slaughter, they'd claimed. Fran sighed and wiped the perspiration from her forehead. The sweat ran between her breasts and her underarms felt sticky. No one else in the café looked as hot as her. She picked up the menu, studied it and then laid it down again. If Ewan Galbreith hadn't sent the friend request, then who had?

'Don't get too involved,' Mike had warned her. 'It was fifteen years ago. He's done his time. She can afford private security.'

'But what if we'd got the wrong man, Mike?' she'd said finally, voicing the thought she'd carried around with her for years.

'We didn't.'

'He swore he was innocent.'

Mike had laughed.

'How many do you know have held their hands up and said, "I did it"? You read too many trashy thrillers.'

'But what if the real killer is threatening her?'

'It's taken him a long time,' said Mike.

He was right. Of course he was.

Fran sighed and sipped her tea. The smell of frying bacon was making her hungry.

'Can I have a bacon roll?' she asked a passing waitress.

The words hit her brain like a bolt of lightning, sending her back to fifteen years earlier. She's in Padley's chippy where Ewan Galbreith is asking, 'Can I have a bacon roll?'

———

'Ewan Galbreith,' Fran said.

'Yeah, who wants to know?'

He didn't turn around.

'Sergeant Fran Marshall, I'd like to ask you a few questions.'

'I've got nothing else to say to the police.'

His mouth twisted with anger. He took his bacon roll and walked past her.

'A portion of chips, please,' Fran called to the chippy. 'I've one question for you, Ewan,' she said, following him.

He stopped and took a bite from his roll.

'What did you say to Libby Owen that night that got her so scared?'

'I didn't say anything to her.'

'We know she saw you the night of the murder.'

'Yeah, she saw me. I've never denied that.'

'I believe she saw you shoot her aunt and uncle in cold blood.'

'Not possible.'

'And that you would have shot her,' she continued. 'Except, Libby ran. What did you shout at her?'

'She's not said it was me.'

He started to walk away from her. Fran took her chips and followed him.

'She saw you.'

'She saw someone. Not me.'

'Your fingerprints were all over the gun.'

He stopped. She watched as he chewed his lip.

'They would be. I use those shotguns all the time. I've already told the police that. I found the gun and picked it up.'

'That was a bit stupid. You don't seem the stupid type.'

'Thanks.'

'So who do you think shot them?'

His lips curled.

'It could have been anyone. Edward Owen had a lot of enemies. He wasn't popular. He was brash and ruthless in business. How do you think he got to be so rich? Have you questioned everyone who has threatened him over the years?'

'Don't worry, we'll get to everyone.'

'You should,' he said, his eyes narrowing.

'Shame about the horse,' she said, hoping to take him by surprise. 'You must have been upset.'

Ewan Galbreith took another bite of the roll and threw the remains into a bin.

'Not upset enough to kill him, if that's what you're trying to say.'

He gave her one last look and then walked away.

'You had the motive,' she called after him.

'Owen bloody deserved it,' said a voice from behind her.

She turned to the group that had congregated outside the fish and chip shop to watch her exchange with Galbreith.

'If any of you know anything you'd be wise to come forward. Withholding evidence is a criminal offence.'

No one spoke. Fran took her chips and left the shop. Twenty-four hours later Galbreith was arrested for the murder of Edward and Rose Owen. Libby Owen had finally admitted seeing him shoot her uncle.

CHAPTER FIFTEEN

PRESENT DAY

The footpath was weedy and the window at the front of the house was covered in ivy.

'Makes it a bit dark inside,' said Grant, the agent, grimacing. 'You'd think someone would cut it down.'

He unlocked the door and kicked aside the pile of letters on the doormat.

'This is the entrance to the flat,' he said, turning to a simple white door to the right of them. 'Those stairs lead up to the first floor. There's an old lady up there. You won't get much noise from her.'

It was dark inside. Grant switched on the light. 'It's the ivy that's the problem,' he said.

Ewan looked around. It was dingy and smelt of something he couldn't place.

'Needs a bit of airing,' said Grant, wrinkling his nose. 'It's been empty a while. It's no Buckingham Palace but it's cheap and that was what you said you wanted.'

Ewan nodded.

'Cheap and cheerful, mate, you can't get better than that. No long-term contracts. Ideal. You got a job down here then?'

Ewan nodded. 'Yeah.'

'Better than a guest house. More private isn't it? Basic,' said Grant from behind him as he peered into the bathroom. 'But functional.'

Ewan tightened his jaw.

'You're not overlooked. Properties like this don't come on the market often. It'll be snapped up in no time.'

Ewan raised his eyebrows. He wished Grant would shut up. He stared back at his reflection in the bathroom mirror. There were dark rings under his eyes.

'When can I move in?' he asked.

'As soon as you want, as you can see the flat is vacant. I'll get the contracts together.'

'I'll pay the three months in advance,' said Ewan.

'Oh right,' said Grant, surprised. 'Less complications.' He wiped the sweat from his brow. 'At least you won't have to worry about the heating, not if this bloody heatwave continues.'

He noticed Ewan wasn't perspiring at all. Lucky guy, Grant thought. He hated this weather.

'Thanks,' said Ewan walking past him to the door. 'I'd like to move in next week.'

'Oh, that soon?' said Grant, taken by surprise. 'I'll need to get the paperwork done then.'

Ewan didn't respond. Grant wasn't sure he liked the guy. There was something odd about him. He was relieved when they were back outside and the door was closed and locked behind them. Ewan stood looking at the windows.

'I'm sure if you asked, the landlord would get someone to cut that back. You could probably do it yourself if you wanted,' said Grant.

'I like it as it is,' said Ewan.

'I'll be in touch then,' said Grant as he watched Ewan climb into his car. He was relieved when he'd driven off. Some people don't half give you the creeps, he thought.

CHAPTER SIXTEEN

PRESENT DAY

Libby

The lighting in the underground car park is dim. I sit in my car, aware he could be anywhere. There are plenty of dark corners. He could pounce at any time. He surely couldn't have discovered where I live, I try to reassure myself. It couldn't have been him that sent the friend request. How would he have known my surname? He'd be looking for Libby Owen, not Elisabeth Warren. Besides, hadn't Fran said he was in Padley? They'd know if he came to London, wouldn't they? They would let her know. They'd have to. Maybe I should get a bodyguard. No, I shan't. I won't let him take away my freedom. Isn't it enough that I only have a handful of friends? I open the door and step out. The hot sticky air hits me. A car alarm sounds and I jump, dropping my handbag. My head is too much in the past. I should go back and face the ghosts, clear Manstead once and for all. The vultures have been after it for years.

It takes twenty seconds to walk through the car park, the clicking of my heels echoing on the concrete floor. I enter the air-conditioned lift and lean my head against its cool interior.

Once inside the flat I secure the locks on the door. Merlin looks up sleepily from his cat box. He meows as I take a carton of cat milk from the fridge and help myself to a beer. The beer is cold and refreshing and I drink it from the bottle. My phone bleeps and I take it through to the lounge. It's a text from Donna.

Have you phoned him?

I'd hoped Donna might have forgotten about Simon Wane. I drop the phone onto a chair and turn on the air conditioning. Could I phone him? Could I take a chance? He doesn't know who I am. I push the idea from my mind, grab my phone again and log into Facebook. My heart is thumping. There are no new friend requests. By the time I've finished the beer I'm feeling confident enough to phone Simon. I dial and wait, and am about to hang up when he answers. His voice is soft and curious to my ears. He doesn't know who is calling. I'd deliberately withheld my number.

'Hi, is that Simon?' I ask.

'Yes, who is this?'

'Libby Warren. We met the other night at Donna and Joel's. You probably don't remember me...'

'Yes I do. How are you?'

'I hope you don't mind me calling. Donna gave me your number.'

'I don't mind at all.'

I can't tell if he's smiling or grimacing.

'I was wondering. If you're free tonight perhaps you'd like to meet for a drink? It's a gorgeous night and there's a nice place by the embankment. The Duchess, do you know it?'

'Not very well but I'll trust your judgement. Sounds great. What time shall I meet you?'

I'm already regretting my impulsiveness.

'Say, in an hour?'

'See you then.'

He hangs up before I can say goodbye.

The wardrobe is stuffed with designer clothes and I pull out dress after dress. Nothing seems right. What am I doing? It's craziness to think I can form a relationship. It's too awkward and the last thing I need is another one-night stand. A drunken fumble followed by a quick meaningless fuck. I'd had far too many of them. The men that had counted for anything hadn't lasted once I'd told them the truth. They'd either been too afraid, worried that the 'nutter' would come after them, or were morbidly fascinated, wanting me to retell the horror. While others had viewed me as some kind of freak, which I suppose in an odd kind of way, is what I am. I'm an object of fascination, someone who has witnessed a horror. It's enough I relive that night in my nightmares without retelling it for someone else's entertainment. That terrible thudding sound as Uncle Edward's body had slammed against the wall. Aunty Rose's terrified screams. The sickening gurgle in Uncle Edward's throat and the spinning of the room as I tried to comprehend what was happening. The deafening shotgun blasts had left my ears ringing, and the blood, so much blood... his voice calling 'Libby'. It had seemed to take forever to reach the main doors. The hallway was never-ending. I ran but never seemed to reach the door, like a surreal scene from a horror movie. I ran and ran with the image of Aunt Rose's breast hanging from her nightie where the force of the shot had ripped the material from her chest. My feet, cut, raw and bruised, becoming numb beneath me.

I shake my head viciously to stop the memories. One drink, that's all I'll have. There's no harm in one drink. It's a warm night. It'll be nice to stroll along the embankment. The place will be heaving on a night like this. It's what I need. Galbreith won't be able to hurt me while there are people around me. I'll be damned if I'll stay in.

I finally choose a thin print dress from the rail and accessorise it with a lace cape and pearl stud earrings. I'll take a woollen wrap with me in case it gets chilly. I decide against make-up and style my hair in a loose knot at the nape of my neck. Donna knows Simon. I'll be safe. All the same, I slip a rape alarm into my handbag.

I deliberate for a few seconds before taking a sharp kitchen knife from the drawer and dropping it into my handbag. When Ewan Galbreith does come for me I'm going to be ready.

———

The embankment is buzzing just as I had anticipated. I pay the cab driver and walk towards The Duchess. The boat is heaving with people and I strain to see Simon. He's standing outside watching the boats on the Thames. His electric-blue eyes sparkle on seeing me. Music drifts out from The Duchess and he nods towards the door.

'It's rather packed inside,' he says. 'Even worse there.' He points to The Duchess's adjoining boat. 'Shall we go somewhere else?'

'Sure,' I say.

I'm regretting being here already. I feel like things are sliding out of my control. The Duchess had been ideal. There were lots of people. There is safety in numbers.

'There's another bar further up,' he suggests. 'It's a bit quieter.'

'Great,' I say.

We stroll along the embankment, the breeze from the

Thames cool on my face. It's too noisy to make conversation, so we don't. The woollen wrap feels heavy and hot over my arm. I think of the cold beer in my fridge and Merlin curled up on the windowsill and I just want to go home. This is pointless. I'm edgy. My mind is on Ewan Galbreith. Is he among the throng here on the embankment? Is he watching me from afar? Damn him. Damn him to hell. I'm not looking where I'm going and I bump into someone. Simon puts out a hand to steady me.

'You okay?' he asks, his hand strong and supportive on my arm.

'Yes,' I say, stepping away from him.

'What would you like?' he asks as we reach the bar.

'A white wine would be great.'

At that moment a couple step away from a table and I hurry towards it, dropping my woollen wrap on the bench beside me. Everyone around me seems to be checking their phones. I check mine and scroll into Facebook. There are no new friend requests. I should come off it, but it is good for keeping in touch with clients. Simon is at the back of the queue and he waves. I scan the faces around me, looking for Ewan. Would I recognise him? He could be watching me right now. I glance behind nervously. When I look back Simon has gone. He must have moved further to the front. My throat feels tight and my mouth is dry. There's the trilling of a phone and I realise it is mine. I fish in my handbag and my hand touches the knife. I feel comforted. The call is from a withheld number. Adrenaline rushes through my body.

'Hello,' I say.

No one speaks. It's so noisy that I can't tell if there is anyone at the other end of the line. I push the phone closer to my ear but hear nothing. I hang up and am about to throw it back into my bag when a voicemail notification pops onto the screen. I tap into it and listen but there's only silence. I sigh heavily and throw the phone into my handbag.

How can the police do nothing? How can he intimidate me like this and they do nothing? My hands are trembling and I clench them together. There's still no sign of Simon. I shiver even though it's a hot humid night. I stand up to leave when my phone trills again and this time my breath catches in my throat when I see it is a withheld number again.

'Who is this?' I demand.

There's a hissing sound and then a husky, breathy voice says, 'It's Rose. Help me.'

I gasp.

'Aunty Rose?' I whisper.

It can't be. It can't possibly be.

I look at the screen. The caller has hung up. The phone vibrates in my hand, making me start that I almost drop it. It's a picture message. I wipe the perspiration from my forehead and click into it. Aunty Rose's bloodied body fills the screen. I reel back with a sob. The phone slips through my sweaty fingers and drops to the ground, shattering the screen with the impact.

'Libby?'

I look up to see Simon. He places a tray of drinks onto the table before picking up my phone.

'Libby, are you okay? You look like you've seen a ghost.'

That's because I have.

CHAPTER SEVENTEEN

PRESENT DAY

Ewan clicked off his phone and made his way back into the living room where the squeals of his niece and nephew jarred on his nerves.

'Dinner's been on the table for almost ten minutes,' chided Dianne. 'The kids are getting irritable.'

'Sorry. It was an important call.'

Greg raised his eyebrows and Dianne ignored him. She knew what he meant. How the hell could Ewan have important calls when he'd only just got out of the nick?

'We don't like dinner to get cold,' said Greg.

Ewan turned to look at Greg and Dianne sighed.

'No one asked you to wait for me,' he said, scraping a chair back. 'It was a job offer. I had to take it.'

Dianne winced. He'd heard her reprimand the kids a thousand times for scraping their chairs back. Why the hell did he do it? She dished up the spaghetti and thrust plates towards the kids.

'What job is it?' she asked.

'I've got a place in London,' Ewan said.

'What the fu...?' began Dianne but was stopped by Greg's

nod towards the children.

'Are you asking for trouble?' she said.

'I don't know what you mean,' Ewan said as he poured water into his glass.

'You know she's in London.'

'I don't know anything. You've just heard rumours. She could be in Mexico for all you know.'

'What's wrong with Padley?' asked Greg.

'There are better prospects in London. No one knows me for a start,' Ewan said with a twisted smile.

Greg shook the parmesan over his sauce.

'You've got to let it go, Ewan.'

'I've let it go,' he snapped, slamming his glass on the table. 'I want to go to London. There's no work here–'

'Of course there is,' interrupted Dianne. 'You've just got to give it time.'

'I've got myself a place there. I'll be coming back occasionally. I'm still looking for a position on the land but until something comes up...'

'But London?' she said.

'Like I said, there's more work there.'

'The police will be on your back,' she argued.

'Yeah, well they should get off my back,' he said, twirling spaghetti around his fork.

'I agree,' said Greg, taking a large gulp of his beer. 'When you've done your time, you've done it.'

Dianne flicked her hair back from her face.

'Chloe, sit forward at the table please. You're getting spaghetti on your top.'

She looked at her brother and felt her heart might break.

'I know it's hard, Ewan...'

'You don't know anything,' he said quietly.

'You can't change it now.'

'She saw the wrong man,' he said flatly.

'She was in shock.'

'That's enough, Dianne,' said Greg. 'It's nothing to do with us. Haven't we been through enough? If Ewan wants to go to London then that suits me.'

'Greg,' exclaimed Dianne.

'He's right,' said Ewan, standing up. 'It's not good for you, Greg and the kids for me to be here. I'll leave tomorrow.'

'That's silly, we've coped...'

'Obscenities painted on our front door. Windows smashed. You and the kids being abused in the street. It wasn't easy, Dianne. I don't call that coping,' growled Greg.

'He's my brother,' she said softly.

'You don't owe me anything, Di,' said Ewan. 'I'm grateful to you both for taking me in and giving me a job. I know it can't have been easy.'

'Those people who did that stuff weren't our friends,' she said. 'I don't give a shit about them.'

'It's better that I go,' said Ewan. 'Better for all of us and it's not like I won't be back. Greg's right. You've been through enough because of me.'

'You're not going to try and find her, are you?'

'She put me in prison,' he said bitterly.

'She was young and scared,' said Greg. 'The police wanted a conviction. They put words into her mouth if you want my opinion.'

'Can we talk about this another time?' Dianne said, inclining her head towards the children. Dianne knew that Ewan was the talk of Padley. It had been two months since his release and still the locals spoke in whispers when she passed. She didn't want the children to suffer. Maybe it was for the best, Ewan going to London. If only he'd let things be. It couldn't have been easy for Libby either, losing all her family in one night. Rumours were that it had turned her head. All the same, it couldn't have been possible that she saw Ewan murder them. Ewan wouldn't hurt anyone. He had a short temper admittedly, but so did a lot of people. He couldn't shoot someone, not like that, not in cold blood.

'You'll give us your address then?' Dianne said to Ewan.

'It's best to give you a PO box number.'

'Do what?' she exclaimed. 'You don't want us to know where you are?'

Ewan shook his head, his lips tight. 'The police can't hassle you then. You can't give them an address in London if you don't know it.'

'You are going to see her, aren't you?' Dianne said wearily. 'In that case you're right, it's best we don't know where you are.'

CHAPTER EIGHTEEN

PRESENT DAY

Libby

'The screen's broken,' Simon says, handing me my phone.

I try to steady my hands, but I know he's aware of how shaky they are. I look at the screen, expecting to see Aunty Rose's bloodstained body but the screen is now black. I turn it on and the home screen flashes at me. I remember those horrid photos. I had to look at them in court and listen to the experts as they coldly gave their evidence and opinions on how Aunty Rose and Uncle Edward were murdered. The judge ruled the photos were not to be used by the media, but of course some sick bastard got them onto the internet.

There's raucous laughter around us. People are enjoying the heatwave. They're sipping Pimms and taking drags from their cigarettes. Some are studying their phones and I struggle to see their faces. Which one is Ewan Galbreith?

'I hope that wasn't bad news,' Simon says.

I look up at him. For a moment I had forgotten he was there.

'What?' I say.

'The phone call.'

I glance at the phone in my bag.

'No,' I say, forcing a smile. 'It was just me being paranoid.'

'I thought you looked a bit shook up.'

'I'm fine,' I say, zipping up my bag.

He looks unconvinced but doesn't push it.

'Thanks for coming,' he says with a smile. 'It's a perfect night and I probably would have worked if you hadn't called.'

'I don't normally call men,' I say, finding my eyes pulled back to the phone in my handbag. I'm expecting it to ring any moment. I hear a deep laugh and then a Scottish accent. Its deep resonant tones make me shiver. I twist in my seat and listen attentively.

'Are you okay?' Simon asks, looking at me oddly. I scan the crowd for the man with the Scottish accent. I see him, but he is short and bald. It isn't Ewan Galbreith.

'I kind of have a stalker problem,' I say, surprising myself.

I don't know why I'm telling him this. I don't normally share my story on a first date. When I say something about my past they usually look at me in horror and then proceed to study me as if they expect to find some kind of mark on me. Then they'll ask what happened, even though they admit to having read the whole gruesome story. Everyone knows the story from the newspapers. But somehow there's nothing quite like the real thing is there – the surviving victim sitting right in front of you like some kind of freak show?

Simon looks at me with concern etched on his face.

'What are the police doing about it?' he asks.

I laugh cynically.

'They say they can't do anything until he acts.'

'That's not very helpful is it?'

I shrug and lift the wine glass to my lips only to discover I'd finished it.

'I'll get us another,' he says, standing up.

'Oh it's fine,' I say, not wanting to be left alone. 'You'll have to get in the queue again. We could walk along the embankment.'

I stand up and realise my legs have turned to jelly. Ewan knows where I am. He has my mobile number. I feel myself shudder when it occurs to me that he probably knows where I live. My eyes scan the faces as we pass, looking for him.

'Did he phone you just now?' Simon asks, breaking into my thoughts. 'Is that why you dropped the phone?'

'Yes,' I say quietly.

My mind is reeling. I should warn the concierge. I will tell him not to give any information to anyone, and to call the police if anyone asks about me. I need to phone Fran. Damn him.

'Shall we go to The Barbican?' he asks as he hails a cab. 'Get a drink there?'

I nod. The Barbican will be packed with people. I'll be safe there. I sit in silence as we weave through the backstreets of London. Simon holds the door for me and tips the cabbie. Inside, several couples sit at tables, but it's not packed. It's cool in the bar. I discreetly glance around. No one has followed us in and I allow myself to relax. I excuse myself and head to the ladies while Simon gets our drinks. My heart races as I wait for my phone to ring. If Galbreith is watching me then he'll know I'm alone, but it doesn't bleep. It's quiet in the loo and I'm able to hear the voice message more clearly. It is Aunty Rose. My hands shake as I drop the phone back into my bag. I must not let him intimidate me. If he's watching I must not let him see I am afraid. My face is pale and I pinch my cheeks. If only my heart would stop hammering in my chest. I leave the ladies, paste a smile onto my face and walk to the bar. The same couples are sitting at the tables and now there is a dark-haired man alone by the bar. I look directly at him. Our eyes meet and at that moment my phone bleeps. I glance at the screen. It's a text message.

I am watching you.

I snap my head up. The man's hand rests on a mobile phone. I stride towards him. He stands. I fumble in my bag for my rape alarm and grasp it tightly. He takes a step forward and my heart jumps into my mouth. I lift the alarm from the bag.

'Sorry I'm late,' says a voice from behind me.

A brunette rushes past me and into the arms of the man. I stop, and the alarm slips from my trembling fingers back into the bag.

'No worries,' he says.

There's no sign of a Scottish accent. I turn, flustered. Simon is walking back from the bar. I hurry to the table.

'He's watching me,' I say.

I hand my phone to Simon and he glances at the screen.

'Do you want me to call it?'

I nod nervously.

He taps the number into his phone, listens and then hands it to me.

'The number you have dialled has not been recognised,' announces a mechanical voice.

'Damn,' I curse. I should have known. Ewan Galbreith isn't a fool. Uncle Edward didn't employ fools and if he did, they never lasted long. Uncle Edward didn't tolerate fools, everyone knew that. I grimace and throw back the wine from the glass that Simon hands me. After the murders, strangers offered to adopt me. The poor orphan girl. Wasn't it enough she'd lost her parents and now this, they said. What evil bastard would do such a thing and leave her abandoned? Of course, it wasn't me they were interested in. It was my inheritance. No one really cared about the poor orphan girl. A pain shoots through the side of my face and I realise I'm clenching my jaw.

'It's probably pay-as-you-go,' says Simon.

I nod.

'I'll report it tomorrow,' I say, trying to sound casual.

I probably won't. There seems little point. I have to deal with Ewan Galbreith myself. Simon and I sit silently. I pick at some nuts Simon had brought back from the bar. I can't relax.

'I'm sorry,' I say. 'I'm useless company.'

'It's fine.' Simon smiles.

'Would you mind awfully seeing me home?' I ask.

His eyes widen. God, if he thinks I'm up for sex he can think again.

'I'm really not feeling great after that phone message.'

'Of course,' he says, draining his beer.

Donna is going to kill me. I'm the world's worst date.

'It isn't you,' I say as we step outside.

'Well, I'm pleased to hear that.' He grins.

The lilt in his voice suddenly seems stronger.

'What's your accent?' I say bluntly.

'What?' he says, clearly taken aback.

I curse as a cab flies past.

'Your accent, what is it?'

I study his face. He wrinkles his nose and sighs.

'Ah, you've spotted it. I'm from Yorkshire. I'm not your typical Yorkshireman though.'

'Yorkshire,' I say, like I've never heard of the place.

'It's up north,' he says, mimicking the accent and grinning at me.

I'm paranoid. I've got to stop this.

'Here we go,' he says, as the cab's brakes squeak behind me.

I'll phone Fran when I get home. Ask her to visit Galbreith. He has to know that I won't be intimidated. I glance again at the broken face of my phone. There are no messages. Tomorrow I'll change my number.

CHAPTER NINETEEN

PRESENT DAY

Libby

We reach the entrance to the flats and a wave of relief washes over me. Soon I'll be inside with the locks tightly secure.

'Here we are,' says Simon.

He has a nice smile. It's warm and he has a confidence that makes me feel safe.

'Thank you,' I say, glancing again at the phone in my bag.

'Will you be okay?' he asks.

I could invite him in for a drink. I have an alarm in both the bedroom and the living room. The concierge will see him. I'm quite safe. I don't want to be alone with my phone. Not just yet. I hesitate. Don't make yourself vulnerable, whispers a voice in my head. Don't make mistakes.

'Would you like to come up for a coffee?' I hear myself asking.

My voice is strained.

'That would be nice,' he says hesitantly. 'Are you sure? I don't want you to feel anxious.'

'Absolutely sure,' I say with forced confidence.

I push open the entrance doors and smile at the concierge.

'Good evening, madam,' he says politely.

'This is Mr Wane,' I say, nodding to Simon.

'Good evening, sir.'

'Good evening, Ian,' says Simon.

I turn, surprised and then remember the name pin on the concierge's jacket. The concierge smiles and pushes the lift button. We step into the lift and I'm suddenly conscious of Simon's body close to mine. I take a deep breath and step from the lift as soon as the doors open onto the fourth floor.

'It's a nice complex,' he says, stepping out.

'Where do you live?' I ask, realising that I have no idea.

'Not in an apartment block like this.' He smiles.

We reach my door and I push the key in the lock. I'm already regretting asking him to come up. I never have people in the flat, let alone men.

Merlin greets us with a meow and I scoop him up into my arms.

'Impressive,' says Simon looking around the flat.

I click on the air conditioning and he smiles.

'Even more impressive.'

I close the door and secure the locks. It's like a reflex and I do it without thinking. Simon looks but doesn't comment. I throw my bag onto the couch and am about to offer him a drink when the knife slides from the bag onto the floor. We both look at it.

There's silence.

'Right,' says Simon, finally.

I lick my lips and pick up the knife.

'I... I'm very nervous when I go out,' I say apologetically.

'It's against the law to carry a knife,' he says.

'I know,' I say simply.

I take the knife into the kitchen.

'What would you like to drink,' I call. 'I can make coffee, or there's white wine, beer, red wine.'

'White wine,' he says, making me jump. He'd followed me to the kitchen.

'It's not just the stalker is it?' he says. 'There's more to it than that.'

I take the wine from the fridge and realise my hands are shaking. I flex my neck and fill two glasses.

'No.'

He follows me into the living room and casually glances around. His eyes land on the triple locks on the front door.

'So, where's the panic button?' he says with a smile.

'Under the coffee table and another one at the side of my bed,' I say flatly.

He nods.

'You're clearly expecting him.'

I sip my wine and feel myself relax.

'He'll come.'

'Maybe he won't.'

I nod emphatically.

'He'll come.'

He sits on the couch opposite me and stretches his legs out in front of him. He opens them slightly and I force my eyes away from his crotch.

'Are we going to see each other again?' he asks.

'I...' I'm taken aback by the question. The truth is I have no idea.

'Because if we are, I'd like to know just how dangerous your stalker is, and why you're so sure he is coming for you.'

I clench and unclench my fists before saying, 'Ewan Galbreith was released from prison a few weeks back. He's served fifteen years for murdering my aunt and uncle, Rose and

Edward Owen. He threatened me as they took him down to serve his sentence. "I'll get you, all of you", he shouted. "Don't think you're safe because I'm going down. I'll be out one day and then you'll all be sorry". It seems he's keeping to his words.'

Just saying the words brings everything back and for a moment I see Ewan's handsome face, twisted and angry as he spat out the words. His eyes had met mine and I'd grasped Fran tightly by the arm and then he was gone. I never saw his face again apart from when I searched for him on the internet.

'That was fifteen years ago,' Simon says, breaking into my thoughts.

I give a scornful laugh.

'Ewan Galbreith doesn't go back on anything he says.'

CHAPTER TWENTY

FIFTEEN YEARS EARLIER

Ewan carefully sliced the Stanley knife through the plaster cast and gently flexed the muscles in his arms. He could see the lights from the promenade and beyond that the blackness of the sea. The smell of seaweed reached his nostrils and he let out a long breath. The cold air stung his face. Putting the binoculars to his eyes he studied the bay carefully. The beach was deserted. Only fools would be on the beach at this time of year. But you always got the odd fool and he was conscious of that. It was almost eight o'clock. He had ten minutes. He was prepared. His hands were steady. He'd have a whisky later and take some painkillers. He would most likely need them. He'd had to hold off all day. He didn't want to make any mistakes. But damn it, he could do with a drink. He lifted the rifle, smarting as he pressed it against his shoulder. He carefully adjusted the sights until his eye focused on the target. The boat bobbed gently on the water. It was a calm night, perfect weather for night fishing. He slid his hand over the safety catch and wrinkled his brow as he studied the target. Ben was laughing with his mates on the jetty. Ewan waited. It wasn't time. He lowered the gun and looked again through the binoculars, ignoring the pain that shot down his arm. He then sat down on the grassy hill and laid the rifle at his side. It was a popular spot during the day, but no one bothered to come at night. It was too windy and cold, but it was the perfect spot for what he had planned. It was a clear night and the light from the full moon was bright, just as he had hoped. He ran his hands through his hair. He now had five minutes.

———

'I'm meeting that chick tomorrow. You know, the one I told you about,' said Matt, rubbing his hands together.

'You dirty bastard.' Ben laughed.

'She's here for a week for some conference.' Matt smiled. 'She's definitely up for it.'

'Make sure you get the fish off your fingers, mate,' said Adam with a grin. 'No tart wants a fish finger on her clit.'

Ben roared with laughter as he dropped the fishing tackle onto the deck.

'Let's make a killing,' he said, climbing in. 'The weather's getting too fucking cold for much more.'

Matt and Adam followed him into the boat and pulled on their oilskin fishing jackets. Ben untied the mooring and the boat drifted out into the bay.

'I reckon...' Ben began, but he never got any further as a thud hit the side of the boat.

'What the fuck was that?' he asked, as a second thud made the helm windshield shatter.

Matt shone a torch around the boat

'What the hell?' he asked nervously.

A loud crack came from the radar pole, knocking it off the side of the boat, and then another smashed the port-side lamp.

'I can't see anything,' said Matt in a trembling voice.

'Probably...' Ben began, but before he could speak two more thuds tore at the boat and Matt began hopping from one foot to the other and waving his arms around like a marionette.

'What the fuck's happening?' he cried, rubbing his neck. 'What's on the boat with us?'

Three more thuds shook the boat. Ben flashed his torch and saw water pouring in through holes in the hull.

'Shit,' he yelled. 'Pull the fucker in.'

But no one was listening to him. Adam had covered his head in fear and Matt was cowering in a corner, the torch sending quivering flashes of light where his hand shook.

'Someone's fucking shooting at us,' yelled Adam.

Two more bullets hit the hull and then Ben heard a screech as another bullet flew over his head. His heart was hammering and his breathing had become laboured.

'Christ,' cried Matt. 'I'm getting off.'

He was about to jump into the water when a thud at the side of the boat paralysed him.

'We're going to be killed,' screamed Adam.

'Fucking Jesus Christ,' Matt moaned as a bullet grazed his ear. All three men dived from the boat and swam to the bay. Ben cursed. He knew the shooter had to be Ewan Galbreith. Everyone knew what an excellent marksman he was. No animal was injured when Galbreith went hunting. He killed them outright, hitting his target exactly where he planned. Ben turned to watch his boat sinking in the bay. The bastard had hit his target all right.

'Christ,' groaned Adam clinging to the jetty. 'How the fuck do we go fishing now?'

'We don't, you moron. That was the plan.'

'He shot my fucking ear off,' Adam cried.

Ben laughed.

'You'd know if he shot your ear off. It's fucking Galbreith,' he said. 'It's repayment. We should have finished the fucker off when we had the chance.'

He looked upwards to the top of the hill.

'Fuck you, Galbreith,' he roared.

———

Ewan fell back on the grass and wiped the sweat from his forehead. The pain from his shoulder was excruciating and his ribs ached. He pulled the bottle of painkillers from his bag and swallowed three before putting the binoculars to his eyes. Matt and Adam were hurrying away from the jetty. Ewan laughed. He'd enjoyed it. If his arm hadn't been hurting so much he'd have put them through a bit more. In the stillness he could hear Ben cursing like a madman. Ewan packed up the hunting rifle and made his way down the hill. He'd drop the rifle in the boot of the car and then drive to the hospital to get his arm re-plastered and then go to the pub. After a few glasses of whisky he'd be fine.

CHAPTER TWENTY-ONE

Libby

I wake lazily. The flat is quiet and I savour the peacefulness of early morning. As I reach for my phone I remember the text from last night and feel the calmness drain from my body. My trembling hand clicks into the text with the horrific picture of Aunty Rose and my finger hovers over the delete button. But this is evidence, I should show Fran, I should show her what a sick bastard Ewan is and maybe then she will do something. I fumble with the phone and press the speed dial for Fran.

'Libby?' she says.

Her voice sounds tired. Is she weary of me already?

'He's intimidating me,' I say bluntly.

I don't see the point in niceties. She's supposed to be protecting me.

'Ewan Galbreith?' she questions.

'He's phoning me and texting me. Yesterday, he sent a photo of Aunt Rose's body. He said he's watching me and...'

'Libby,' she breaks in. 'Can you prove they are from Ewan?'

'Of course not,' I snap. 'He's not a fool. He never was a fool.

He knows exactly what he's doing. He won't make any mistakes.'

I hear her sigh.

'Can we borrow the SIM card? We may be able to run some checks.'

'You can keep it,' I say angrily. 'I'm getting a new phone today.'

'Okay, if you can drop it into a police station we can get someone to look at it.'

I fall back onto the pillows.

'You're not going to do anything are you?'

'It's not like that, Libby.'

I laugh cynically and hang up without saying goodbye.

Later, I stand under the shower and feel the warmth of the water trickling over my breasts. I think of Ewan Galbreith and soap myself down. It's as I step naked into the bedroom that it occurs to me. I grab a towel and look out of the window at the flats opposite the living room. What if he's there? What if he has a flat overlooking mine? He only needs a pair of binoculars. I pull the living-room blinds down, hurry to the bedroom and pull those down too. My skin tingles at the thought of his eyes on my naked body. My phone by the bedside is flashing and my heart starts to race. I click it on and Simon's name lights up the screen.

> Thanks for a lovely night. Are you free for a repeat tomorrow evening, maybe we could get dinner this time?

I scroll through my messages. There are several banal emails, a meeting reminder and a text from Fran:

> Let me know the station.

I scroll into Simon's message and punch a reply:

> That sounds great. I'm free, where shall we meet?

I consider suggesting a restaurant but think better of it. It's expensive. I have no idea how much he earns. No doubt he will check me out, if he hasn't already, and will realise I'm loaded. And so begin the doubts. Is he with me for me, or for my money?

I dress and pull the blinds up. I see several people leave the entrance of the apartment block opposite. Is one of them Ewan? How hard can it be to find out who lives there? There's no point asking Fran. It's an invasion of privacy, she'll no doubt tell me. Never mind how much Ewan is invading mine. I have an hour before my meeting. Excitement ripples through me as I make my plans. I throw on a pair of jeans and a thin shirt. The sun is shining through the windows and it already feels hot.

The concierge greets me, and I fumble for the right words.

'Good morning,' I say. 'I need to tell you... well, there is someone stalking me.'

'Yes madam,' he says.

He doesn't even blink. It's as though stalkers are normal for him.

'Do you have a photo, madam?'

'Not a recent one but I can get an old picture.'

'That would be helpful, madam.'

'I don't want any information given out about me and if any strange gentleman asks for my flat number, please let me know?'

'Of course, Miss Warren, and does that include the gentleman you were with last night?'

I hesitate. Do I know Simon well enough? Joel and Donna know him. I'm being paranoid.

'No, that's fine, thank you.'

'I'll pass the word on, madam.'

I leave the block and cross the road. The building is similar to mine. That should mean there will be two flats on the fourth floor. I prepare a little speech for the concierge but there isn't one. I study the nameplates. The fourth floor houses flats 22 and 23. If I've worked it out right, 23 will be the flat opposite mine. The nameplate reads 'G. Newman'. I pause for a moment and then push the buzzer.

CHAPTER TWENTY-TWO

Libby watched as Rose studied her reflection in the bedroom mirror. Rose couldn't help thinking the dress was too much. It was the staff party after all. She didn't want to look overdressed.

'Maybe something simpler,' she muttered.

'I think it's lovely,' said Libby.

It was two weeks before Christmas and traditionally Edward and Rose Owen held the staff party at this time.

'We should go down,' said Edward as he strolled into the room. 'We don't want them arriving with us not there to greet them.'

'I'm overdressed,' she said.

He cocked his head and she smiled. He looked very attractive in his dress shirt and bow tie.

'Well, look at you.' She smiled.

'Exactly.' He grinned. 'We have to make the effort. There is no such thing as overdressed. You look lovely and it's exactly what would be expected.'

'Would you help me, dear, and unclip this necklace?' she asked Libby.

Libby unclipped the necklace and Rose studied herself again.

'Yes, that's better.'

'I was wondering, could I wear my mother's pearls tonight?' Libby asked.

'I don't see why not,' Rose said, looking at Edward for confirmation.

Rose opened the safe and removed the pearls from their box and Libby's eyes widened in pleasure. Her blue chiffon dress shimmered as she walked towards her aunt.

'Now, let's go,' said Edward impatiently.

Libby and Rose followed Edward down the stairs where Ewan was waiting at the dining-room entrance.

'Evening, Ewan,' Edward said. 'Did you check the horses?'

Ewan nodded.

'I'm not happy with Princess,' he said. 'She's not her usual self. I'll see how she is after the festivities. We may need to call Neil.'

'The vet?' snapped Edward. 'Over Christmas? He'll rip us off left right and centre.'

'Unfortunately the horses don't know it's Christmas,' Ewan said dryly.

Libby hid her smile. Ewan had made an effort for the party and was wearing a white shirt tucked into his jeans. His hair was freshly washed, Libby could smell the shampoo. His eyelid was still slightly swollen but looked better.

As though reading her mind Edward said, 'How's the arm?'

'Better.' Ewan smiled.

'Must be if you went hunting yesterday,' Libby said.

'Hunting?' questioned Edward.

'It wasn't me you saw,' said Ewan.

'But...' began Libby.

Her eyes met Ewan's and he winked at her. She knew that it

had been him. She saw him leaving the tradesman's entrance with a rifle over his shoulder. She had wondered about it. Ewan didn't normally hunt that late in the day.

'Anyway, Merry Christmas,' Ewan said, holding out his hand to Edward.

'And a Merry Christmas to you,' Edward responded, shaking his hand warmly.

Rose leant forward and kissed him on the cheek.

'Merry Christmas, Ewan.'

Molly joined them a short time later along with Kevin the gardener and the rest of the staff. Libby gave out the presents from under the tree. Ewan stood by the roaring fire nursing a whisky in his hand. Libby found his present and handed it to him. He took it with a nod.

'Maybe now you'll stop stealing mine,' said Edward with a smile as Ewan unwrapped a single malt.

'Thanks for that.' Ewan grinned.

'There's another one,' said Libby.

Ewan took the gift and pulled off the wrapping. Libby watched him and stroked her pearls self-consciously.

'Your favourite,' said Molly, smiling.

Ewan grinned at the sight of the CD.

'Brilliant, thanks a lot.'

'I chose that one,' said Libby.

'Good choice.' He smiled. 'Thanks.'

He liked it. Libby felt all warm inside.

The dining table had been laid expertly by the caterers and the staff looked at it wide-eyed as they did every year, except for Ewan who never seemed impressed. Libby sat between Molly and Ewan, and his fresh fragrance wafted over to her. His knee touched hers and she blushed profusely. He seemed not to notice. She'd heard the gardening staff gossiping about him and

Patti, the woman from the village. One said they saw them doing it against the wall by the chip shop. Uncle Edward said it was her husband who'd beaten Ewan up in the barn. Libby glanced sideways at him and felt her hands tremble. She pictured him thrusting inside Patti and became breathless. Her hand reached for a glass of water, knocking it over. Ewan quickly stopped it before too much damage was done and handed it to her. His hand brushed hers and she thought she might faint.

'I hear Ben Mitchell's boat got wrecked,' said Kevin after consuming several glasses of champagne. 'Someone shot at it. Serves the bugger right, I say. He sabotaged old man Miles's nets more than once just so he could get the best haul.'

Ewan helped himself to more turkey.

'Shot it?' said Edward.

'Full of holes. It's like a bloody colander,' said Kevin, laughing.

'Language,' said Molly softly.

'Right, sorry,' said Kevin.

'You hear that, Ewan?' said Edward with a grin.

'I did. I can't think who'd want to go doing that.'

Libby looked at him.

'Well, we know it wasn't you,' said Molly. 'You can't do anything with that arm.'

'That's right,' said Ewan, meeting Libby's eyes.

His leg brushed hers and she pulled it away. He smiled indulgently and reached for a dish.

'Stuffing?' he asked her, a curl to his lips.

Libby blushed and shook her head. It was Ewan who shot the boat and she felt sure her uncle knew it too.

'May I be excused?' she asked.

Her uncle nodded. Libby rushed to the loo. Once inside, she

slid her hand into her panties and pictured Ewan thrusting inside the woman called Patti until gasping, she came. She'd see Patrick tomorrow. Perhaps he'd do it to her again. But she couldn't help wondering if Ewan did it better.

CHAPTER TWENTY-THREE

PRESENT DAY

Libby

I wait but there's no reply. I push the buzzer again.

'Hello,' says a faint voice through the crackly speaker. I can't distinguish an accent.

'Hello, I live in the apartment across the road. I wonder...'

'How can I help you?' the voice snaps back.

'Could I come up?'

The buzzer sounds, and I push open the door. I hurry to the lift as someone comes out of it. The lift ascends, and I study my reflection in the lift mirror. Will Ewan recognise me? Surely not; I look very different to the teenager he knew fifteen years ago. The lift pings and I step out. My legs have turned to jelly. I've completely forgotten what I'd rehearsed. The door of number 23 opens and I take a deep breath. A man of about twenty opens the door. It isn't Galbreith and I'm not sure if I'm relieved or disappointed.

'You want to see me?' he asks.

His voice is deep. It doesn't match his boyish face.

'I... I live in the block opposite,' I say, pointing into the flat.

'Yes, you said.'

'I have a stalker,' I say abruptly. This wasn't how I had planned it. 'Could I look to see if your apartment overlooks mine?'

He wrinkles his brow.

'Are you accusing me of stalking?'

I shake my head emphatically.

'No, not at all. It's just the man stalking me is sending me messages saying he's watching me.'

He rubs at his chin.

'I've got a flatmate but...'

My stomach tightens.

'Do the police know?' he asks.

I nod.

'You can have a look,' he says uncertainly.

He opens the door to his flat. I step inside cautiously. The flat smells of weed. I wrinkle my nose and follow him into an untidy living room.

'Your flatmate...' I begin.

'He's at work.'

'What's his name?'

He rubs his chin again.

'I don't think...'

'Is he Scottish?'

He stares at me for a second and then bursts out laughing.

'Scottish? He's from East London.'

I look out of the window.

'I'm really sorry about your stalker and everything but you've got the wrong flat.'

I look across to my flat. I recognise the blinds at my kitchen window, but I can't see anything inside the living room. The inside of the flat looks dark against the sunshine outside.

'What's your flatmate's name?' I ask, turning to look at him.

He bites his lip.

'Look, I don't think...'

'If I have to send the police here then I will,' I say firmly, reaching in my handbag for the rape alarm.

'It's Dave,' he says.

'How long has he been your flatmate?'

I glance around the room.

'Eighteen months. Look, no one in this flat is stalking you...'

'Eighteen months?' I repeat, my hand dropping the alarm.

'Yes.'

I feel deflated. I take one last look out of the window and walk to the door.

'I made a mistake, I'm sorry.'

'But...'

'There's no way my stalker could have been living here for eighteen months.'

I open the door as my phone bleeps. The door is slammed shut behind me. I step into the lift, pull out my phone and squint to read the message through the crack in the screen. There is a dark picture, the silhouette of a woman in a doorway. The text message simply reads

> Every move you make and every step you take
> I'll be watching you.

I rub the screen and look again, and realise the woman in the picture is me. The photo is of me entering the building.

CHAPTER TWENTY-FOUR

FIFTEEN YEARS EARLIER

Libby watched as her aunt nodded at Uncle Edward. She knew they were about to leave. They always left the party just as it got going. Libby felt her heart sink. She knew everyone had had too much to drink, but it was Christmas after all. Why shouldn't they have a good time? Just like previous years they were making the most of it and Libby enjoyed seeing them having fun. Molly's cheeks were bright red and strands of hair from her perfectly coiffured bun were hanging around her face, making her look a little wild. Libby liked Molly. She was kind. Libby guessed her to be about thirty. Her boyfriend worked at The Pleasure Gardens in town and was very handsome.

'We'll leave you to it,' said Uncle Edward, downing the last of his whisky.

'Don't fancy Twister then?' Ewan grinned.

Libby saw Molly cringe. Everyone thought Ewan pushed things too far with the Owens.

'Thanks, but no thanks.' Edward smiled. 'I'm surprised you're up for it with that arm.'

Molly stood up.

'Thank you for a lovely dinner, sir,' she said, and for a moment Libby thought she was going to curtsy.

Rose smiled. 'We're very pleased you enjoyed it. We're very grateful for all that you do.'

'The pheasant was mighty tasty,' added Kevin.

'Excellent,' said Edward. 'You carry on with the festivities. Graham will drive you home whenever you're ready.'

Rose beckoned to Libby who stood reluctantly.

'Are you leaving too?' said Peter, the stable lad.

'Well... I...'

'Goodnight,' said Rose, taking Libby by the hand.

'I could stay a little bit longer,' Libby said, looking pleadingly at her aunt.

'Well...' said Rose.

'I'll make sure she's in bed before midnight,' said Ewan, winking at Libby.

Libby blushed and hated herself for it.

'I'm sure she'll be fine,' Edward said to Rose.

'Brilliant,' cried Peter.

Libby rolled her eyes. He was the same age as her and she knew he liked her. She didn't go for boys her own age. Libby preferred a more mature man. One who knew what he was doing. There was a moment of silence after Rose and Edward left and then Molly jumped up, grabbing Ewan by the arm.

'Let's have some music,' she said.

Ewan went over to Uncle Edward's music system and sorted through the CDs.

'Fancy a game?' Peter asked, pointing at the Twister mat.

'Okay,' said Libby, looking at Ewan.

'Come on, Ewan,' goaded Peter.

'I've got an unfair handicap with this arm and not to mention the sore ribs,' protested Ewan but he stepped onto the mat anyway. Peter threw the dice and Ewan struggled to reach the squares. His leg crossed over Libby's and his eyes met hers.

'Enjoying yourself?' he asked.

'Yes,' she said breathlessly.

'I'll change the music,' said Molly. 'Let's put your CD on, Ewan.'

Ewan's warm hand touched Libby's foot as he moved to take his go. She wobbled and her other foot got caught up in his. Suddenly she was on her back with Ewan on top of her. His whisky breath wafting over her. He laughed, showing her his even white teeth. At that moment Molly changed the music. Ewan's eyes looked into Libby's as 'Every Breath you Take' played through the speakers.

CHAPTER TWENTY-FIVE

PRESENT DAY

Libby

I'm so hot. I can feel the sweat running from my underarms. My throat is so dry that I can barely swallow. I don't want him to know how scared I am. I wrap my hand around the rape alarm and pull it from my bag.

I wave at three cabs before one finally stops. I've got one hour before my meeting. I rest my throbbing head for a few moments before taking the phone from my bag. A picture message with a sound-file attachment shows on the screen. It's the eighties song, 'Every Breath you Take'. There's no doubt that this is Ewan.

I feel sick and my head is spinning. The cabbie glances at me in his mirror.

'Are you okay there?'

'I'm fine. It's the heat.'

'You look a bit pale. I'll turn the air con up.'

'Thanks.'

Ewan Galbreith knows my surname. He knows where I live.

He knows what I look like. I tap into my phone and google private security firms.

'Can you stop at Fulham Police Station please?'

I'll hand my phone in and let Fran know when I get my new number. I won't let him get to me. He'll do something stupid and then they'll throw him back inside. I won't let him intimidate me. I won't.

'Excuse me?' asks the cabbie.

I realise I've spoken my thoughts out loud.

'Nothing,' I say, looking out of the window.

Is he following me now? The text sits menacingly on my phone. I hesitate for a few seconds and then type *who is this*? I wait for the message received notification but there is nothing. Damn him, damn him to hell. Simon was right. He is no doubt using pay-as-you-go mobiles.

I turn my phone off and breathe deeply. He's playing with me. Anyone who remembers Ewan Galbreith knows what a marksman he is. If he gets hold of a gun I won't stand a chance.

———

'That's if you're interested,' says Anna.

My eyes are fixed on the man entering the restaurant. He's wearing a blue hooded jacket. It's like the one Ewan used to wear. I tighten my grip on my wine glass. The man looks over and I hold my breath. It isn't Ewan.

'Libby?'

I turn back to Anna.

'I'm sorry.'

'Are you okay, Libby? You seem distant.'

I force a smile.

'I'm sorry. I've not been sleeping well.'

'Oh, poor you. Do you need something? I've got this great doctor; he gives me everything.'

'Oh no, that's fine.'

I never want to be out of control, especially at night.

'Shall we talk about it another time?' Anna asks.

'No, absolutely not,' I say resolutely.

I wave to the waiter and order coffee. I need to pull myself together. I can't let Ewan destroy me. It took a lot of work to build my new identity and even more work to set up my business. I'm a success and I won't let him ruin that.

'The new venture sounds fabulous and I'd love to do the designs,' I say with a smile.

'Brilliant,' says Anna enthusiastically. 'Let's celebrate with lunch and then I'll take you to see the development.'

'I have a new mobile number,' I say, pulling an iPhone from my bag.

'Love the handbag,' she says, enviously eyeing up my Gucci.

'Thanks, it's one of my favourites.'

She covets it with jealous eyes and I make a mental note to have one sent to her from Harrods the next day. Clients love that kind of thing. I allow myself a glass of champagne with lunch and begin to relax. My phone doesn't bleep. No one knows my new number, except for Fran. The sales assistant was able to restore my contacts list for me, which was a great help. The restaurant is getting busy and Anna and I have difficulty hearing one another. I preferred it when the place was empty. I could keep tabs on the people coming in. Now it's almost impossible.

'Shall we go to the development?' Anna asks.

I nod and we make our way to the doors. I look at the diners but I only see strangers. Anna has a car waiting. I look down again at my phone and sigh with satisfaction. I feel better and less anxious than earlier. I'll go to Harrods later and treat myself to some retail therapy. That always helps. I'll buy a new dress for my date with Simon tomorrow. The security company aren't coming until nine, so I have plenty of time. I'm my own boss. There's no one to say I can't go shopping at three in the afternoon. I'll make sure there are lots of people around. He can't get to me that way.

'I'm delighted you're on board,' says Anna.

'Me too,' I say.

'We're having a small function to celebrate the opening. I do hope you can make it. It's next Tuesday at eight. It's in the penthouse suite of the development. Do feel free to bring your partner.'

'Lovely, thank you.'

Maybe I'll ask Simon. I'll see how tomorrow goes.

CHAPTER TWENTY-SIX

F ran zoomed in on the photo of Rose Owen. She recognised it. It was one of the photos that had been posted online by a sick bastard. She topped up her wine glass. The wine was sharp and vinegary. Bloody cheap plonk, but it did the trick. If the photo jarred memories for her, what must it have done to Libby? Fran and a number of other officers had been the first on the scene and the sight that greeted them had etched itself on their brains forever. One newbie had to rush out to throw up. Fran remembered fighting back the nausea. The sight of Rose Owen's body had tortured her ever since. The look of horror shown on her dead face as she must have faced the gunman is something Fran could not get out of her mind. The naked breast hanging over her red dress had disturbed Fran the most. It was a final humiliation. Fran had wanted to cover it, but she couldn't touch the body. She remembered seeing Galbreith as he'd sat in the hallway, his head buried in his hands. That's how he'd found them, he said. He was still holding the shotgun while maintaining his innocence. He looked after the Owen's hunting guns and was a trained marksman. Everyone knew it. He'd been twenty-four years old. Libby must be terrified. If Galbreith got hold of a rifle he could shoot her through the heart from five hundred yards. Jesus, what must she be going through?

She offered the bottle to Mike.

'Do me a favour,' he said, pulling a face. 'Meths would taste better than that shit you call wine.'

He fumbled in his jacket and pulled out a hip flask. Fran had bought it for him last Christmas.

'You use it?' she said, surprised.

'Wasn't that why you gave it to me?'

She smiled and popped a cracker into her mouth and then slid Libby's phone across to him.

'What do you think?' she asked.

Mike took a swig from the flask and looked thoughtful.

'Galbreith is no fool. That's something I remember about him. I don't understand why he's doing this, if it is him.'

'Who else would it be?' Fran said.

Mike shook his head.

'How would I know? Someone out to get Libby or out to get Galbreith?'

'It's Galbreith,' said Fran with certainty. 'You heard his threats as they took him down.'

'He's also done fifteen years inside. No one who gets out is going to want to go back, now are they? He was younger then. He had no previous convictions. Why would he walk straight back into trouble?'

Fran shrugged. 'We know he sunk Ben Mitchell's boat.'

'There was no proof. Mitchell never filed a complaint.'

Fran sighed. 'We have to protect her, Mike. She's already been through a lot. The poor bitch has lost everything. First her parents in a car crash, killed by a drunk driver. Can you imagine? Then being taken in by her aunt and uncle only to have some maniac shoot them dead in a moment of rage. I don't know how she managed to come out of this sane.'

'I expect the money helped,' he scoffed.

'You're too cynical.' She smiled.

'Yep, that's me. Anyway, anyone could have sent that photo and voicemail. There are home videos on YouTube, of their shoots and parties afterwards. Anyone could have edited Rose Owen saying, "It's Rose, help me".'

'I know,' Fran said through a sigh.

Mike shook the hip flask. 'I don't suppose you've got anything decent in this place?' he said, peering into the empty flask.

Fran shook her head. She was surprised Mike had come over. She'd phoned him for advice about Libby and expected him to tell her to hand it over to Scotland Yard, but he hadn't. He'd offered to come to her place and discuss it. She would have got a bottle of whisky in if she'd known.

'Let me have another look at that mobile,' he said, nodding to the phone.

Fran pushed it across the table. Mike silently studied the text messages and photos.

'Have you spoken to him?' Mike asked.

'Not recently. I can't accuse him. It's not hard to make an untraceable call these days. There must be a dozen apps that will do it.'

'There are a lot of weirdos out there still obsessed by her story,' Mike reminded her. 'It may be coincidence that Galbreith's just out of prison.'

'Libby is convinced,' said Fran.

'Any trace on the Facebook page?'

'It was closed down after she got the request. The mobiles are black market disposables.'

'It's a lot of trouble to go to,' said Mike cynically.

'Well, she's not making it up,' Fran said irritably.

'I'm playing devil's advocate,' said Mike. 'Someone's got to.'

'I know,' said Fran.

He slid the phone across the table.

'She can afford a security guard. She's less vulnerable than some.'

Fran grimaced at him.

'I'm just saying if she's really that scared then she can afford her own cover, CCTV, panic button, I don't know. We can't bang up Galbreith because she thinks it's him. We need proof.'

'We'll just wait until he blows her head off, shall we?' Fran said, getting up. 'Do you want some pizza?'

He nodded. 'You put it in the oven and I'll go and get some decent booze from the off-licence.'

Fran failed to hide her surprise.

'Don't you have to get back?'

'Oh, didn't I tell you? Barb and I have separated.'

Fran gaped at him. Shit, she thought. Only fifteen years too late.

CHAPTER TWENTY-SEVEN

PRESENT DAY

Libby

Ian greets me as I enter my apartment building. It's almost eight o'clock. I have one hour before the security guy arrives.

'Evening, Miss Warren. Would you like me to take those for you?' he says nodding at my Harrods bags.

'That would be great, thank you.'

'I have a parcel for you. It was delivered at lunchtime.'

'A parcel?' I repeat. 'Do you know who delivered it?' I say, sounding anxious.

'I believe it was the florist. Their name is on the packet.'

He disappears into his office and returns with a large box. I stare at it and turn to the doors. Is he watching? Is he frustrated that he can't call my mobile? I don't touch the box but study the sender's details: *Gabriella's flower shop, Knightsbridge.* It must be from Simon.

'Could you bring it up please?'

'Of course.'

'I'm expecting someone at nine. Could you let me know when he arrives?'

I collect my post and Ian joins me in the lift. My eyes don't leave the box. Ian carefully places the bags in the hallway and I give him an extravagant tip before closing the door and locking it. I stare at the box before taking my Harrods bags to the bedroom. Would Simon send me flowers after one date? It seems unlikely but what other explanation could there be? It enters my head that the box may contain a bomb, but I dismiss the idea immediately. It has the florist's name on it.

'He could easily have got a box,' whispers a voice in my head.

No, a bomb is too intricate for Ewan. If he's going to get violent, he'll use a gun. That's where he's skilled. I glance out of the window to the apartment block opposite. The lights are on. I pull the blinds and sigh. A hot bath is what I need, and I run the taps, sprinkling a large amount of bath salts. The fragrance relaxes me. I've just enough time for a soak before the security guy arrives. I pass the box on my way to the fridge and it's only after the bath is ready and I've poured myself a large glass of wine that I decide to open it. I take my time but I don't know why. All kinds of thoughts enter my head. Wild imaginings of what may be inside. I glide the scissors around the edges and carefully lift the top. A large mound of tissue paper is protecting whatever is inside. I take a sip of wine before removing the paper and revealing a crystal glass vase. It's surrounded by two bunches of lilies, carefully wrapped in cellophane. My hands are shaking and I curse. There's an envelope in the box. I leave it unopened and refill my wine glass. I take a large gulp of wine and slit open the envelope. A small card with a black cat on the front slips out. Inside it simply says, *For Libby*. It doesn't say who the flowers are from. It's a thoughtful and extravagant gift. With a feeling of relief, I take the lilies out of the cellophane and arrange them in the vase. Merlin sniffs them and sneezes. I laugh.

'Aren't they gorgeous?' I say, petting him.

I text Simon my new number, but I don't mention the flowers. I'll thank him tomorrow.

Great, thanks, he texts back. *I'll see you tomorrow. I'm looking forward to it.*

I try to picture his face but all I see is Ewan Galbreith's. Is he still good-looking, I wonder? Does he still have that animal magnetism or have the years in prison changed him? Is he watching me? I shiver and climb into the bath. I won't think about him. I refuse to.

CHAPTER TWENTY-EIGHT

PRESENT DAY

'Hello, Dianne,' said Fran after Dianne opened the door.
Recognition flitted across Dianne's face and her expression changed. She frowned.

'He doesn't live here anymore.'

Fran nodded.

'Do you have an address for him?'

Dianne lowered her head and sighed.

'He's not been out that long. Why are you harassing him? Greg told me you went to the garage.'

'I'm not harassing him,' said Fran.

Dianne opened the door wider. 'The kids are at school otherwise I wouldn't let you in,' she said, stepping back into the hall. Fran followed her to the kitchen. Dianne's hair was pulled back in the same messy bun she wore the last time Fran saw her all those years ago. Dianne's eyes fastened on Fran's and she said, 'He's not in trouble, is he?'

Fran licked her lips. She was thirsty. Was this heatwave ever going to break? Although she knew most of her thirst was due to the hangover.

'I couldn't have some water could I? This heat is...'

'Yeah, it's getting tedious,' said Dianne, filling a glass.

'Thanks,' said Fran, throwing it back. She handed Dianne the glass with a grateful nod.

'Libby Owen has reported that someone is harassing her. She's been getting messages and threatening texts. It started shortly after Ewan was released.'

Dianne pulled out a chair and sat down.

'There are plenty of nutcases out there. I imagine she has weirdos contacting her all the time.'

Fran looked down at Dianne's hands. The knuckles were white where she was clenching them.

'She feels sure this is Ewan,' said Fran.

'Why would he want to do that? He's just got out.'

'He threatened her before he went down. He threatened a lot of us.'

'He was distraught. He was going down for something he didn't do.'

'He was found guilty, Dianne.'

'While the real murderer went free,' said Dianne, standing up. 'Owen had enemies.'

Fran sighed.

'It was fifteen years ago, Dianne. I accept that Ewan has done his time, but I still have to follow up the charges, even if it is to eliminate Ewan from the case. Can you tell me where he's living now?'

Dianne shook her head.

'I honestly don't know. But... I think he's working in London.'

'London?' repeated Fran. 'How long has he been in London?'

'I'll have to ask you to leave. If Greg knows I've let you in he'll go mental,' she said and walked to the door.

'How long has he been in London?' Fran asked, with her

hand on the door.

'I'm not sure. I haven't heard from him in a bit.'

'I'll find out where it is. You could save me some time by letting me have the address.'

'I don't know the London address.'

Fran didn't believe her.

'Thanks, sorry to have troubled you.'

'No, you're not,' said Dianne before slamming the door in Fran's face.

———

Fran climbed into her car and fumbled with the air conditioning. As she drove to Padley Pier she wondered if Mike had left the flat or if he would be there when she got back. She doubted it. He had stayed the night, but it wasn't quite how she'd dreamt it. He'd had far too much whisky and she'd had too much wine. Neither of them could have driven, although Mike was up for it.

'Do you want to throw your job away as well as your marriage?' Fran had said. 'I've got a spare bedroom. You can sleep in there.'

It had driven her mad knowing he was in the next room, so near and yet so far away. She had almost gone to him, but something had held her back. The truth was she was afraid Mike would reject her. She pushed the thought of him away and parked her car outside The Crown. It was busy. Holidaymakers were filling up the beach already. How they could enjoy sitting out in this heat Fran would never know.

The pub was heaving. She pushed through the queue and flashed her badge at anyone who got in her way.

'Where's Luke?' she asked the barmaid.

'He's in the cellar.'

'Can you get him out of the cellar,' said Fran flashing her badge.

It was too hot in the pub. All those sweaty bodies were making her feel sick. The barmaid hurried off and a group of irritated customers grumbled.

Luke appeared and frowned at the sight of her.

'Can I have a word?' she said. 'In private?'

'You'd better come out the back,' he said, leading the way and showing her into a pokey office. She sat in front of a fan, the coolness making her feel better.

'You're busy today,' she said.

'It's the holiday season. I'd be worried if I weren't. So, why would a police officer need to talk to me?' he asked cautiously. 'You wouldn't pay me a visit over a parking ticket.'

'I hear Ewan Galbreith has a place in London.'

Fran noticed how quickly his expression changed.

'Is that right, I wouldn't know. Anyway, what's it to you? He's done his time.'

Fran nodded.

'He has done his time. I would just like a word with him. I need the address.'

'I don't have it.'

Fran had no idea if he knew the address or not. She'd most likely have to try all of Ewan's old contacts. That was all she needed in this weather, to traipse all over Padley.

'You'll be obstructing the police if you do know it and don't tell me,' she said sharply.

'We all felt for Libby Owen you know. It was a terrible thing. No girl of seventeen should have gone through that. But Ewan... maybe did things he shouldn't, but murder? I just don't see that.'

'Maybe you didn't know him as well as you thought you did.'

117

He nodded.

'Maybe not.'

'Where does Molly Richards work now?'

'In the café on the sea front.'

'Sally Anne's?' asked Fran.

'Yeah and I doubt she'll know where Ewan is.'

'Thanks,' said Fran and pushed her way back through the throng.

Sally Anne's was less busy. Most of the patrons were sitting out in the sun.

'Bloody fools,' muttered Fran.

Molly was wiping tables. Fran remembered her from the murder investigation all those years ago. Molly turned to smile at Fran and then froze.

'Hello Molly,' Fran said, sitting at a table.

Molly didn't reply.

'Can I have a Diet Coke and a minute of your time?'

Molly looked at the woman behind the counter. Fran, realising it was most likely her boss, got up and flashed her badge.

'I won't keep her long. It's nothing she's done. I just want to ask her some questions.'

'Ten minutes at the most,' said the woman.

Molly took a Diet Coke from the fridge and a glass from behind the counter before walking towards Fran.

'I hear Ewan Galbreith has gone to London.'

'I don't know where Ewan goes,' Molly said quietly.

'I need that London address.'

Molly wrung her hands and fidgeted on her feet.

'If I don't give it to you?'

'I think you know the answer to that.'

'He's not doing anything wrong,' Molly said sullenly. 'But he said if you pestered, then we were to give the address.'

'Why would he think we'd pester?' said Fran.

'Because you already have, that's why.'

She pulled a pen from the pocket of her apron and wrote on her notepad.

'That's the address. He needs work. We all do.'

Fran took it and glanced at the address.

'Thanks,' she said.

'Yeah, sure,' said Molly before walking away.

Fran folded the paper and pushed it into her pocket. The last thing she wanted to do was travel to London, unless of course Mike came with her. It was a possibility. Her heart fluttered at the thought.

CHAPTER TWENTY-NINE

FIFTEEN YEARS EARLIER

'Go on, just a drop,' said Peter, pushing the whisky under her nose.

Libby looked at Ewan and Kevin as they prepared to arm wrestle. Ewan had rolled up the sleeves of his shirt. Kevin laughed.

'Those muscles don't scare me, Galbreith.'

'Go on,' said Peter again.

Libby took the bottle from him. The whisky stung her lips and burnt her tongue.

'Let's watch,' he said, pulling her to where the men were arm wrestling.

'What's the prize?' Ewan asked.

'A kiss under the mistletoe,' said Molly, 'from us girls.'

She nudged Libby who reddened immediately. She should really leave. They were staff, after all, and family were supposed to leave the party for the staff to enjoy. Aunty Rose always knew the right time to leave but somehow Libby couldn't. She was having fun.

'Sounds like a good prize to me,' said Kevin with a laugh. 'Are you on. Ewan?'

Ewan looked up at Molly.

'Are you sure about this?' He grinned.

'It's a kiss, Ewan, nothing else.' She giggled.

'Okay, why not,' said Ewan, resting his elbow on the table.

'I thought you'd be up for it,' said Kevin.

'On my count of three,' said Peter.

Libby watched in fascination at the men's concentration as they fought for victory. She could see the muscles ripple in Ewan's arm as he strained against Kevin. Libby didn't fancy Kevin kissing her. He had bad breath, but she'd agreed, and she only hoped Ewan would win. Ewan had his eyes fixed on Kevin's, and for a moment it looked like he was losing. His hand shook as he pushed against Kevin's. Libby and Molly held their breath while Peter cheered them both on. With one final push Ewan got the better of Kevin and slowly pushed his arm down. His jaw twitched with the effort. Peter cheered as Kevin's arm thumped to the table.

'Well played,' said Kevin rubbing his arm. 'Next go is with your bad arm.'

'I'd still beat you,' Ewan said confidently. He took a large swig of whisky and looked at Molly.

'What about that snog then?' he asked.

'A kiss under the mistletoe is all.' She smiled.

Libby stepped back as he stood and drew Molly to him, his arms encircling her waist. He then dipped her backwards and holding her by one arm kissed her passionately on the lips. Libby watched and could feel her face reddening and her nipples hardening.

Ewan released Molly who slapped him playfully.

'You're a cheeky bugger you are.'

He turned to Libby and winked.

'Still up for it?' he asked.

She nodded shyly and stepped under the mistletoe. Much

to her chagrin he didn't encircle her waist with his strong arm or dip her backwards. He barely touched her at all. His lips brushed hers lightly and then it was over. She wanted to cry. Did he not like her in the same way as Molly? Was she unattractive to him? She turned to look at him, but he was already at the door.

'I'm going to check on the horses,' he said.

'You're mad you are,' said Kevin. 'It's sodding Christmas. They'll be all right.'

'I'm checking on the horses,' Ewan said again, firmly.

Libby decided it was time for her to go. She felt too upset to stay.

'It's getting late, I should go,' she said.

'Not yet,' said Peter, disappointment evident in his voice.

'She doesn't want to spend the whole evening with us,' said Molly. 'It's not etiquette for a start.'

Libby didn't think Molly would be saying this if she'd been sober.

'We're going to play charades,' said Peter. 'Can't you stay for that?'

Libby hesitated.

'I'd best not,' she said, picking up her clutch bag.

'I need some air,' said Kevin.

'Me too,' said Molly, following him.

'I wish you weren't going,' said Peter, stepping closer to her.

Libby felt nervous being alone with him. He'd had too much to drink. She realised she was standing under the mistletoe and went to walk away when his hands grasped her wrists.

'I could beat Ewan you know? Don't you think I deserve a kiss under the mistletoe too?'

'I have to go now,' she said, struggling to pull her hands out of his grasp.

He released one hand and pulled her roughly to him, his lips crushing hers. She fought against him.

'Peter, please. If my uncle...'

But his lips silenced her and with one arm he pulled her closer while the other hand fumbled with the buttons of her dress. She heard it rip and gasped. She slapped at his chest, but her slaps were futile. The door creaked open and she prayed it was Kevin and Molly. His hand touched her breast and he groaned. She was about to bring her knee up when Peter released his grip.

'What are you doing, Peter?'

Ewan pushed him roughly and Peter fell to the floor. Ewan looked at Libby's torn dress and her exposed breast. He pulled her dress together and she felt his hand brush her nipple.

'It's time for you to go,' he said roughly. 'Peter's drank too much. He meant no harm. There's no need to tell your uncle.'

Peter grunted something from the floor.

'You'd be best to keep quiet, mate,' said Ewan.

'I wouldn't have told my uncle,' Libby said, clutching her dress to cover her breast.

Ewan frowned and said, 'Do you want me to escort you home?'

She shook her head while her body screamed yes.

'Thanks anyway. Goodnight Peter.'

She walked from the room, trying to keep her head held high. Why couldn't it have been Ewan that had torn her dress, she thought.

CHAPTER THIRTY

FIFTEEN YEARS EARLIER

Ben looked at his boat. The damage was worse than he'd thought. Damn it. It would be months before he got it back out to sea and what the hell were they supposed to do in the meantime?

Adam looked at the holes and cursed.

'How long do you reckon?' he asked. 'Will it be ready next week?'

Ben laughed mirthlessly.

'Are you a fucking joker? Am I God? The fucker has finished us for the winter.'

'I need the extra income, Ben. I've got kids.'

'I can't wave a magic wand,' Ben snapped. 'It needs money that I don't have. I'll have to repair the damn thing myself and that's going to take time.'

It was going to cost enough to fix the damn thing. There's no way he'd have enough to rent a boat in the meantime.

'Fuck it,' he snarled, kicking out at the boat.

'You should demand Edward fucking Owen pays,' said Adam. 'It's his bloody employee and his guns he used. He should take some fucking responsibility.'

Ben's eyes glistened. Why hadn't he thought of that?

'That's not such a bad idea,' he said. 'If I get enough to rent a boat I'll be able to do the repairs myself. That would help. That'll show Galbreith.'

'I wasn't really serious,' said Adam doubtfully. 'He'll just tell you to fuck off after what we did to Ewan.'

Ben looked at the boat.

'I've got fuck all to lose,' he said, pushing his woollen hat onto his head. 'Owen's loaded. What's a few hundred quid to him?'

Adam watched Ben march to his old pickup truck. He had some nerve he thought. It would be good if Owen did pay up. He'd have a drink and wait. Ben shouldn't be that long.

———

The gates to Manstead Manor were always open. Ben reached them and brought his truck to a sharp halt. He had his doubts about approaching Owen now that he was here. Hadn't he threatened to shoot his head off if he ever stepped on his land again? That fuck Galbreith would get away with murder if someone didn't stop him. He shouldn't be allowed to use those guns. Ben felt that he really should have reported it to the police, but he knew what would happen if he did. Owen would accuse him of trespassing on his land and assaulting his niece. The stupid bugger always stood by Ewan. He'd live to regret that one day.

He'd do things properly. He could be polite when needed.

He drove through the gates and slowly along the drive, parking the pickup outside the main doors. He climbed from the truck expecting a bullet to whizz by his head any minute. From the corner of his eye he saw Galbreith at the back of the house. He had a saddle in his good hand. He eyed Ben and then walked towards the stables. Ben took a deep breath and headed for the doors. He pulled the bell and waited.

'I've come to see Mr Owen. Is he home?' Ben said bluntly to Molly.

'If you'd like to wait,' she said, stepping aside so he could enter.

'Tell him it's Ben Mitchell.'

'I know who you are,' said Molly.

Ben had never been inside Manstead Manor. He looked around the grand hall and at the huge Christmas tree that stood in the centre and sniffed. He lifted his head to look at the painted ceiling.

'Jesus,' he muttered, the sight taking his breath away.

Ben knew that Rose Owen had inherited the house from her titled family. Ben bit his lip and wondered if he should ask to speak with her. He decided Owen himself was the best bet. He'd made a fortune over the years with his property lettings as well as his corrupt business dealings. It was all wrong, rich landlords and crooked business deals when people like him had to sweat just to keep their head above water.

A door to the right opened and Libby strolled into the hall in her riding gear. He nodded at her and she smiled. Then her expression changed to one of horror. She'd recognised him. She turned and rushed from the hallway. To tell her uncle, no doubt, thought Ben. Molly came back and beckoned him to follow her. He was briskly led into a reception room where Edward Owen sat behind a heavy oak desk.

'Thank you, Molly,' he said. 'To what do I owe this visit?' Edward then said without rising from his chair.

Ben glanced around the room. Christmas cards hung elegantly from the fireplace. A roaring open fire and a perfectly decorated Christmas tree in the corner completed the festive ambience.

'Galbreith shot my boat to bits,' he said.

Edward's face remained impassive.

'I'm not sure what that has got to do with me,' he said dismissively, glancing down at some papers.

'He used one of your rifles is what it's got to do with you. It's criminal damage,' said Ben sharply.

Edward looked up.

'You have proof, do you?'

'There's not many around these parts that can hit a target like Ewan Galbreith.'

Edward stood up and walked to a drinks cabinet.

'Can I offer you anything?' Edward asked.

Ben nodded.

'Yeah, you can offer me five hundred in cash so I can repair the damage to my boat.'

Edward smiled.

'Am I right in recalling that you trespassed on my land not long ago? And if I remember rightly, you not only beat up a valuable member of staff, whose two arms I very much needed, but you also assaulted my niece.'

'He shouldn't be allowed use of those guns when he's not on your land. The police might be interested to know how he wanders around the village carrying one of your guns.'

'Are you threatening me?'

'Galbreith was fucking my wife,' Ben snarled.

Edward smirked and stepped towards Ben. Looking him in the eye he said, 'It's a man's weakness if he can't satisfy his wife. Ewan did you a favour.'

Ben pushed his hands into his pockets to stop himself from punching Edward Owen.

'He's dangerous with those guns of yours. He'll kill somebody.'

'Best not get in his way then.'

'I can't work, thanks to him. It's Christmas.'

'I can see our Christmas tree,' said Edward blandly.

'Fuck you,' snarled Ben, turning to the door.

'I'll give you three hundred and that's it,' said Edward as Ben put his hand on the door handle.

'You're paying me off?'

'I'm being generous. Take it or leave it, but that settles the matter. I'll throw in a pheasant for your Christmas Day dinner. Your wife will like that.'

'Five hundred,' bartered Ben.

'Two hundred.'

'You said three, you cheating bastard.'

'You argued about it.'

Ben wished he had a shotgun. The bastards always had the upper hand. He waited while Edward unlocked a drawer in the desk and removed a wad of notes. He counted out two hundred and handed them to Ben.

'Cash, as you requested. There's no way to trace that back to me. If you tell anyone I gave it to you I'll deny it.'

Ben snatched the notes before Edward could change his mind.

'Don't set foot on my property again.'

Ben shrugged and opened the door. Molly was waiting outside, and she led him back to the hall and opened the main doors. Shots rang out above his head as he climbed into the pickup. Ewan was never happier than when he was killing things, Ben thought. He sat and counted the money. He wasn't going to be swindled. If it was short of a fiver he was going back. It was all there. He folded the notes and shoved them into his pocket. He started the engine and accelerated out of Manstead, his tyres scattering the gravel.

'Two hundred quid,' he muttered. 'The bastard could afford a lot more than that.'

He'd fix the boat and then he'd get his own back.

CHAPTER THIRTY-ONE

PRESENT DAY

Ewan was early. He preferred it that way. It gave him time to make his checks. You didn't spend fifteen years in the clink without learning a few things. It was a rough area. That didn't bother him. He could handle himself. Always could. He was good with his fists. He looked at the map and stepped cautiously into the alleyway. He pulled up his hood and walked slowly. The third door on the right, said the map. It was covered in coarse graffiti and Ewan wrinkled his nose before knocking.

There was the sound of footsteps on stairs and then a voice said, 'Yeah?'

'It's Ewan Galbreith. Leon is expecting me.'

There was the sound of bolts being shot back and the door squeaked open. A smartly dressed black man smiled widely at Ewan and slapped him on the back.

'Hey wazzup?'

He high-fived Ewan.

'I need your expertise,' said Ewan.

'Sure, I owe you one. Come on up.'

Ewan followed Leon up a dark stairwell and into a flat. It was nicely decorated with white leather couches draped in brown fur blankets. One corner of the room was filled with computer equipment.

'Impressive,' said Ewan.

'You're talking about my toys, right, and not the sofas?' Leon laughed, exposing a row of even white teeth.

Ewan nodded. 'I need you to hack into an email account.'

'Is that all?' Leon smiled. 'And whose account do I have the pleasure of hacking?'

———

Libby

I hurry from the shower to answer my phone. I smile. It's Anna. She has received the handbag.

'Hi Anna,' I say cheerfully.

I feel more relaxed. I know Ewan can't reach me on this number.

'Libby,' she says softly, and seems to hesitate.

'Is everything okay?' I ask.

My stomach does a little churn but I've no idea why.

'Thank you for the lovely handbag but I really can't accept such an expensive gift.'

'Don't be silly, of course you can. It's my pleasure and...'

'I'm going to have to pull out of our agreement. I can't sign the contracts. I'm so sorry, Libby.'

'I don't understand, Anna. Why? I thought we had agreed...'

'The email you sent, Libby,' she says, interrupting. 'It has caused a lot of upset.'

I struggle to understand what's happening. What email? I haven't sent her an email.

'I don't know what email we're talking about.'

She sighs.

'The email you sent to the development committee. It arrived this morning. Carl Walter's daughter saw the photo you attached and, she's only six...'

The room spins around me.

'I don't understand...'

'I'm so sorry but we really can't get involved in that kind of gruesome publicity. It will pull away completely from what we're trying to achieve. It's not all about you, Libby, and we won't be pressured in this way.'

'But...'

'I'll have the bag returned to you.'

I go to speak but she has hung up. I try to get my breathing under control, but it comes in gasps. I pull my laptop towards me and with shaking hands click into my Outlook account. I hit the sent items and stare at the email I'd apparently sent last night. It was sent to all my business contacts.

'Oh God,' I groan, clicking into it.

Dear Colleague

I have decided to make some changes in our marketing strategy. You've heard the axiom, 'there's no such thing as bad publicity', well, I believe we have a great resource to put me into the public eye again. Recently, the man who was convicted of murdering my aunt and uncle has been released from prison and is on the loose in London. He wants to destroy me and my business, which makes my personal story of interest again. You, as my partners, are part of this. For those who don't know my story, I have attached the newspaper clip of my aunt and uncle's murder. I have also attached photos of their bodies, which, as part of your contact with me, I would expect you to share on social media. As partners I am asking you to fight with me against the injustice that this murderer is on the loose. The

message should be that 'out of tragedy one woman prospers'. If you
want to continue as partners then I insist on your loyalty – this is not
negotiable.

  Regards
  Libby Warren
  (Previously Libby Owen).

I drop my head into my hands. I feel defeated. Every one of by
business contacts has received the email. They now all know I
am Libby Owen. Tears rain down my cheeks. That bastard, that
fucking bastard has hacked into my account. I frantically check
my sent items again. That was the most recent. My inbox is
filling up with the responses to it. I don't need to read them to
know what they say. If he's hacked into this account what else
has he hacked into? It can't be Ewan; his skill isn't computers. I
grab my phone and punch in Fran's number. It rings for too long
and panic begins to well up in me. Finally she answers.

'You took a long time,' I say accusingly.

'Libby, you sound frantic, what's the matter?'

'He's hacked into my email account. You've got to do
something. I don't know what kind of email he'll send next.
Please, Fran. He's emailed all the contacts in my business
address book. I've lost nearly all my contracts. He's trying to
destroy me. I don't know what he's going to do next. I'm getting
a security guard, he starts today; but I can't stop Ewan Galbreith
hacking my email account.'

'Have you closed the account?' says Fran, her voice urgent.

'No... I...'

'Do it now, right now, while I'm on the phone to you.'

With trembling hands I click back into my Outlook account
and gasp. There's a new email. The sender is 'Every Breath'

'Oh God, he's emailed me,' I say.

'Open it.'

I click into the email and a photograph pops onto the screen. It's Ewan. It's an old photo. He's smiling.

My heart somersaults. He looks handsome, self-assured. The message attached reads *Hello Libby. How time passes.*

'It's a photo of him and a message. Do I still delete the account?'

'Shit. We don't want to lose that email.'

I wait for her to tell me what to do and as I wait I watch in horror as a window pops onto the screen and then disappears before my eyes. The music player flashes onto the screen and then the PC starts to play 'Every Breath You Take' through the tinny speaker.

'Shit.'

'Libby, what's happening?'

'Everything's opening up and then just disappearing in front of me. My photos have now gone and now my documents are disappearing.'

'Fuck,' groans Fran. 'Can you close it?'

I try to close the page, but I can't move the mouse.

'The cursor is moving on its own,' I say with a little sob.

'That email must have had a virus. Switch off the laptop. I'm sending Scotland Yard over.'

I press the off button, but nothing happens. I sit frozen in front of my laptop, helpless to do anything as I watch everything disappear until finally there is just Ewan's photo on the screen. I stare into his eyes and then it's gone.

CHAPTER THIRTY-TWO

FIFTEEN YEARS EARLIER

Patrick swaggered towards her. His brown hair was pulled up into a ponytail. He took a deep drag of his roll-up and then threw it to the ground.

'You're late,' Libby said.

'The kids, you know how it is. Then again, you're just one yourself, aren't you, darling?'

She hated it when he referred to her as a kid. She was almost eighteen. But, compared to Patrick she was a kid. He stroked her bum and she felt the excitement build up in her loins. Ever since Ewan had kissed her at the party she'd been bursting for relief.

'I've only got an hour. I've got the kids in a bit. She's going out with the girls.'

Libby bit back her retort. She didn't want to ruin things. An hour was enough and it would be worth it. Patrick always made it worth it. Her time with him was exciting. The deceit and the sordidness of it made it all the more appealing to her. If her uncle ever discovered she was shagging a twenty-seven-year-old married gypsy, he'd have a stroke. The fact they did it just a few feet from where his wife was in her caravan excited them. Libby would orgasm several times knowing she could catch them anytime. She loved the filth Patrick spewed into her ear, the way he made her beg for release. His fingers would toy with her and she'd imagine they were Ewan's fingers and she'd come so quickly that it took Patrick by surprise. Tonight was no different.

'God, you're hot tonight,' Patrick said.

The throbbing music from the pier reached her ears and she wondered if Ewan was down there with his friends. Patrick rolled off her and lit a cigarette.

'Christ Libs, you wear me out, you know that.'

Libby pulled her hair up and straightened her clothes.

'It will be New Year soon,' she said.

'Not for a while.' He laughed.

'We should celebrate together,' she said excitedly.

'I'll be with Lil and the girls.'

She pouted. 'We can celebrate after New Year then,' she said, kissing his rough cheek and then stroking it.

He caught her hand in his and said, 'We may be moving on in the New Year.'

'Moving on?' she said, shocked. 'Moving on where?'

He sighed. 'Back home to Australia.'

'Australia?' she echoed, pulling her hand out of his. 'You can't go to Australia.'

'I'm a gypo, Libby, we don't stay put for long. Besides, my visa runs out soon.'

'When does it run out?'

'In a few weeks.'

She sighed. She'd talk him out of it. There was time. She'd convince him to leave his stupid wife and she could go to Australia with him.

'How can you afford to go to Australia?' she asked scathingly.

He shook his head at her. 'We'll manage.'

'I love you,' she said.

She wasn't sure if she did, but it was nice saying it.

'Love you too, chick,' he said with a smile, sliding his hand down her blouse.

'It's cold,' she said.

'Yeah, you should get back to that roaring fire of yours.'

She slapped his hand.

'Don't mock me.'

'As if.' He laughed.

They got up from the ground and Libby pulled her coat around her. It was funny how she didn't feel the cold when they were doing it. She didn't seem to feel anything except wonderful sensations.

'See you, babe,' said Patrick.

'When?' asked Libby.

'I'll send you a text. It won't be long.' He winked.

Libby smiled and watched him walk away. She decided to get some chips. Maybe she'd see Ewan at the chip shop.

CHAPTER THIRTY-THREE

PRESENT DAY

Libby

I arrive twenty minutes late for my lunch date with Donna. I look terrible. My hair is greasy and I'd dragged it back with a hairband. There wasn't time to put on make-up and my eyes are still swollen from crying. Donna waves from her table. She's smiling, and I sigh with relief. Ewan hasn't got to her yet then. I've time to warn her. Her expression changes on seeing me and she hugs me.

'What's happened?' she asks, looking at me, concerned.

'He's... he's...' I stammer.

Donna sits me down and beckons to a waiter.

'Can we have two brandies please?'

I slip off my scarf and take a breath.

'He's made contact. He's been texting me and sending me photos. He says he's watching me and he is. He's taken photos of me and sent them minutes later.'

I take the brandy from the waitress and sip the liquid, its warmth comforting.

'You've told the police, obviously?'

I nod towards the doors.

'I've got a bodyguard. Ewan's destroyed my career. He sent an email to all my business contacts. I'm surprised you didn't get it.'

'I did,' she says, sitting back in her seat.

I stare at her.

'But...'

'I wanted to discuss it with you. I couldn't believe you would send it. I know how hard you've tried to hide your story. It seemed to go against everything I know about you.'

'He hacked into my email account and then sent a virus which destroyed everything I had on my laptop. He's got all my documents, photos... everything.'

'Jesus,' says Donna, throwing back the brandy and asking the waitress for more. 'What are the police doing?'

I take another sip of brandy and say, 'He's in London.'

'Oh Libby,' she says.

'I told you he would come.'

I see her hand is shaking as she lifts the glass to her lips.

'I can contact everyone cc'd on that email list. They may believe me. It might get you some contracts back.'

'Would you?' I ask hopefully.

'Of course,' she says, glancing at the door. 'Do you know where in London he's living?'

I shake my head.

'They won't tell me.'

'Bastards,' she says angrily.

'Has Simon contacted you?' I ask.

'Simon?'

'Do you know if he got an email? I can't check and... we're meeting tonight for dinner.'

She nods.

'I can send him a message. Try to get a feel of whether he did or not.'

'Oh Donna,' I say, reaching for her hand. 'I'd be so grateful.'

She grasps my hand and I see tears well up in her eyes.

'Oh Libby, as if you haven't been through enough.'

I cling onto her hand like it's a life raft.

'I'll email everyone and I'll let you know. I'm sure they won't cancel their contracts once they know the truth. Go out tonight with Simon, enjoy yourself. Don't think about him. He'll make a mistake sooner or later and then they'll get him.'

'Ewan doesn't make mistakes,' I say and down the last of my brandy.

CHAPTER THIRTY-FOUR

PRESENT DAY

'Dingy,' said Mike, looking at the house.

Fran didn't like London and she particularly didn't like this area. Mike checked his watch.

'He should be here soon.'

'We should have gone to that nightclub where he's working,' said Fran biting her nails.

Mike turned in his seat to look at her.

'We don't know if it is him harassing Libby. We can't barge into his place of work. He's every right to come to London and every right to get a job. It's a clean slate for him. It's not for us to bugger that up. If he was to lose his job through us elbowing our way in there without evidence, he could do us. You've got to keep an open mind, Fran.'

'This bloody heat,' she complained.

'We'll get a drink later and sort out a place to stay, with air conditioning.'

'Stay?' repeated Fran. 'I didn't know we were staying overnight.'

'It's nearly six already and we've still to have dinner. I'm not driving back unless you want to.'

She shook her head. Fran would never turn down an evening with Mike.

'There is only one reason and one reason alone that Ewan Galbreith would come to London,' she said.

'Yeah, to find work. Let's face it, Padley is dead and everyone knew him. Who do you imagine would employ him, apart from his brother-in-law? Maybe he wanted a new start. Libby Owen did.'

An old Nissan Micra turned the corner and parked in front of them. Fran recognised the man as Ewan. He pulled two shopping bags from the boot and walked to the front door. Mike climbed from the car and called, 'Ewan, okay to have a word?'

Ewan turned and smiled.

'All the way from Padley,' he drawled. 'I'm honoured.'

'He's not fazed,' said Fran.

Ewan turned back to the door, opened it and walked in. Mike looked at Fran.

'I presume that means yes. Let's go.'

Ewan was in the kitchen packing away the contents of his carrier bags.

'It's not air-conditioned I'm afraid,' he said, opening a window.

It was clean though, Fran noted.

'Have you been expecting us?' asked Mike.

'Molly said you'd bullied her for my address.'

'She wasn't bullied,' said Fran.

'So, what's London got to offer that Padley hasn't?' asked Mike.

Ewan laughed.

'That's a trick question, right?'

Mike smiled.

'I don't know where she lives. I don't care much either. I'm here to work and to get some money. Any other questions?' said Ewan flatly.

'I don't want to hassle you. We just have to follow things up, you know how it is. Libby had an email from someone called *Every Breath*. They sent a photo of you,' said Mike.

'That's nice of them. Maybe they thought she'd like one.'

'They hacked her email account.'

Ewan clicked on the kettle.

'You can't be too careful opening attachments, can you?' he said, sucking through his teeth.

'I never said there was an attachment,' said Mike.

'You don't get a virus any other way, not as far as I know. Can I offer you guys tea? I learnt how to make a good cuppa in prison.'

'What else did you learn, Ewan?' asked Fran.

'No tea then,' said Ewan, dropping a teabag into a mug. 'I didn't learn about computers if that's what you're asking. We weren't allowed them inside.'

'You must have learnt some things while inside,' persisted Fran.

Mike pulled out a chair and sat down. 'I'm not as young as I once was.' He smiled.

Ewan stood by the sink, his face expressionless.

'Nice little flat,' said Mike. 'Any particular reason you came to London?'

'Any particular reason you want to know?' replied Ewan. 'This is beginning to feel a bit like harassment.'

Fran bit her lip. She'd leave this to Mike.

'Not harassment, Ewan. I'm of the mind that when a man has done his time, that's it, he's done it. You've got as much right as I have to come to London. My problem is that I have someone accusing you of harassment. I have to look into it. I don't like it.

But... you did threaten people in court and now you're out and one of those people is getting threatening messages...'

'Libby Owen is who you're talking about,' said Ewan, his expression hardening.

Fran saw his lips tighten and recognised the angry young man of fifteen years ago.

'I wouldn't touch her with a bargepole. It's more than my freedom is worth and like I said, I know bugger all about computers.'

Mike nodded and stood up.

'That's good to hear, Ewan. I wouldn't want to have to come back.'

'It's a long way from Padley.' Ewan grinned, opening the door.

———

'I don't believe him,' Fran said as they sat in the car.

'I do,' he said. 'You're too taken up with Libby Owen. I don't believe Galbreith is stupid enough. You need to look elsewhere. It isn't him.'

CHAPTER THIRTY-FIVE

FIVE YEARS EARLIER

Belmarsh Prison

L eon Lapotaire was determined to stay out of trouble. He'd got ten years for fraud and he had decided he was going to get out in six. So when he went to clean out the showers and found shit strewn all over one of them, he had to make a choice, clean it up or refuse to. He chose to clean it up. He knew there were a couple of bastards who had a problem with a black man getting out early. He wasn't going to let them fuck it up for him. If it meant cleaning up shit, then that's what he'd do.

'Shit yourself again, black boy?' someone yelled.

There was laughter. He ignored it and carried on mopping. The shower stank. It would take him longer today. He couldn't lose it. Leon Lapotaire was a big man. He enjoyed exercise. Men knew to take him on would be suicide. They also knew he was determined to get out. It was common knowledge that you could push him to the limit and he wouldn't retaliate. Not now, not with his appeal so close.

Ewan Galbreith watched as the men ridiculed Leon. He knew better than to get involved. He had his own appeal coming up. He walked into his cell and picked up the amateur dramatics society script he'd been studying and covered his ears with headphones.

The same thing happened every day and by Friday Leon had had enough. Three showers were covered in shit and his temper was rising.

'Do you need someone to plug up that shitty hole of yours?' yelled Fat Diamond.

Leon turned to face him.

'I've a good mind to smash that fat fucking face of yours in the bog,' snarled Leon.

'Yeah, come and do it then.'

A small group formed around Fat Diamond, and Ewan, seeing it from his room, sauntered out. He sighed. Leon took a step towards the group as Ewan walked through it.

'What are you doing, Leon? Don't let this scum get to you.'

'Who are you calling scum, Galbreith? The only scum in this place is you.'

Ewan ignored them and met Leon's eyes.

'It's three weeks before your appeal. Don't mess it up. Don't let them rankle you.'

Leon cracked his knuckles and took a step back.

'Do you need a hand?' Ewan asked, nodding at the shitty showers.

'Nah,' said Leon. 'Thanks, mate.'

'Aw, ain't that sweet,' mocked Fat Diamond.

The men laughed.

'Why don't you two lovebirds have some fun while we watch?'

Ewan felt something snap inside him. The bastard had been tormenting Leon for weeks and everyone let him get away with it.

'Ewan,' warned Leon, but it was too late.

Ewan already had Fat Diamond by the throat. The other men moved forward but Leon's stare held them back.

'You shut that filthy mouth of yours once and for all or I'll have to ram your teeth down your throat so you won't be able to talk,' Ewan snarled.

Fat Diamond struggled to free himself, but Ewan Galbreith was strong and determined. Fat Diamond lifted his knee and rammed it hard into Galbreith's groin. The men cheered as Ewan groaned and staggered back.

'Ewan,' said Leon, stepping forward.

'Stay out of it,' snapped Ewan.

'Fucking shirt-lifter,' said Fat Diamond with a laugh. 'You ain't got a shotgun now, so what you going to do?'

He laughed again and turned to the group surrounding them. They laughed with him, but no one came forward.

'I'm going to ram that head of yours in the shit you threw in the shower,' said Ewan, grabbing Fat Diamond around the throat with one hand and his groin with the other. Fat Diamond fought for release, but he was too unfit for Ewan. He called to the men around him, but they just stared, too afraid to take on Ewan and Leon. Fat Diamond was dragged into the shower. Leon walked out and closed the door behind him, moving quietly on to the next shower.

The men waited until Leon was out of the way before opening the door. Fat Diamond was squirming under Ewan's grip. Ewan wrinkled his nose and pushed Fat Diamond's face into the faeces, feeling him retch.

'Don't make a bigger mess you fat pussy. It's you that's going to clear it up.'

The men laughed and releasing Diamond roughly, Ewan turned to face them.

'Anyone else?' he asked.

The men backed away, disgusted at Fat Diamond's sobs.

'You'd better clean this up,' barked Ewan, throwing him a mop. He turned to leave the shower as the prison wardens barged in. Ewan sighed and held up his hands.

'Didn't you have an appeal coming up?' The warden smiled.

'Fuck you,' said Ewan.

Leon, watching from the doors of the shower, gave Ewan the thumbs up and Ewan smiled.

'I owe you one,' said Leon.

CHAPTER THIRTY-SIX

Libby

F ran had phoned to say that my laptop was with an IT
expert but that she didn't hold out much hope of them
being able to restore it. I'll need to buy a new one. I've already
bought a new phone. What else can he destroy? *Your life*,
whispers a voice in my head. I fight the urge to drink some wine.
Simon will be here soon. I don't want him smelling alcohol on
my breath. The last thing I feel like is food. Ewan has ruined my
appetite even though Donna had got half of my contracts back.
But only half, which means Ewan has won.

'We're on our way back from London,' Fran had said on the
phone.

'You saw him?'

'Yes, he denies contacting you. His words were he wouldn't
touch you with a bargepole.'

'You believe him?'

'My colleague does. I'm not so sure. Have you got your
bodyguard?'

'Why? Do you think I need one?' I ask anxiously.

'I never said that, Libby.'

'Yes, I have.'

'Good.'

I don't mention that I'd cancelled him tonight. I'll be perfectly safe with Simon. Ewan wouldn't dare approach us. He won't want witnesses. The buzzer sounds, making me jump. I push the intercom.

'Yes.'

'Mr Wane is here.'

'Thank you. I'll come down.'

I slip my wrap around my shoulders and pick up my bag. I need to pull myself together. Simon is waiting in the foyer and smiles on seeing me.

'You look nice,' he says.

'Thank you.'

'I've got a cab waiting.'

'Donna said you've been having a bit of trouble,' he says as we drive off.

'I've hired a personal bodyguard.'

He looks out of the cab's rear window.

'Not tonight.' I smile. 'Where's the restaurant?' I ask, trying not to sound anxious.

'I've booked a Chinese restaurant in Stratford. It was recommended, and I tried it last week. It's very good.'

'Oh right,' I say.

'It's also safe.'

He senses my anxiety and I feel embarrassed.

'I'll protect you,' he says with a smile and something about his confidence reassures me. I turn to look at him. His blue eyes meet mine.

'Where in Yorkshire are you from?' I ask.

'Ripon,' he says without hesitation.

I nod. The cab stops outside a restaurant. It looks tacky and cheap. It's the last place I want to have dinner, but I don't want to seem a snob.

'I hope this is okay,' Simon says. 'The food is really good.'

'It's great,' I lie.

The waiter takes my wrap and I place my handbag on the chair next to me. I can see the rape alarm at the top of the bag and feel strangely comforted. The waiter gives us menus and takes our drinks order. I ask for a large white wine.

'The duck here is very good, if you fancy sharing a starter?' says Simon.

'Sounds great.'

I choose a chow mein dish for the main course and force myself to relax. Simon said he would protect me and I believe him. The wine arrives, and I take a large gulp. Simon sits back in his chair.

'Has he bothered you again?' he asks. His body is relaxed while mine is like a tightly wound spring.

'Yes... I... I don't want to bore you.'

I brush my hair from my face and feel his eyes on me. His stare makes me uncomfortable, but I don't know why.

'Where did you say you lived?' I ask.

I don't know what's happening to me. I'm suspicious of everyone and everything. He laughs but his eyes are serious.

'I hope you will be able to relax with me, Libby,' he says.

I feel myself blush.

'I'm sorry,' I say.

'I have a flat in Knightsbridge, not far from Harrods.'

The waiter brings the duck and the sight of it restores my dwindling appetite.

'I have a house in Padley, Cornwall,' I say, picking up my wine glass and realising I've already drained it.

'I'll order another,' he says, finishing his beer.

'The house where the murder happened?' he asks after ordering our drinks.

I nod. The waiter brings the wine and I sip at it. I'm drinking it way too fast and my head is already fuzzy.

'I'm thinking of selling it.'

He sits forward, his eyes glistening with interest.

'It's been empty for fifteen years. The gardens will be overgrown and the house in a terrible state...' I trail off.

'I could look it over for you,' he says. 'I know about property. I can tell you what it's worth in its present condition.'

'I don't know,' I say doubtfully.

The thought of going back to Manstead cripples me, especially now that Ewan is out.

'It needs clearing. I just don't think...'

'With someone to help you wouldn't it be easier?'

'I...'

'I'm happy to help, just let me know.'

I play with my duck before saying, 'I was planning on visiting William and Caroline at the weekend. I didn't want to go to the house, but...'

'William and Caroline?' he questions.

'William is my lawyer. He and his wife Caroline took me in after the murders.'

He nods.

'I could have a look at the house and advise you,' he suggests.

I chew my lip. The thought of going back to Manstead makes my stomach churn. It would be easier though, going with someone else. The ghosts might not be so terrifying if I'm not alone. But there's Ewan... Still, if he's in London maybe this is the best time to go back to Manstead.

'The thing is...'

'I'll be with you,' he says reassuringly as though reading my mind. 'You can take your bodyguard too if that helps.'

I smile.

'Ewan is an extremely capable person. He fears nothing and is a skilled marksman with a gun. He's not a fool.'

'Then he isn't going to come after you in broad daylight at the house where the murder happened, especially if you're with someone.'

I nod. He's quite right and I've got to go back sometime. I can't put it off forever. 'Okay, if you're sure?'

Our main meals arrive, and he settles back in his seat.

'I'd love to come. It's the perfect weather for a day at the seaside.'

——————

By the time we arrive back at the flat I'm quite tipsy.

'I'll see you to your door,' Simon says.

'Won't you come up for a coffee,' I say.

He hesitates.

'If you're sure? I wouldn't mind using your loo.'

'Of course,' I say, walking ahead.

It's a different concierge and my heart beats a little faster. I've not seen him before.

'Good evening, madam.' He smiles.

'I thought Ian would be on this evening,' I say cautiously.

'He's off sick, madam.'

'He seemed fine this morning,' I say.

'I wouldn't know about that, madam.'

'Good evening, Lee,' says Simon, noting the name badge on Lee's lapel.

'Good evening, sir.'

Simon pushes the lift button and then we're on our way up.

'I was expecting Ian,' I say, realising I sound paranoid.

'I expect he needs a break.' Simon smiles.

'If it's not Ian then it's...'

I realise I don't know the name of the other concierge.

'Bernie,' says Simon.

'Bernie?' I repeat in a shaky voice.

'That's the name of the other concierge.'

'Oh, is it?'

'Ian told me.'

Simon smiles and walks to my door. I fumble for the keys, pulling out the rape alarm as I do so.

Simon raises his eyebrows.

'I always carry it,' I say.

He nods. God, he must think I'm such a neurotic. Last time a knife fell out of my bag.

'Let me,' he says taking the keys. 'Sorry to be in a rush,' he smiles, 'but I badly need your loo.'

'I'll need to turn off the alarm,' I say quickly.

He waits while I punch in the numbers and then rushes to the bathroom. I close the door and lean against it feeling relieved to be back in the safety of my own flat.

CHAPTER THIRTY-SEVEN

FIFTEEN YEARS EARLIER

Ewan frowned as he watched Ben's truck speed down the driveway. He strolled back to the house and entered through the back door. Molly looked up from the pastry she was making.

'Ewan,' she acknowledged. 'Was that you shooting?'

He looked at his arm.

'It's the hunt from Widcombe, come for their annual pheasant shoot.'

'No one told me. I haven't prepared refreshments,' she said worriedly.

'Don't look so panic-stricken.' He smiled. 'Edward's taking them out for lunch.'

She let out a sigh of relief.

'Is he in the morning room?' Ewan asked.

She nodded and pulled a tray of mince pies from the oven. He whistled in appreciation and reached out for one.

'No way, Ewan Galbreith,' she reprimanded, but he already had one in his hand.

'Serve you right if you burn your mouth.'

He blew her a kiss and walked out of the kitchen to the morning room. He knocked on the door and waited.

'Come in,' Edward barked.

Edward was sitting on the couch, a pile of papers on his lap.

'Bloody paperwork. How's the horse?'

'I've called the vet,' said Ewan, stuffing the last of the pie into his mouth.

Edward sighed.

'The man's a rip-off merchant.'

'He's good at his job,' said Ewan.

'Princess is an old horse.'

'She's not finished yet,' Ewan disagreed.

Edward got up and poured himself a brandy. He nodded to the bottle.

'How's the arm?'

'Not great.'

'I guess this will help then. You might as well. You help yourself to everything else,' Edward said as he handed a glass of brandy to Ewan. 'So, what's the problem?'

'I saw Ben Mitchell leaving here. I figured he came to ask you for money.'

Edward nodded and sat behind the desk. 'You used our gun to shoot his boat.'

Ewan looked down at his glass.

'Are you going to deny it?'

'No.'

'So,' said Edward sitting back in his chair. 'If he decided to press charges, then it would come out that you used my gun irresponsibly. I'd have to let you go and... well, it then gets messy. It was only two hundred. The bugger no doubt deserved what you did but I wish you'd use a little self-control sometimes.'

Ewan finished the brandy, turned to leave and then hesitated.

'Something else?' Edward asked.

'It's Libby.'

'What about her?'

'There are some gypsies in town. They've not caused any trouble. I just think she's going to get herself in hot water.'

Edward sighed.

'She's taken with one of them. Patrick is his name. He's got three kids. No money. He's from Australia.'

'That's just perfect,' said Edward.

'She's lonely, you know that. She'd be out with our crowd if she could...'

'God forbid.'

Ewan gave a scornful laugh. 'She'd be a lot safer than with those gypsies.'

'A bloody job is what she needs,' Edward said, checking his watch. 'I've got that shooting party to take to lunch. I need your advice on something. Pop back and see me tonight. I will want an update on Princess too.'

'Sure, and thanks.'

'I didn't have a lot of choice did I, Ewan? It's a good job I think you're worth it.'

Ewan smiled and closed the door.

CHAPTER THIRTY-EIGHT

PRESENT DAY

Libby

I click on the air conditioning and pull off my wrap. I can hear Simon running the tap in the bathroom. The phone bleeps again and I take it from my bag. My heart skips when I see it is a text from an unknown number. It's a photo. I can barely look at it. But it's innocent enough. I'm expecting something gruesome, but it isn't, and it takes me several seconds to realise what I'm looking at. It's a picture of the lilies in their box. I click into the second message.

> Did you like my flowers?

'I'll put the kettle on, shall I?' Simon says as he comes out of the bathroom.

'What?' I say distractedly.

'Shall I make the coffee?'

'Oh, yes, if you don't mind.'

'Sure, do you want one?'

I hear him bustling around in the kitchen. My phone bleeps again. Simon didn't send the flowers, so who did?

'I didn't add sugar,' says Simon, wandering in with the coffees.

'You didn't send the flowers?' I ask.

He looks baffled and then follows my eyes to the lilies.

'I...' He looks embarrassed. 'No, I'm sorry I didn't.'

I fall onto the couch and hand my phone to him.

'I thought it had to be you. I don't know anyone else that would send me flowers. It was Ewan then, he did it.'

He takes my phone.

'There's another text on here,' he says.

'From him?'

'It's a Goodreads recommendation.'

I stare at him.

'A Goodreads recommendation?' I repeat.

He hands me the phone and I click into the link. My ears buzz when the book cover pops up onto the screen. A blonde curvaceous woman wearing a long red chiffon dress stares back at me and my breathing quickens as I recall the book.

I don't need to read the book title. I know it well enough. '*Lay Her Among The Lilies*,' I whisper.

It was one of Uncle Edward's favourites. The book had been found on the floor the night of the murder. It had been splattered with his blood. It had been evidence, shown to the jury. Is that what Ewan has planned for me? Laying me among the blood and lilies? I shudder.

Simon takes the phone from me and calls the unknown number. He puts it onto speakerphone and an automated voice tells me the number is not recognised. I want to scream in frustration.

'How did he get my number? It's a new phone,' I say, struggling to breathe.

'Did you load the backup from your old phone?'

'Yes,' I mutter.

'I don't know, but if you had a virus on the old phone then it may have been transferred onto this one.'

'I need to phone Fran,' I say.

'It's midnight,' he says softly.

I take my phone from him and check the time. How did it get to be so late? I jump up and pull the flowers from the vases.

'He's trying to frighten you,' he says.

'He's succeeding,' I say, tears pricking my eyelids.

'Let me take these,' he says, carefully removing the flowers from my hands. 'I ought to be going. I'll throw them away on my way out.'

'Thank you,' I say, trying to control the anger that is shaking my whole body. He taps me on the shoulder and I turn to face him. I wait for his kiss, but it doesn't come.

'I'll phone you. Let me know if you change your number in the meantime. I've got a lot of meetings this week so it may not be until the weekend,' he says apologetically.

'That's okay,' I say, feeling shaken and lost.

'I'll pick you up Saturday, say about ten? We can have a leisurely drive to Cornwall.'

'Oh yes,' I say, forgetting that I had agreed he could come. I close the door after him and secure the locks before falling onto the couch and bursting into tears.

CHAPTER THIRTY-NINE

FIFTEEN YEARS EARLIER

The Bible felt cool in her hands. Its leather worn and faded. She wondered how many other people had sworn on this bible, to tell the truth, the whole truth and nothing but the truth. She looked at the barrister and then back at the bible. The lights in the courtroom were too bright. They were giving her a headache.

'Could I have some water please?' she asked.

The barrister looked at the judge. He must have nodded because someone brought a glass of water. She took it and then the bible was pushed into her hands again.

'You need to swear,' the barrister said softly.

He was a nice man with a soft voice, but she couldn't remember his name. The other one wasn't so gentle. He was aggressive with her, nasty. She suspected that it was him that had given her the headache.

'Please state your full name for the court.'

'Elisabeth Jane Owen.'

'Miss Owen, can you tell us in your own words what happened on the night that your aunt and uncle died?'

She could feel Ewan's eyes boring through her. Always she

could feel those eyes. Her shoulders ached where she had hunched them and her neck felt stiff. She forced herself to glance his way. Her eyes met his. He was staring straight at her. His body tense. His usual handsome features were not smiling at her. His eyes were hard, his mouth set in a firm line. He was frowning, waiting to hear what she had to say.

She took a deep breath and started to speak but the words caught in her throat and she coughed. Someone handed her a glass of water. She thought she heard someone on the jury sigh.

'You went to a party that night, didn't you?'

'Yes...' She faltered. 'Yes, I went to Laura's. She's my friend. It was at her house.'

'Where was that?'

'Baywater Heights.'

'That's close to the beachfront isn't it?'

Libby nodded.

'Could you answer the question please, Miss Owen.'

'Yes,' she said.

'Do you remember what time you left the party?'

Libby shrugged.

'Not exactly, but it was after midnight because we'd celebrated the millennium.'

'Did your aunt and uncle go out that evening?'

'No, they were going to have a dinner party but my aunt had a migraine so they cancelled it.'

'So the staff at Manstead Manor would have known they hadn't gone out?'

'Objection. That's a leading question, Your Honour.'

'Please rephrase the question, Mr Fosh.'

'Did any of the staff work that evening?'

'Yes, there was a lot of clearing up to do. Aunty Rose had ordered all the food. Molly had to wrap it all and freeze it and...'

'Did you see Mr Galbreith before the shootings, earlier in the evening, for instance?'

'Yes, I went to see the horses before I went out. He was with them in the stables.'

'Roughly what time was that?'

'About seven thirty, I think. I don't remember. I was meeting Laura at eight. We were going to a pub in Exeter and then back to hers for the party.'

'Was there a problem with one of the horses?'

Libby nodded, and tears sprang to her eyes.

'Princess was sick. She'd not been well for a while, since before Christmas.'

'I see. And were you upset about it?'

'Yes, and so was Ewan. He loved Princess.'

'Had the vet been?'

'Ewan said he was coming later.'

'Did Mr Galbreith at any time mention having the horse put down?'

'Oh yes,' she said emphatically. 'That was why the vet was coming back.'

'Did you agree with that?'

'Yes, I did,' she said, looking at Ewan. 'Ewan knew horses.'

'Did the vet come?'

'I didn't see him. I went out after that.'

'Thank you, Miss Owen.'

Libby felt her legs give way. She didn't want to think about that night. She didn't want to think about Princess and what happened to her. Ewan must have been out of his mind.

CHAPTER FORTY

Libby

I wake in a sweat and throw the duvet off me. It's just starting to get light. I fumble for my phone to see what time it is and then remember I had switched it off. I'm afraid to turn it on in case there is another message from Ewan. I consider calling Fran to tell her about the lilies but decide against it. What would be the point? She'll only ask if I can prove it is Ewan. I lean over for my wrap and slide out of bed.

I scoop Merlin into my arms and take him back to bed where I pull the duvet over us. I then pull my new laptop towards me and turn it on. Using the landline, I call the security company's number and book the bodyguard for the rest of the week.

'He's already at your building, Miss Warren,' says the efficient receptionist.

There are no suspicious emails. I let out a sigh of relief and click into my graphics folder on the Cloud. I won't think about Ewan Galbreith. I need to get the first draft of my graphics concept ready for Anna. I promised to have them ready by tomorrow. I flip back into my emails and check the diary. Damn it, I'd forgotten that the Swift Corporation's opening party was tomorrow. I'd meant to ask Simon if he'd like to come. I glance nervously at my phone. What if Simon was right and there had been a virus on the phone? What if Ewan was tracking my location from my phone, or even, watching me through the camera? I grow hot. God, is he is watching me now? Did he see me crying last night? Has he seen me undress? I throw the phone down as if it was a hot coal. Fuck! I can't be without a phone. I'll have to buy another one, but this time I won't restore my backup. I won't phone Fran. I won't contact the police either. I'll track Ewan down myself. I'll find a private investigator. They will be able to tell me where Ewan is. I have every right to know. How dare the police keep that from me? A quick search on Google brings up several private investigators in London. I call one from the landline and make an appointment for this afternoon.

'Work,' I say, picking up Merlin. 'I've got a few hours before lunch.'

———

Jimmy, the bodyguard is waiting in his car. I ask him to take me to the sushi bar where I am meeting Donna for lunch. Several people brush by me on the street. I look across the road to the bus stop where a man waits. He's reading a newspaper. I study him for a second and then get into the car. I'm taking no chances now. I have the kitchen knife in my handbag along with the rape alarm, and a pepper spray. If I have to finish off Ewan Galbreith before he does me then that's exactly what I intend to do. He ruined my life. Took my future away from me and now he wants revenge. I had no choice but to put him away. I couldn't let him get away with what he did. Ewan Galbreith threatened me.

Ewan Galbreith carries out his threats. I thought Fran Marshall knew that.

Donna smiles at the sight of me. I'd made an effort. Her expression changes however when she sees Jimmy.

'Do you really think that's necessary?' she asks, glancing at him.

'It's the only way I feel safe,' I reply.

Jimmy seems inconspicuous in the corner of the restaurant, but I know he is watching everyone. I feel more relaxed knowing he is with me.

'It's no life, Libby.'

I glare at her.

'Do you think I want this?'

'Of course not,' she says, taken aback.

'I'm sorry,' I say. 'My nerves are ragged. Let's eat.'

She nods, and we choose our dishes. I ask the waitress to take something over to Jimmy and then sit back in my seat to enjoy lunch.

'Thanks for all you did, Donna,' I say gratefully. 'I thought I was going to lose everything.'

'Don't be silly. I only told them the truth.'

I sigh. 'It's just a shame they have to know.'

'It's not a shame, Libby.'

I smile gratefully.

'So what are the police doing about all this?'

I shrug. 'I don't think there is much they can do. They don't seem to believe it is Ewan. Or at least they don't want to confront him unless they have a hundred per cent proof. So, I've decided not to tell them anything that happens now. He's managed to get my new phone number and I think he's put a virus on it. He sent me flowers too. I thought they were from Simon, but I now know they weren't. I'm going to get my own investigator. I want to see what Ewan looks like now and where he is.'

Donna puts down her fork, a concerned look on her face.

'Is that a wise move, Libby? He shot your family. Surely you should keep the police updated.'

'What's the point? They don't do anything. He's one step ahead of me all the time. I want that to stop, Donna. I need to be one step ahead of him.'

'Perhaps he'll get fed up.' Donna smiled, her tone hopeful.

I reach a hand across to hers.

'Ewan doesn't give up. Don't worry. Now I've made the decision to be more in control I feel much better.'

My trembling hand belies my words.

'Please be careful,' Donna warns.

'I will. I'm going to Cornwall at the weekend. I've decided to sell the house. Get shot of it. Simon has offered to come with me.'

'Oh good,' she says, her face brightening. 'You'll feel safe with him, won't you?'

'Yes.' I smile.

If only things were that simple.

————

I hand over the photo of Ewan. It's an old photo. It was the one the newspapers used when Ewan was arrested.

'Ah, I think I remember this case,' says the investigator.

He's short and fat, a perfect specimen of someone who eats too much and never exercises. He introduces himself as 'Raymond Little, but call me Ray.' I have no intention of calling him Ray.

'He's recently been released,' I say. 'It was my aunt and uncle that he shot.'

Raymond Little raises his eyebrows ever so slightly.

'Ah,' he says.

'He threatened me as he was taken down. He said he would get me. I've had threatening text messages with photos of my dead aunt, and my computer was hacked. He says he is watching me.'

Raymond Little opened a paper bag and pulled a ham and tomato sandwich from it.

'Do you mind? I've not had lunch.'

I shake my head.

'Thing is,' he says through a mouthful of ham. 'If it's a bodyguard you need then it's the police you should be talking to.'

'I have my own bodyguard. What I want to know is where Ewan Galbreith lives in London or if he's living in Padley. Where he works and how often he comes near my flat.'

Raymond Little wipes his hands on a soiled tissue.

'That doesn't sound like a difficult job. How often would you like a report?'

'Whenever you have something to tell me.'

He grins.

'Well, the costs...'

'Money isn't an issue.'

He pushes a toothpick into his mouth.

'I'll just need a few particulars. What prison he was in, when he came out, family names, that kind of thing.'

'I can give you those.'

'That's great. I'll get on it ASAP.' He holds out a greasy hand to me. I ignore it and stand up.

'I look forward to hearing from you,' I say and walk to the door.

I take a deep breath and step out into the summer heat. I finally feel back in control and decide to do some shopping.

CHAPTER FORTY-ONE

FIFTEEN YEARS EARLIER

L ibby and Laura giggled as they walked around Ann Summers. The shop had only recently opened in Exeter and Libby couldn't wait to see it. She considered buying a few things, but she couldn't very well do so while Laura was with her. How would she explain why she needed them?

Libby hadn't told anyone about Patrick. She was too afraid the word would get back to her uncle and then that would be it.

'Ooh look at these,' said Laura, pointing to the vibrators.

'Have you done it yet?' Libby asked.

'Not all the way,' admitted Laura. 'What about you?'

Libby nodded.

'You haven't,' gasped Laura. 'Oh my God, who with?'

'I'm not going to tell you.'

'Why not? I won't tell anyone.'

'But what if you do and then they tell someone else. It will get back to Uncle Edward and then I'll be in big trouble.'

Laura tucked her arm into Libby's.

'Is it Ewan? God, you lucky cow if it is.'

Libby sighed.

'No.'

'Let's get a milkshake.' Laura grinned. 'I'll get it out of you.'

They walked from Ann Summers towards the milkshake shop when Laura squeezed Libby's arm.

'Guess who just passed us,' she whispered.

'Who?' asked Libby looking behind her.

'Molly, your housekeeper, she's just gone into Ann Summers.'

They both giggled and backtracked to see what Molly was looking at.

'The vibrators,' whispered Libby.

'She's got Aunty Rose's handbag,' said Libby, surprised.

'No way!'

Molly spotted them and hurried from the shop.

'I needed a birthday card for a friend,' said Molly.

'Isn't that Aunty Rose's bag?' asked Libby.

Molly's face coloured.

'She said I could borrow it.'

'Oh,' said Libby, disbelieving.

Aunty Rose would never let Libby borrow the Gucci handbag.

'I'd better hurry. I'll miss my bus,' said Molly.

'Bye,' said Laura.

They watched Molly hurry away.

'I bet her boyfriend is good at it. Have you seen him?' said Laura. 'He's a knockout. Come on, you've got to tell me who you did it with and what it was like.'

Libby decided she would tell what it was like but not who with.

———

Patrick drained the last of his beer and considered whether there was time for another. He ought to get back. Lil would be creating. When didn't she create? He stumbled to the pub door and pulled it open. The cold air knocked him back and it took him a few seconds to steady himself.

He walked along the promenade, the wind cutting through him. It'd be bloody cold in the caravan, he thought and hoped Lil had the heaters on. They'd have to move on soon. He'd heard there had been complaints. There were always complaints. They'd have a few more weeks. It always takes forever before the law pushes them on. He needed to get a bit of work soon too. Money was tight. Still, if he played his cards right, there would be money. Libby Owen was a soft touch with a rich uncle. He wouldn't miss a few thousand. It was timing it right. He also didn't fancy going up to that big house. They most likely had vicious dogs. He didn't want his leg chewed off. He needed to think this through. Plan it. Maybe he'd do that tomorrow.

It was a fair walk to the caravan and he wished he'd jumped on the bus. His hands were numb and the cosy feeling the beer had given him had been blown away by the cold harsh wind. He bloody hated it by the sea. He'd only come here for Lil. Still, it had been a good move by all accounts. He just had to play his cards right. He climbed the gate leading to the field and saw the caravans ahead. He was so focused on getting into the warm that he didn't see the shadowy figure by the fence.

'Patrick?' the man questioned, stepping in front of him.

Patrick thought he was vaguely familiar.

'Yeah,' he said suspiciously.

The man smiled and Patrick remembered. He was the gamekeeper at Manstead Manor. He'd won the darts championship. He'd watched that night. He'd mentioned it to Libby and she had been proud when telling him that Ewan was her uncle's gamekeeper.

'Can I have a word?' asked Ewan.

'It's fucking freezing,' said Patrick. 'How long will it take?'

'That's up to you,' said Ewan.

He couldn't have been waiting long, Patrick thought. He didn't look in the least cold. His arm was in plaster. Patrick couldn't help wondering how Ewan had done that. For a moment he felt scared but only for a moment.

'What's this about?' asked Patrick.

They weren't on Owen's land, he was sure of that. There could be only one reason why Owen's gamekeeper wanted a word and that reason was Libby.

'Edward Owen isn't happy about your relationship with his niece.'

Patrick smirked.

'Is that right?'

Patrick's drunken brain wouldn't let him think clearly. All he could think was maybe this was his chance. Perhaps he wouldn't need to get his leg chewed off by some fucking wild dog. He'd just tell Ewan what he wanted and he could pass it on.

'That's right,' said Ewan softly. 'Edward Owen has other ideas for his niece. You know the sort, a decent, hard-working type of guy.'

Patrick scoffed.

'Are you saying I'm riff-raff?'

'I'm saying it as it is.'

He's calm, thought Patrick. What he doesn't realise is that I only have to call and he'd be surrounded by more so-called riff-raff.

'Libby and I love each other,' said Patrick.

Ewan laughed.

'That's funny,' he said. 'Don't you have a wife and three

kids? Or have you forgotten about them? Mr Owen doesn't want you seeing Libby again.'

'That's tough, because I will be.'

Ewan was so quick that Patrick didn't have time to take a step backwards. He hadn't even seen the shotgun. But he saw it now all right. It was aimed at his groin.

'Jesus fucking Christ,' he groaned. 'What are you going to do?'

'Nothing,' said Ewan calmly.

'I've got kids.' Patrick trembled.

'You've remembered them now have you?'

'Is that thing loaded?' asked Patrick, quivering now.

'It may be.' Ewan grinned. 'You'll just have to keep guessing won't you? What you do know though, is that Libby's only seventeen. She's just a kid and you're taking advantage of her. No one would care if I ended your sex life, right here, right now.'

'I... I... she told me she was nineteen,' lied Patrick.

'I don't believe you,' said Ewan, moving the gun.

'All right, all right,' Patrick yelled. 'I knew her age.'

Patrick struggled to breathe. He hated himself for being so scared. He'd yell for help, but no one would come once they saw the shotgun.

'You're on private property. You need to move out, right out of Cornwall,' Ewan said. 'You understand what I'm saying.'

Patrick figured he had nothing to lose. This was a hundred times worse than a vicious dog. If he was going to ask, it might as well be now.

'I don't have any money. Not enough for diesel even. I'll need a couple of thousand if I'm to get off the land. Can't Owen help me out a bit?'

He heard Ewan sigh.

'Edward Owen's not a charity.'

'I'm not joking. I don't have any money. I spent the last tonight in the pub.'

'That was responsible,' said Ewan cynically.

'Just a few hundred then, to help a bloke out, just so I can get myself sorted. I'll go back to Oz.'

Ewan gave him a shove. Patrick tried to stay upright but the beer running through his veins coupled with his jelly legs made it impossible and he fell onto the muddy ground.

'I'll ask for you,' said Ewan.

Patrick waited for the kicking in the ribs, but it never came. There was no crack from the gun There was just silence and he realised Ewan Galbreith had gone. He staggered to the caravan, his eyes darting all over the place. Jesus, he never expected someone to come at him with a shotgun. Libby was a dangerous person to hang around with. That Edward Owen thought he was something, intimidating innocent men like that. He flung open the door of the caravan, the smell of baby vomit hitting his nostrils. The place always seemed to smell of sick and sweat. He wished Lil would clean up sometimes. God knows she didn't have to do it every day. He couldn't honestly think what she did all day long.

She gets up from the couch, the baby still stuck to her nipple.

'Where the fuck have you been?' she drawled.

The floor was littered with fish and chip wrapping paper and empty beer cans. He wasn't going to tell her that some Scottish bastard had threatened to shoot his cock off because he'd been dipping it well above his station.

'Why don't you clean up?' he said instead.

'Why don't you get a job?' she countered.

He dropped his trembling body onto a torn couch, a baby's rattle stuck into his arse and he cursed.

'I've got some money coming soon. We can move on then.'

She looked at him suspiciously.

'Money coming from where?' she asked.

'Does it matter?'

She shrugged.

'You'll come a cropper one day.'

CHAPTER FORTY-TWO

Libby

The guy in the iPhone store is doing his best to be useful but I can tell he thinks I am an overanxious, paranoid female.

'You can track with Google map tracker, or the friend tracker, on your iPhone. Of course, your boyfriend needs to have an iPhone too for the friend tracker. We have a special on today – buy one and get the other for half price. I can go over the app with you.'

'No, thank you anyway. But supposing my boyfriend is the computer hacker type and he deliberately puts a virus onto my phone, through my laptop. If I change the SIM will the virus carry over?'

He gives a thoughtful 'Hmm,' and then says, 'Why would he want to do that?'

I smile.

'I suppose if that happens you'd be best to get another phone and enter everything manually.'

'Right,' I say.

This is getting ridiculous.

'I need a phone then,' I say.

I spend the evening entering my contacts and anything else I need on my phone. It's time-consuming and irritating and I curse Ewan the whole time. The highlight of the evening was Little's phone call on the landline.

'He's living in Forest Gate,' he said. 'I'm emailing the report over to you now.'

'No, don't email it,' I said. 'I want everything sent by post.'

'That's a bit outdated,' he said.

'Well, that's how I want it. No emails. Texts are okay and if you can't manage that then maybe I need to hire someone else.'

'Whoa, hold your horses. I can do it. It'll take longer, that's all.'

'I don't mind that.'

I'm not taking any risks. I don't want Ewan knowing I'm onto him.

'Forest Gate,' I said. 'Are you sure it's him? I was expecting him to be in West London.'

'It's all London. You can check for yourself,' said Little, clearly affronted. 'But if you don't want to go to his place in Forest Gate then you can always clock him at Heaven Scent, the nightclub. He works there. He does all kinds of odd jobs. He's on the door on a Tuesday and a Friday night. It's in Stratford.'

I can imagine Ewan as a nightclub bouncer. He'd be able to throw his weight around to his heart's content. It also means that he'll be mixing with people who can get hold of guns.

Swift's new development party is this evening. They'd liked my graphics. I ought to go, to be seen as a team player, especially after Ewan hacked my account and sent that dreadful email. It's going to be uncomfortable meeting the people who saw that email and that gruesome photo, but I can't let Anna down. I'll go to Stratford afterwards. I don't want to wait. It's

Tuesday and I want to see what Ewan now looks like. I can dress down before I leave. I pull a pair of jeans and a thin beige blouse from the wardrobe and fold them neatly into an overnight bag along with my cleanser and some cotton wool. I don't want to go to Stratford with my make-up on and wearing a cocktail dress. I stare at the blouse and then pull it out of the bag. It doesn't do me justice. This is ridiculous. I don't want Ewan to see me. But part of me wants to look good just in case he does. I take a more flattering blouse from the wardrobe and fold it into the bag.

I look at my phone to see if Simon has answered my text. It would be so much nicer having company at the party this evening and I'd feel so much more confident going to Heaven Scent, if he were with me, but there's nothing. I sigh and go into the bathroom with Merlin at my heels. I'll have a long relaxing soak and then I'll get ready. It most likely isn't Ewan at all and all this anxiety will have been for nothing.

I'm about to climb into the tub when my phone bleeps. I grab it hopefully. It's a text from Simon.

> That would have been great. Sadly I'm out for dinner with a client in Henley. I'm looking forward to Saturday though.

I step into the bath as disappointment washes over me. Merlin meows and I lean over to pet him.

'I wish I could take you, sweetie,' I say, hugging Merlin close. But I'll have Jimmy and that's more than enough. The warmth from the bath relaxes me and I push Ewan from my mind and think about the graphics I had done for the new complex. It would be good to discuss them tonight. There's no reason why I can't have a good time.

———

The party is in the penthouse suite. I check my hair in the lift mirror as it travels up to the suite. The doors open, and I step out where champagne is flowing and people are talking loudly. I look for a familiar face but don't see one. Jimmy blends into the background and I'm left alone.

'Madam,' says a voice.

I turn to a waiter carrying a tray of hors d'oeuvres.

'No, thank you,' I say, nausea rising in me at the sight of them.

I see another with a tray of drinks and walk towards him.

'Wine, madam?' he asks on seeing me. I nod and take a white wine from the tray. There are so many people. The smell of expensive perfume permeates the room. The women are wearing designer dresses and expensive jewellery.

'Hello.'

I turn to the voice. He's young. No older than twenty. I suddenly feel very old.

'Hello.' I smile.

'Adrian Swift,' he says offering his hand. 'My dad's the founder.'

'Yes, I know. I'm Libby Warren. I designed the graphics for the new project.'

'Ah,' he says, looking at me curiously. He knows about the email. I feel myself blush and want the floor to open up and swallow me.

'Have you seen Anna?' I ask.

'Your graphics are brilliant.' He smiles.

'Thank you.'

'Anna's over there,' he says, clearly sensing my discomfort.

I follow his eyes and see Anna, dressed in a flowing blue chiffon dress talking to a well-built man in a tuxedo.

'Shall we go over?' says Adrian.

I nod and follow him. Anna's eyes light up and she nods at me.

'Oh great, I'd been looking out for you. When did you arrive?'

'Not long ago.'

'You've met Adrian?'

'Yes,' I say, nodding at him.

He looks down at my glass.

'You're empty. Let me get you another one.'

I hadn't even remembered drinking the wine.

'Libby,' says Anna, 'this is Clive Swift, the founder. This is Libby Warren who did those fabulous graphics for us.'

He smiles, there's no curiosity in his eyes. But he must have read the email. He's a stocky man with strong features.

'Very nice work,' he says. 'We're very glad to have you on board.'

'Thank you.'

Adrian returns with my drink. He's accompanied by a tall wiry man who looks at me suspiciously. I feel my neck muscles tighten.

'This is Carl Walters,' says Anna. 'He's the CEO.'

My face grows hot.

'This is Libby Warren.'

I hold my hand out nervously. There's a second before he accepts it.

'I'm so sorry about the email and the fact that your daughter saw it,' I say.

His face is impassive.

'It wasn't your fault, it seems. But it was unfortunate.'

He's judging me, and I hate him for it.

'Have you tried the crab?' Anna asks, lightening up the mood.

'No, I haven't.'

'You must, come on.'

I allow her to lead me away. My face is flushed. Everyone here is going to judge me and for that I hate Ewan Galbreith with all my being.

———

I make my escape at eleven. It's still early but I tell Anna I have a terrible migraine. She seems to believe me and offers to see me to my car. I have to explain who Jimmy is and she seems shocked.

'Have things got worse?' she asks.

'The police advised it,' I say.

'Thanks so much for coming. Your graphics are brilliant and I'm so looking forward to working with you in the coming months.'

She kisses me on the cheek and I climb into the car. I wait patiently until she disappears back into the building and then step inside the foyer again. In the downstairs toilet I remove my make-up and change into my jeans. I pull my hair out of its neat bun and brush my hair around my face. Jimmy doesn't bat an eyelid at the change in my appearance or at the fact that I ask him to take me to Heaven Scent in Stratford. As we travel through the London streets I check and double-check that the knife is in my handbag and that the rape alarm and spray are easy to grab. Heaven Scent is on the outskirts. Jimmy asks where I'd like him to park and I say opposite the entrance.

'Chances are we'll get moved on,' he says, parking the car where I can see the entrance to the club and the people queuing outside it. I put my face to the window and strain to see the bouncers at the doors. My mouth is dry and my hands are shaking. I feel sick and I wish my heart would stop racing so much. He can't hurt me. I'd like to think he won't recognise me but of course he will. He has that advantage over me. It's too difficult to see the men's faces even this close. I have no choice but to go nearer. I realise I'm perspiring and wipe the sweat from my forehead. I pull my denim jacket on and lift the collar.

'I'm getting out,' I say. 'Can you stay close?'

'It would be better to move the car somewhere else,' he suggests.

I nod and stay in the car while he drives it around the corner to a parking space. I get out and walk slowly back to the entrance with Jimmy behind me. I walk along the queue when someone yells at me.

'Hey you, no jumping the queue, missy.'

'Sorry,' I say quietly. 'I'm not going in. I'm just looking for someone.'

They give me disbelieving looks. I continue walking and then stop several feet from the men on the door. I pretend to look around as though I'm waiting for someone. After a while I feel confident to look up at the men. One of them is hidden in the shadows but the other I can see clearly. He's olive-skinned and of muscular build. Ewan was never that big. The girls in the queue are screeching loudly and it's difficult to hear the man's voice but finally I do.

'What's this?' he asks a girl, pulling something from her handbag.

'They're my 'eadache pills,' she says.

'You can't take them in.'

He has a cockney accent. It isn't Ewan.

I let out a little sigh and then the other man speaks and my legs give way.

'Oh,' I utter, feeling myself go.

'Shit,' says a girl in the queue, grabbing me. ''ave you taken something?'

I shake my head and take a step backwards. It's Ewan. I'd recognise that accent anywhere. My heart pounds in my chest and I take several deep breaths to calm it. I have to see him. I have to see what he looks like now.

CHAPTER FORTY-THREE

FIFTEEN YEARS EARLIER

'Have you ever seen Mr Galbreith lose his temper, Miss Owen?'

Libby shook her head.

'I need you to answer the question,' said the judge softly.

'No, I never saw him lose his temper.'

'But you did see him get beaten up in the barn by Mr Mitchell and his associates?'

'Yes.'

'Did he tell you that he wanted to get even with Mr Mitchell for that night?'

'No.'

'But you knew he took your uncle's firearms from the gun cabinet for reasons other than hunting?'

'I only thought he took them for hunting.'

'Didn't he threaten a friend of yours with one of your uncle's shotguns?'

Libby blushed but didn't reply.

'He threatened to shoot Patrick O'Leary in the genitals if he continued seeing you. Mr Galbreith claims this was on your uncle's orders. Did Patrick tell you about this?'

'Yes, he did.'

She looked at Patrick who was holding on tightly to Lil's hand. She wasn't at all what Libby had imagined. She was pretty and fresh-faced, not haggard and ugly like Patrick had said. He'd lied to her, but she still loved him. She wouldn't let him go to prison. She couldn't bear to think of a free spirit like him locked up.

'So, Mr Galbreith wasn't out hunting that day, was he?'

'No.'

'Was your uncle aware of Mr Galbreith's use of his guns?'

'Yes I think he was. He didn't seem to mind.'

'It seems his loyalty to Ewan Galbreith backfired on him, would you agree?'

The barrister defending Ewan jumped up.

'Objection. Your Honour, counsel is putting words into the witness's mouth.'

'Please rephrase the question.'

Libby's head spun. She didn't understand the courtroom jargon and never fully understood if it was her that had said something wrong.

'Miss Owen, what was your relationship with Patrick O'Leary?'

'We were friends.'

'Just friends?'

She nodded.

'Please answer the question.'

'Yes,' she said but her cheeks turned red.

'But your uncle didn't approve of this friendship clearly. Why would he send Ewan Galbreith to warn him off?'

'Uncle Edward didn't like gypsies.'

'Let's go back to the night of the murder, Miss Owen.'

'Objection. The question is suggesting the circumstances of the victims' death.'

'They were clearly murdered.' The barrister smiled.

'Counsel, would you rephrase your question please,' said the judge.

Libby's heart began to pound in her chest and she reached for her glass of water.

'So, on the night your aunt and uncle died, you left the party after midnight and walked back to Manstead Manor. Is that right, Miss Owen?'

'Yes.'

'Can you describe what happened when you got to the house? Take your time.'

Libby licked her lips and clenched the fingers of one hand in the other. She squeezed them tightly.

'I opened the front door and I heard music. My shoes had sand in them, so I took them off in the hallway and then walked through the hall to the morning room where the music was coming from.'

'Did you sense anything was wrong at this point?'

'I don't remember. Everything happened so quickly.'

'So you went into the morning room and then what happened?'

'I was about to open the door when I heard a shot and...'

Her legs gave way and she fell onto the bench behind her.

'Would you like a few minutes?' the judge asked quietly.

Ewan's eyes were boring into hers. He was sitting forward, the veins in his neck prominent as he strained to look at her. His lips were tight. He looked nothing like the Ewan she knew. His whole being was focused on her words and she was scared to utter more.

'I...'

The barrister looked over at Ewan and said, 'You're quite safe here. No one can hurt you.'

Tears fell unbidden from Libby's eyes and her hands began to shake.

'We'll take a short break and resume in thirty minutes. The court will rise,' said the judge.

Libby sighed with relief and saw Ewan crack his knuckles.

Libby stepped from the witness box. She had thirty minutes to recover and then she'd have to tell them.

CHAPTER FORTY-FOUR

FIFTEEN YEARS EARLIER

'I'm not giving that scum my money,' roared Edward.

Ewan looked to the door.

'Libby's in the kitchen,' he said quietly.

'I don't give a shit. Everyone wants a piece of me. I'm not doing it.'

Ewan shrugged.

'Fair enough.'

Edward rubbed his eyes tiredly.

'I've got those bloody investors threatening to sue me. Did you see that? It's in the bloody papers. One of them has even threatened my family – lowlife. All of them, nothing but lowlives thinking someone else owes them a living. How did she meet this toad anyway?'

'No idea.'

Edward sighed.

'How much?'

'That's up to you. He wanted a couple of thousand but...'

Edward roared with laughter. The door opened, and his eyes met Ewan's. It was Rose. She was dressed for going out. She looked from one to the other and smiled.

'You two look like you're conspiring. How's the arm, Ewan?'

'It's getting there.'

'He's all right,' snapped Edward.

'How's Princess?' asked Rose.

'I'm keeping an eye on her. The medication doesn't seem to be helping much.'

'Give it bloody time,' said Edward.

Rose walked to the bookcase and removed a large volume.

'Well, I'll leave you to your meeting. Are you doing anything special for the millennium, Ewan?'

He smiled.

'No. I'll maybe go to the pub.'

'Wise man.' Edward grinned. 'We're having people over. Not my idea of fun.'

'You'll enjoy it.' Rose smiled. 'Libby and I are going to the history talk in the village. I thought I'd take our little family history with us.' She nodded at the book in her hand.

Ewan waited until she had left.

'He says he doesn't have enough money for diesel, but according to those in the pub he's been talking about going back to Australia.'

'He no doubt expects me to pay for that.'

'He'll be out of Libby's way.'

'Maybe you're right but I'm not giving him any money. I can make life very difficult for him and his family. Make sure he knows that. Whose land is he on?'

'Farmer Davis, I think he...'

'Owes me money,' finishes Edward. 'I bought pigs for his pig farm. Maybe it's time to have those pigs slaughtered. Just in time for Christmas...'

'I don't think...'

'You tell Farmer Davis to get them gypos off that land or he won't have much of a farm left.'

Ewan fought back a sigh.

'You'll have to tell him yourself.'

Edward's hard eyes met Ewan's.

'What did you say?'

'I'm not doing that. I warned Patrick off. I think he's bad for Libby. I didn't mind doing that. But Farmer Davis is okay. He's paying you back. It's hard for most people.'

'My heart bleeds, Ewan.'

Ewan turned to the door.

'Maybe you don't appreciate this job enough,' said Edward, his words halting Ewan.

Ewan shook his head and gave Edward a sad look.

'If you're not happy with me I can pack up my stuff. There are plenty of jobs for a man not afraid to work.'

'Not many with cottages though.'

'I'll always find somewhere,' said Ewan opening the door.

Edward stepped up behind him and slammed the door shut.

'Don't be bloody stupid. I'll talk to Davis. I'm not paying a gypo money unless I have to. Did you give any thought to that other business I asked you about?'

Ewan nodded. 'I think it's a sensible thing to do.'

Edward agreed. 'Yes. I'll look into it.'

Libby suddenly burst into the room and they both struggled not to look uncomfortable.

'Aunty Rose left her handbag,' she said, picking it up from the floor.

Ewan couldn't help wondering if she had been listening at the door. She smiled at him and he nodded in return. Poor cow, he thought, all she wants is for someone to love her.

CHAPTER FORTY-FIVE

Libby

'Are you going in?' asks a girl with pink hair, tapping me on the shoulder.

I shake my head.

'You can go on ahead of me,' she offers.

It's difficult to see Ewan's face. He's turned away from me. He speaks again and now I have no doubt it is him. His body is stockier but still firm and a little shiver runs down my back. I'm shoved forward by the crowd and suddenly Jimmy is there grabbing two of them by the arm.

'Get off,' cries one of the men.

I gesture to Jimmy and he follows me to the back of the queue.

'It's not the best place,' he grunts.

'I'm fine. I just want to watch someone for a little while.'

Ewan is checking handbags. He's focused on what he's doing. I can't take my eyes off him. His accent is as strong as ever. I can't see his face and wish he would turn so I can get a good look at him. Have the years treated him well?

'Thanks gorgeous,' says one of the girls, clearly flirting with him.

'Have a good evening,' he says, barely looking at her.

It is him. I know it is.

The queue is dwindling slowly and soon I will be conspicuous. I cross the road with Jimmy behind me. Jimmy opens the car door and I slide inside. I lean my head against the window and study Ewan from there. He's smiling at someone and my heart skips a beat. He still has the animal magnetism. The queue ends, and he runs his hand through his hair and says something to the other bouncer. I'm too far away now so that when he glances over my way I can't see his features clearly. I'm sure it is Ewan. He is looking at the car. I can't pull my eyes away from him. I know we should go but I can't. He cocks his head to one side as though trying to figure something out. I gasp as he steps forward into the road and begins to walk towards us. I slide down in my seat.

'Go,' I say to Jimmy. 'Hurry.'

Jimmy puts the car into gear and shoots forward. I have trouble breathing. Had he seen me? I hope he had. He'll know I'm no longer afraid of him. Is that true though, I ask myself, am I really no longer afraid of him? Jimmy gives me confidence, but the truth is I do fear Ewan and he knows it.

'Can you take me to Fox Lane Road? It's somewhere in Forest Gate,' I ask Jimmy.

There isn't a better time to check out Ewan's place than while he is working. I'm taken aback when I see the house. I had been expecting a block of flats. I wait in the car for a few minutes. I'm fearful that Ewan may have followed us. After several minutes have passed I get out and walk to the front of the house. Jimmy follows me and waits by the gate.

'I'm not going in,' I say.

I turn on my phone torch to see the flat numbers. Ewan's is

the one downstairs. The lights are off. I try to see in through the windows, but ivy is in the way. It's a tatty place. I remember the gamekeeper's cottage on the estate. Ewan had kept that so nice. He was always tidy. William told me that Dianne had come to collect Ewan's stuff, shortly after he was sentenced. I wonder if he has any of it here in this flat. I peek again through the window but it's impossible to see anything with the lights off. A car speeds around the corner with music booming and I freeze. The next one could be Ewan's. I get back into the car.

'Home please,' I tell Jimmy.

I know where Ewan lives. I know where he works. I have more money than he does. I have more power than he does. If this is a battle then I will surely win. I have a new laptop and a new phone. The other one is at home. If he is tracking me, then that's where he'll think I am. It occurs to me that I should take it out with me some days, just in case he gets suspicious. He won't know I've been to his house and he won't know I was at the nightclub. I wish I'd left a calling card. I want him to know that I'm now one step ahead. Ewan Galbreith needs to know he can't intimidate me.

CHAPTER FORTY-SIX

Christmas

L ibby opened her present and feigned surprise at the Marc Jacobs handbag and Chanel wallet. She'd been expecting exactly this. When Aunty Rose had asked her what she'd like for Christmas, Libby had shaken her head and said she had no idea. But when they'd gone Christmas shopping together she'd looked lovingly at the handbag and purses and knew that Aunty Rose had bought them while Libby was in the ladies' room.

They were perfect and she couldn't hide her delight. She'd take them tonight when she met Patrick, providing he could get away. He hadn't promised but she'd tantalised him with hints of her present to him. She knew he wouldn't be able to resist.

'I'm so pleased you like them.' Aunty Rose smiled.

Libby had told her aunt and uncle that her friends were meeting up later to celebrate Christmas. Edward hadn't seemed happy about her going.

'But you've got your friends here for the evening. I'll be bored to death,' Libby had protested.

'She's quite right, Edward, she will be,' agreed Aunty Rose.

Libby could always rely on Aunty Rose to stand up for her. Never having children themselves, Libby had become a daughter to her. Uncle Edward, on the other hand, was much tougher. He didn't have much time for the fairer sex. They were too weak and whimsical for his liking.

Now, she was getting ready to meet Patrick. She was trembling with the excitement of seeing him. She pulled on the new jumper she had bought. It was loose-fitting and Patrick could slide his hands under it easily. She shivered at the thought. Patrick liked her hair up, so she twisted it at the neck and knotted it with a hairband. She couldn't put too much make-up on in case Uncle Edward saw her. She could do that in the loo at the pub where she was meeting Patrick. She stroked the handbag and slid the bottle of whisky into it. Patrick would like that. It was single malt and expensive. Libby didn't think Patrick had ever had his own bottle. She wondered if he had bought her something; probably not. He never had much money. If only she could get him a job at Manstead Manor. She sighed. She knew that would never work. She hesitated and then slid open her bedroom drawer and removed a card and a small box and then left her room. Aunty Rose was preparing the table in the dining room.

'You look nice,' she said.

'I'm off, thank you for the lovely handbag. I adore it.'

'Good, I'm glad. Have a nice time.'

Libby nodded.

'You too.'

'Do you need a lift into town?'

'I phoned for a taxi.'

Libby didn't want Aunty Rose taking her anywhere. Uncle Edward could easily get that information out of her and she didn't want that.

'Okay darling, take care,' said Rose, distracted by the table layout.

Libby hurried to the front door to see if the taxi had arrived. It was waiting for her.

'The town centre,' she said. 'But can you stop at the gamekeeper's cottage. It's left along the drive.'

Through a gap in the trees she could see the lights were on in Ewan's cottage. She'd felt sure Ewan wouldn't be home tonight.

'Won't be a sec,' she said.

She walked slowly towards the cottage. She could see the fire burning in the living room. How sad, she thought, to be all alone over Christmas. She knocked timidly on the front door. It was a while before it opened and for an awful moment she feared she may be interrupting something. What if he had one of his women here? What if they were...?

The door opened and Ewan stood in front of her. He was barefoot. He smelt fresh, as if he had just got out of the shower. Libby sniffed the fragrance.

'Hello,' he said, surprised.

She wondered if he thought she looked pretty.

'Aren't you cold without a coat?' he said.

'I'm on my way out,' she replied, realising that didn't answer his question.

'Right,' he said.

She could hear soft music in the background and strained to see if anyone else was in the cottage.

'I just came to wish you a Merry Christmas, and to give you this.'

She pulled the gift quickly from her handbag before she lost her nerve. She waited for him to invite her in, but he didn't.

'That's very nice of you.' He smiled, but he didn't reach out to take it. She held it towards him.

'You really shouldn't buy me presents,' he said. 'I'm just an employee.'

'Uncle Edward buys you presents,' Libby said haughtily.

'He buys all the staff presents,' said Ewan.

Libby faltered. She didn't know what to do with the gift now that it was in her hand.

'It's personalised,' she said, blushing. 'I can't give it to anyone else.'

'Just this once then.' He smiled, taking the card and present from her. She stood awkwardly on the doorstep for a few moments.

'Your cab's waiting,' Ewan said, nodding towards the car.

'Yes, well Merry Christmas.'

'You too, Libby.'

He could open it, she thought. At least show his appreciation. But he didn't. He just stood there, waiting for her to leave. She bet Peter wouldn't have treated her like this.

'Bye then,' she said and hurried to the cab. She turned to wave but he'd already closed the door. She wondered if he was opening the gift and whether he would use the wallet right away. She hoped he liked it. It had been specially embossed with the shape of stag antlers. She knew how much Ewan loved the stags.

CHAPTER FORTY-SEVEN

PRESENT DAY

Libby

Lee smiles as I enter the lobby. It's almost midnight. I feel confident and in control. I have my life back. My contracts are intact, well, most of them. I'm one step ahead of Ewan Galbreith. I have money, he has nothing. He was a fool to think he could intimidate me. He should have known I would not let him destroy me even more.

'I have a package for you,' Lee says.

I try to ignore the churning stomach that these words produce. I collect the post from my mailbox and see the report from Mr Little among the pile. Lee returns with a bouquet of flowers and my heart sinks. I take them hesitantly and then see the card.

These are from me. Thanks for a lovely evening. I'm looking forward to the weekend. Simon.

I let out a long sigh.

'Is everything all right, madam?' Lee asks.

'Oh yes, everything is perfect. How is Ian?'

'Much better, thank you, madam.'

'Good. Did he mention my stalker problem to you?'

Lee straightens his back.

'No, he didn't.'

'No worries.'

There's no point showing a photo to Lee. Ewan could easily slip into the lift. People visit every day. He knows my address. He isn't about to ask the concierge which flat. I have a bodyguard. I'm one step ahead.

Jimmy presses the lift button and sees me to the apartment.

'What time would you like me in the morning, madam?'

'Ten should be fine.'

He nods and steps into the lift. Merlin greets me as usual. It's hot and stuffy in the flat. I turn off the alarm and switch on the air con. I wrinkle my nose at the smell of Merlin's food.

'Come on, darling,' I say. 'Let's give you something fresh.'

I yawn. It had been a long day and although it's late I'm still feeling exhilarated at the steps I'd taken to deal with Ewan Galbreith.

I grimace at the stench of Merlin's food. It never smells this bad. I click on the light and recoil in shock. I stifle a scream at the sight of the mauled rat on the kitchen floor. The flowers slip from my fingers. Merlin purrs happily around my ankle. I swallow the bile in my throat and rush from the kitchen to the front door when I'm halted in my stride by the sound of music. I can't breathe and my legs won't move. 'Every Breath you Take' is playing somewhere in the flat. My legs are immobile. I feel the tears running down my cheeks. Finally I stretch out a trembling hand to the door of the living room and stumble in. I hit the light switch and brace myself. There's no one here. The music is coming from the kitchen. I retrace my steps and head back. The song is playing on the old phone that sits on the kitchen counter. I snatch it up and turn it off. I can't think. My brain is numb with shock. Ewan has been in my flat, but how? It isn't possible. I rush from the flat, down the stairs and to the foyer where Lee reels back as I yell at him.

'Who has been in my flat? Who the fuck did you let into my flat?'

'I... I didn't let anyone into your flat.'

'You must have. No one has a key apart from me and you.'

'Miss Warren, I assure you I didn't let anyone into your flat.'

'You're lying, you have to be,' I say. 'There's a dead rat in there.'

'You have a cat though, don't you?' Lee says.

'He never goes out,' I say angrily.

I'm distraught. I'm shouting and waving my hands around. I know I should calm down. This is just what Galbreith wants.

'I'll call the police,' he says.

'No,' I snap.

I march back into the lift. How dare he? How fucking dare he? I've lost it. I've looked like a raving lunatic. I've given Ewan exactly what he wanted.

———

The police sergeant looks at me. There is sympathy in her eyes.

'We've searched the flat,' she assures me. 'There are no cameras.'

I sigh with relief.

'Are you sure there is no way your cat could have brought in the rat?'

'I have a stalker,' I say.

'Yes, Inspector Marshall informed us about him.'

'Have you checked his movements?'

'It's not unusual for a cat to bring in a rat.'

'My cat doesn't go out,' I say angrily.

'According to the concierge, no one asked to come into your flat. Have you given keys to anyone?'

'Are you insane? I have a stalker. I'm not in the habit of giving people keys. What about the music on my phone?'

'The song is in your playlist.'

'Of course it is. He sent it to me.'

This is ridiculous.

'There is no sign of forced entry. The concierge insists he didn't let anyone into your flat...'

'He would say that now, wouldn't he?'

'He's extremely distressed by the whole thing. Now, if no one broke into your flat and the concierge didn't let anyone in and you haven't given Ewan keys then we have nothing to accuse him of.'

I stare at her.

'He's intimidating me. He murdered my family,' I say, fighting back tears.

She lays a hand on my shoulder.

'I'm so sorry, but look at it from our side. There's no break-in, there's no cameras. The only crime here seems to be a cat with a rat.'

She gives me a sympathetic look. They think I'm having a breakdown. I'm playing right into Ewan's hands.

'Thank you,' I say, walking to the door.

They're happy to go. I sit back on the couch and clench my fist.

'You fucker. You won't win. You won't fucking win.'

CHAPTER FORTY-EIGHT

PRESENT DAY

Libby

I jump at the sound of the door buzzer, spilling some vodka from my glass. I'd been sitting on the couch ever since the police had left. My mind is numb. I can't seem to think straight. How did Ewan get into my flat? If Lee is telling the truth then there is no way it could have been possible, but somehow a rat found its way in here. Little's report wasn't much help. I already knew where Ewan lived and worked and according to Little, Ewan Galbreith hasn't been near my flat.

The buzzer sounds again and I force myself from my place on the couch.

'Yes,' I say into the intercom.

'Sorry to bother you, Miss Warren,' says Lee, his voice uncertain.

'No problem,' I say.

I feel bad about how I had shouted at him. I'll buy him a bottle of wine as an apology.

'Mr Simon Wane is here.'

'Oh yes, that's fine.'

What is Simon doing here? I thought he had meetings all week. I check my reflection in the mirror, open the door and wait for him. Jimmy has gone home. There seemed little point in him just hanging around. I've got triple locks on the door. Unless Ewan has developed some kind of Houdini skill there is no way he could get inside. The lift pings and Simon steps out. He's carrying a glass of bubbly and some chocolates.

'Donna said you had something of a shock last night. I thought these may help.'

'That's kind, thank you,' I say, opening the door wider.

He sees the vodka and smiles.

'Ah, you're already on the hard stuff.'

'Yes. Can I offer you a drink?'

'I'm driving, so just a small one.'

I fetch a glass from the kitchen and pour a small measure of vodka and top it up with orange juice.

'Are you okay?' he asks, sitting opposite me.

I nod.

'I think so. My brain is still whirring from it all. The police haven't been at all helpful. Thanks for coming over.'

'I did text, but it wasn't received.'

'Oh,' I say, remembering. 'I have a new phone. I meant to send you the number. The other one I've turned off, since the music...'

'The music?' he questions.

I tell him everything that happened last night and then take a large gulp of vodka.

'Do you think he's been in the flat?' I ask.

'Not unless he can walk through walls. Who else has keys to the flat?' he asks.

'No one.'

'It is a bit like Fort Knox in here.' He smiles. 'I thought I'd never make it to the loo in time the other night.'

'Sorry,' I say.

'It's fine. You need to feel safe.'

'I don't understand it. When I came home the door was locked. So how did he get in?'

'Maybe he didn't.'

I nod and top up my glass.

'Am I going mad?' I ask worriedly.

The thought had occurred to me several times. Was the fear and anxiety having a profound effect on me that I no longer knew what I was doing? How could Ewan get through locked doors?

'You're stressed,' he says softly, laying a hand on my arm.

'Merlin had a rat on the kitchen floor. It looked like she'd mauled it. But how could she have had a rat? She doesn't go out. Then my music player started playing on my phone, just out of the blue. It was a particular song; it's a song that Ewan used to play. It's all so coincidental.'

He drank his vodka and orange and then put the glass on the coffee table before taking my hand. His feels warm in mine.

'The rat could have come from anywhere. Have you asked Lee if anyone else in the block has had problems with rats?'

I shake my head.

'What about the music?'

'Maybe Merlin jumped on your phone?'

Why does everything sound so plausible? I'm beginning to feel like a right fool.

'Thank you for the flowers,' I say, changing the subject.

He smells nice. The alcohol has gone to my head, and it's all I can do to keep my hands off him.

'Shall we open the chocolates?' I say, pulling off the wrapper. 'I was going to watch a movie in a bit, to get my mind off things. What do you think?'

He finishes his drink and checks the time on his phone. Surely he's not going already.

'I've got a meeting,' he says apologetically.

'This evening?'

'I'm afraid so. I've freed the weekend so I can go to Padley with you.'

'Oh, right.'

'I'm looking forward to seeing your house.'

I thought he was going to say he was looking forward to spending the weekend with me. I consider asking him if he'd like to stay at William and Caroline's beach house, but it seems a little forward and he does seem reluctant to get involved too quickly. Donna had said something about him getting over a bad relationship, so I guess that is why.

'It will be relaxing,' I say.

He goes to stand up. I lean towards him and he hesitates.

'Thanks so much for coming,' I say.

My lips touch his cheek and the smell of him is so exciting that I have to fight for control. Why doesn't he grab me or kiss me? Instead, he lays a hand on my knee and says, 'Happy to, I'm only sorry I can't stay longer.'

He walks to the door.

'You don't have to see me out. I'll see you Saturday, about ten?'

'Great,' I say.

'We'll do something special when we're there.' He smiles. 'Try not to worry too much.'

'I'd like that.'

The door closes and I turn the key in the lock.

Ewan Galbreith isn't Houdini. I know that, and I don't buy the idea that there are rats in the block. Something odd is going on and I no longer feel one step ahead of Ewan and that bothers me. It bothers me a lot.

CHAPTER FORTY-NINE

Patrick had some money to throw around.

'I won on the games,' he said.

He bought her a decent drink for a change and a kebab as they walked to the old textile shop. It was boarded up, but Patrick said he knew a way in. He kept looking behind as though expecting someone to be following them.

'It's okay,' she said, laughing. 'Everyone's celebrating Christmas. No one is interested in us.'

They climbed over some bins and Patrick carefully removed a plank of wood to reveal a covered entrance.

'It's a bit tight,' he said. 'Watch your clothes. There was some old stock left behind,' he told her. 'I took it. Lil made some nice curtains and...'

She glared at him. The last person she ever wanted to hear about was Lil and his kids. When they were together Libby fantasised about all kinds of things but none of these fantasies included Lil and the kids.

They made love three times and Libby was sated. She imagined the hands stroking her breast were Ewan's and she grabbed Patrick feverishly. The orgasms had overwhelmed her in their intensity. She'd wrapped her legs around Patrick, inviting him inside her, the whole time picturing Ewan's muscular torso.

'I bought you this for Christmas,' she said afterwards, handing him the whisky bottle.

His eyes widened.

'Sweet. Thanks babe.'

A firework exploded outside and he jumped. Libby had noticed he was edgier than usual.

'What was that?' he said, grabbing his jeans.

'Just a firework, Pat. Someone starting their New Year celebrations early, no doubt. What's the matter? You're really nervous tonight.'

'I don't want that Scottish prick catching me with my pants down.'

Libby sat up.

'What Scottish prick?' she asked but she already knew who Patrick meant.

'That gamekeeper of your uncle's, he came to warn me off the other day.'

'What?' said Libby, feeling her heart race. Was Ewan jealous?

Patrick pulled his jeans on and then opened the whisky bottle.

'Your uncle doesn't like me. He thinks I'm not good enough for you. I suppose he's right.'

Libby grasped his arm.

'You are good enough for me. I love you and no one will stop me seeing you.'

'I know, babe.' He smiled before lifting the bottle to his lips.

'I'll tell Ewan to back off,' she said.

'Nah, don't let him know he spooked me.'

He went to stand up, but Libby stopped him.

'Do you have a present for me?' she asked.

He grinned.

'Come on, babe. Where have I got money for presents? My win on the games wasn't that big. I've got to move off that farmer's land or that Scottish prick will shoot me in the fucking balls. I need more money.'

'Ewan threatened to shoot you?' she said, shocked.

'Yeah, he did. Anyway, like I told you, we've got to go back to Australia.'

Libby blushed at the thought of Uncle Edward knowing about her flings with Patrick.

'You can't go to Australia. Please say you won't go.'

Patrick sighed. Libby was getting too clingy for him and she was trouble. He didn't need that Scottish bastard on his back.

'I've got to get back, babe. The kids will expect me home soon. We've still got presents they haven't opened.'

Libby put her fingers in her ears. She didn't want to hear about Patrick's other life. Maybe it would be best if he went to Australia. It was horrid sneaking around like this, but she loved him.

'You're only seventeen, Libby. I don't know, maybe I could get done doing it with you?'

'I'll be eighteen in April,' she protested.

'But you're not eighteen now are you? I shouldn't be doing this.'

'Can you wait until I'm eighteen? I'll come to Australia with you.'

Christ, thought Patrick, that's all I need.

He'd go and see her uncle. Tell him that Libby was obsessed with him. That he'd tried to break it off. He'd say she lied about her age. Surely he'd give him a bit more to get rid of him. The last thing he'd want is a scandal involving his niece. Galbreith wouldn't do anything. It was more than Edward Owen's reputation was worth, and why would Galbreith get himself into deep water for Libby Owen? It was just to frighten him off. He wouldn't use the gun. No, the uncle would pay up and then he'd be on his way Down Under and Libby Owen would be well and truly forgotten.

CHAPTER FIFTY

FIFTEEN YEARS EARLIER

'Miss Owen, you said you heard shots coming from the morning room in the early hours of January 1st this year.'

'Yes,' said Libby.

'How many shots did you hear?'

'I can't remember. I think it was one.'

'So, you heard a shot. Did you hear anyone speaking?'

'Not at first but then I heard Uncle Edward shout and Aunty Rose scream. She sounded petrified.'

'Did you go into the morning room?'

Libby closed her eyes for a second. The courtroom was deathly silent. She could feel Ewan's eyes on her. She didn't want to have to look at him.

'I opened the door. Then I saw Aunty Rose,' she sobbed. 'She was on the floor. I... I stepped in the blood. Her dress was ripped and her... her...'

'Take your time.'

'The dress was ripped off her. Uncle Edward shouted for me to run and then I realised there was a man in the room. He was pointing a shotgun at Uncle Edward.'

'Did you recognise the man holding the shotgun?'

'He had his back to me.'

'Did you recognise him?'

'I...'

'Was the man with the shotgun Ewan Galbreith?'

'Objection!'

'Rephrase the question, Mr Whittaker.'

'Sorry, Your Honour. Miss Owen, did you know the man that was aiming the gun at your uncle?'

'I... I think...'

'Did you or didn't you know the man?'

Libby's legs felt like jelly.

'I... yes, it was Ewan Galbreith.'

'NO!' Ewan shouted.

Libby looked over at Ewan. He'd stood up and was pointing at her. Her hands started to shake.

'She didn't see me. It wasn't me,' he shouted.

Libby's eyes went to Dianne. She was crying.

'Silence in court,' called the judge. 'Mr Galbreith, I must warn you that if you continue to interrupt the witness's evidence then I will have no choice but to remove you from the court and Miss Owen's evidence will continue in your absence.'

Libby bowed her head and wiped tears from her eyes.

'Miss Owen, is it at all possible you saw someone else that night?'

Libby bit her lip.

'Take your time,' said the judge.

'I saw Ewan Galbreith,' Libby said.

This time there was no outcry from Ewan, but she felt his eyes on her and the hatred in them.

'What did you do after seeing Ewan Galbreith with the gun in his hand?'

'I think... I can't remember. I think Uncle Edward turned.

Maybe he was going to phone the police. I don't know. The man...'

'Ewan Galbreith?'

'Shot him in the back. I ran. I didn't even know where I was going. I remember slipping on blood and crying and just wanting to get away. I should have stayed. I should have tried to save them, I should have...' She broke down and fell onto the bench behind her.

'Could we have some water please?'

Libby took the water into her shaking hands and attempted to drink from the glass. She looked up at Ewan. His eyes were hateful. She'd never seen such hate in anyone's eyes before.

'Where did you run to, Libby?'

'The beach, I wanted to get to the beach. I knew there would be lots of people there.'

'Do you remember if Ewan Galbreith chased you?'

'He called my name. I remember feeling scared that he'd seen me.'

'Thank you, Miss Owen. No more questions, Your Honour.'

Libby let out a long breath and lowered her head. She didn't want to look at Ewan or Dianne.

CHAPTER FIFTY-ONE

TEN YEARS EARLIER

E wan sat at the back of the drama class and yawned. These workshops bored his arse off, but he had to attend. All part of his rehabilitation, apparently. Although how acting rehabilitated anyone was beyond his understanding. But it passed a few more hours in this dirty stinking hole.

They'd been studying *Macbeth*. He'd enjoyed that. Today they were going to look at something new. He strolled into the hall with everyone else. It was a different tutor this time. A woman stood at the front of the hall. On tables in front of her were masks, stage make-up and other paraphernalia. On the table lay the script for the play *Strange Case of Dr Jekyll and Mr Hyde*.

'Mr Smith is sick I'm afraid, so I'll be taking the workshop this week. My name is Layla and we are to look at a whole different way to view the theatre.'

'This is going to be boring,' mumbled another inmate.

Ewan smiled and nodded in agreement. But as the workshop wore on he found himself fascinated and enthralled. For the first time in years something interested him.

The workshop lasted for two hours and when they were

asked to give a show of hands for who would like further workshops on the subject, Ewan's hand was the first to go up. He'd taken all the notes from the workshop and ordered books from the library on the subject. His mind was whirring when he returned to his cell.

'Found your vocation, Ewan?' said Jeff, his cellmate.

'Something like that.'

'Are we going to see you in the summer play then?' asked the guard.

'Maybe,' said Ewan with a grin.

That night he lay on his bed and thought back to that night. The night of the millennium, the night his life changed. He thought about it most evenings. His mind would travel first to Libby, and then Ben Mitchell before trying to picture Rose and Edward Owen. Some nights he found it hard to remember their faces. Finally, he would think of Patrick. The hatred that had once been in him had mellowed to resigned acceptance. He had no future, while they were out there living their lives, making the most of everything. He picked up the script for *Jekyll and Hyde* and ran his finger over the title. He thought of Manstead and his cottage. He wondered what had happened to that. Was someone living there now? Dianne had said she thought she saw someone in the garden there but of course, she could have been mistaken. Manstead Manor hadn't been sold, she told him. It was just sitting there like a museum. Libby didn't live there. Dianne didn't know where she lived, she said, when he asked. Why didn't he just forget about her, she wanted to know? Dianne had no idea. No idea at all.

He closed his eyes and pictured the morning room. Edward had been at his most comfortable there. It was fitting he should die there. He could see the heavy oak desk and the drinks cabinet in the far corner. He could almost taste the whisky on his tongue. His eyes then snapped open. How could he have forgotten? He sat upright as a memory, vague to begin with, entered his head.

'Jesus,' he muttered.

Did Edward go through with it? So much had happened afterwards that it had completely gone out of Ewan's mind. But if Edward had... Ewan daren't think about it. Because if he had. God, if Edward had... Damn it. He wouldn't know until the day they let him out of this shithole.

CHAPTER FIFTY-TWO

PRESENT DAY

Libby

I should have known the rat was the beginning of the end. I also should have known that I could never be one step ahead of Ewan Galbreith.

I wake with a raging headache. I'd slept badly. I'd dreamt of the murders and of Manstead. It was probably because I was returning there at the weekend. It has been years since I'd been back. William and Caroline had always visited me. The last time I went to Padley was seven years ago. It had been painful and traumatic. I'd vowed never to go again. I take two painkillers and check my phone and laptop before making breakfast. I've decided to get bad news out of the way first thing. My hands tremble as I turn on the laptop. There's nothing unusual and I breathe a sigh of relief. The phone bleeps as I turn it on. There are messages from an unknown number.

How is Merlin?

I immediately know it's Galbreith. How does he know Merlin's name? He wouldn't hurt him. I know that. Ewan loves animals.

> How many more phones are you going to buy?

And then the tone changes, it becomes insulting and nasty.

> Thought you wouldn't hear me from me again? Stupid bitch that you are. I'm watching you.

I struggle to breathe. There are two messages from Donna.

> I'm meeting a client at 11. Are you about for a coffee at 1?

> Sorry, can we change that to 2?

There's one from the bodyguard agency.

Miss Warren, we received your email that you no longer need a bodyguard. We have confirmed via email and text. Please don't hesitate to contact us if you need assistance in the future.

I hurry to the front door and double-check the locks before looking down at my phone again.

Are you reading these? Or are you too chicken to turn on your phone? I'm watching you.

I angrily throw the phone across the room before checking my emails. Sure enough, there is an email from *Fort Rock Security*, confirming I'd cancelled my contract.

I pick up the phone and stare at it. Can he see me? Is he looking at me right now? I text Donna and agree to meet her at two this afternoon. I then turn the phone off. I glance at the landline phone. If Ewan has been into my flat he might have bugged the phone too. It looks okay but I wouldn't know where a microphone would be hidden.

'Damn him.'

I pick up the receiver and call the security company.

'I have your cancellation email on the screen in front of me,' says the woman at the other end.

'Someone hacked my account,' I say, trying to keep calm. 'Can you please send Jimmy to my flat?'

'I'll just see whether he has been assigned somewhere else.'

I hear her tapping at her computer screen and wring my hands in agitation.

'I can have him with you by this afternoon. Or I can send someone else.'

I don't want someone else.

'That's fine.'

'I'll let you know when he is on his way, Miss Warren.'

I hang up and then disconnect the phone. Merlin meows for food and I force my weary body to the kitchen. I'll make sure all the mobiles are off. I place Merlin's dish onto the floor and suddenly find myself sobbing on the floor beside it.

Merlin rubs himself against me.

'How?' I sob.

How did he get to my phone yet again? How did he get into my flat? I've got to make him stop. I can't stand it. *He can't walk through locked doors,* whispers a voice in my head. *The safest thing is to stay here. Don't go out.* I pull myself up and switch on my phone. It doesn't bleep and my racing heart starts to slow down.

> Donna, do you mind coming to me? PLEASE.

She replies immediately.

> What's wrong? Is it him?

YES.

I'll come to you, no problem.

I sit staring at the phone for what feels like an eternity. Nothing makes sense. It isn't possible that Ewan has my new number. It just isn't possible. I bite my lip nervously and then call Fran.

'He's coming to get me,' I say dramatically.

'Calm down,' says Fran.

'Don't keep telling me to fucking calm down!' I scream. 'The bastard is out of control. He's been in my flat. He's somehow got keys. He's hacked the third phone I bought. He always seems to know the number and...'

'Okay, okay,' she interrupts. 'Get your locks changed. I'll arrange a secure line for you and...'

'I've seen him. He's living in Forest Gate. I know where he lives, if you don't sort this out then I will...'

'Libby...'

'My life is in danger, why won't you lock him up?'

I'm struggling to keep calm. I feel sure she can hear the sobs in my voice.

'Libby, we need proof. We need proof he broke into your flat. The police said there was no sign of a break-in. We've been doing some background checks. He was friendly with a computer hacker when he was inside. We'll send someone to question him to see if he has had any contact with Ewan since his release.'

'I want you to arrest Ewan,' I say bluntly.

'On what grounds, Libby?'

'Harassment.'

'Okay, can you prove he is harassing you? Can you prove it is Ewan?'

'No... I...'

'It could be any number of weirdos. Do you still have your bodyguard?'

'They received an email from me saying I didn't need him anymore. I didn't send it.'

There's silence for a few seconds.

'I'll pay him a visit,' she says.

'Thank you, Fran.'

'Carry on keeping a record of all the messages and threats. But don't, I repeat, don't attempt to see him or meet with him. It could seriously backfire on you, Libby. Promise me that? We still don't know it was Ewan that hacked your computer. It certainly wasn't an interest of his in prison. It seemed his only interest was the theatre and stage make-up. So, promise me you won't do anything silly?'

'I promise,' I say.

Fuck you, I think. *If you imagine I'm going to lie among the lilies and wait for him then you can fucking think again.*

CHAPTER FIFTY-THREE

FIFTEEN YEARS EARLIER

Patrick hesitated at the gates of Manstead Manor. Now he was here he was too chicken to go any further. He knew Libby wasn't at home. He hadn't been stupid. He wasn't about to visit old man Owen with Libby about. He'd been pretty canny about it, he thought. He'd written Edward Owen a letter and waited for the postman to arrive at the gates.

'Deliver this will you?' he'd said.

The postie had looked at him oddly but taken it all the same. Patrick simply had to sit back and wait. Owen soon got in touch.

Come Saturday morning at eleven. Libby will be out riding.

That was it. Nothing to indicate he would give Patrick the money. But Patrick figured he wouldn't have asked him over if he had no intention of giving him something. Of course, he could be waiting with the Scottish bastard. Maybe they were planning to do him over. It was a chance he'd have to take. It could well be that old man Owen was willing to give him a fair bit to keep his mouth shut about his niece. He took a deep breath and walked down the drive. Maybe he'd been a bit too graphic in his descriptions. He didn't want to rile the old bloke, but he wanted him to realise just what kind of dirt Patrick could dish out about his niece. Of course, he was taking the risk they may have police waiting. They could get Libby to cry rape. He stopped uncertainly at the front door. He could turn around now. He and Lil could be away from Padley in a few hours. No one was going to come after them. But supposing... He'd be a fool to leave without anything. His facial muscles twitched with nerves and then he pulled the hand bell. There was a loud ringing throughout the hallway. If no one answered in a few seconds, he'd turn and go back. But before he could take a step the door swung open. A pretty young woman now stood in front of him.

'Yes?' she said.

'I've got a meeting with Edward Owen. He's expecting me. My name's Patrick...'

'Come in,' she said before he had finished.

He didn't take in the grand hallway. He was too shit scared. There was no going back now. Either he was going to get a bullet in his nether regions or a few grand in his pocket.

'I'll let Mr Owen know you're here,' said the woman.

He fidgeted on his feet, his eyes darting about, looking for the Scottish fuck.

'Patrick,' said a deep voice.

He spun round and came face to face with Edward Owen. He was a big man with stern features and steely grey eyes. He was dressed in corduroys and a cabled jumper.

'You're weedier than Ewan described,' he said, turning on

his heel and walking into a room off the hallway. 'You'd better come in.'

Patrick's jaw tightened.

'Not too weedy for your niece,' said Patrick viciously.

Edward stopped suddenly and Patrick found himself walking into him.

'I don't want you mentioning my niece. You got that?'

Patrick fought back the words he wanted to spit in Edward's face. Edward closed the door behind Patrick and said, 'So how much?'

'Five thousand.'

Edward burst out laughing.

'No way, now you know where the front door is. Get out of my sight.'

Patrick was taken aback. His scrambled brain tried to make sense of what was happening.

'I could make a lot of trouble,' he said finally.

Edward walked slowly to his desk and sat in the chair behind it.

'My niece will claim you raped her. It won't be hard to find other young women that you've raped in the time you've been trespassing on private property. Let's face it, only scum trespass like you do. So scum like you are most likely capable of anything.'

'I never raped anyone.'

'Two thousand is all I'm willing to offer. Take it or leave it. If things get dirty just remember I can afford to be dirtier than you. I'm being far too generous.'

'I'll tell the police that Scottish fuck threatened me.'

Edward suddenly sat up, the chair falling backwards with the force. He was round the table before Patrick had time to think. He was grabbed by the shirt and almost lifted from the floor.

'Don't you use that language in my house. How dare you,' growled Edward.

Patrick fell back as Edward released him. Christ, that was a bit of an overreaction.

'I'll give you a cheque for two thousand and I expect you to be gone within the next twenty-four hours.'

'I don't do cheques,' said Patrick defiantly. 'I don't have a bank account. It will have to be cash.'

Edward sighed.

'Why don't you get a job like everyone else?'

Like Libby? Patrick wanted to say but bit his tongue. He didn't want to jeopardise things now. He'd hoped for more, but this was better than nothing.

'That'll just about pay my air fare,' he said. 'I've got a wife and kids.'

Edward gave him a scathing look.

'You're getting two thousand and if you're not off that land by tomorrow you will be very sorry. I can make the rest of your days a living nightmare. I'm owed favours. Do you understand what I'm saying? Some nasty people owe me money. I can call in my debts anytime I want. I'm being lenient with you. Don't push me, lad.'

Patrick nodded. Owen was bluffing, he felt sure of it. He'd get the two thousand and leave when he wanted.

'I've got things to take care of first,' he said.

Edward smirked.

'What things?'

'I've got to sell the caravan for a start and...'

'Twenty-four hours,' repeated Edward, an element of menace in his voice. 'Wait outside.'

Patrick walked to the door, a victorious smile on his face. Two grand, he thought and then there's the money he'd get from the caravan. Just to make it really sweet maybe he'd have one last fuck with Libby. That would be the icing on the cake.

He waited outside the door, his eyes surveying the grand hallway and ornate staircase. How the other half lived. Maybe he'd get another bottle of whisky out of Libby before he went. God knows they could afford it. The door opened and Edward strolled out, an envelope in his hand. He gave it to Patrick.

'It's all there. Count it when you're off my property. You're causing a stench.'

Patrick smiled.

'Don't worry, I'm going.'

'Twenty-four hours,' repeated Edward.

'Yeah, don't worry.'

He tucked the envelope into his jeans pocket. He was as high as a kite. Two grand, just like that. It had been worth fucking Libby Owen. The front door slammed shut behind him. There was no sign of the Scottish bastard. It had been a breeze. He began to whistle. He'd check out flights later. It would be good to get some sunshine.

CHAPTER FIFTY-FOUR

FIFTEEN YEARS EARLIER

'Sergeant Marshall, can you please recount for us the events of 1st January 2000 when you were called to Manstead Manor in Padley, Cornwall?'

Fran looked down at her notepad.

'We took an emergency call at 12.55am. Ewan Galbreith had phoned from Manstead Manor. He said that Rose and Edward Owen had been shot. He believed them to be dead.'

'Ewan Galbreith called the emergency services that night?'

'Yes.'

'Did anyone else call them?'

'Fifteen minutes later at 1.10 there was an emergency call from Alex Phillips. He said that a girl with blood on her had collapsed on the Kaylen Beach. That's a short distance from Manstead Manor.'

'And the girl was Libby Owen, is that correct?'

'Yes.'

'Were there any other calls to the emergency services regarding the incident?'

'No, sir.'

'So Libby Owen didn't call the police to report the shooting of her aunt and uncle.'

'No, but...'

'That's odd, don't you think?'

Fran shrugged.

'No, Libby Owen was in shock. It had only just happened.'

'Or she was covering for someone?'

'Objection.'

'Rephrase the question, Mr Fosh.'

'So, it is a fact that Ewan Galbreith, who is on trial for the murder of Edward and Rose Owen, is the same person that reported the murder.'

'That's correct.'

'You didn't think that odd at the time?'

'No I didn't.'

'Tell us what you saw when you arrived at Manstead Manor on the morning of January the 1st.'

Fran again glanced down at her notepad.

'We arrived at the house at 1.10am. The accused was sitting in the grand hallway holding a shotgun. It was later confirmed that this was the firearm that had killed Edward Owen and his wife Rose. On entering the house Ewan Galbreith informed us that his employers were dead. On questioning, Mr Galbreith said he had heard shots and came running to the house. He found the bodies and the shotgun on the floor of the morning room.'

'Did Mr Galbreith have blood on him?'

'Yes, there was blood on his shoes and his hands.'

'Did he tell you that he had seen the murderer?'

'No, he said the house was empty when he got there.'

'But he told you that he had seen Miss Owen?'

'Yes, he said she looked terrified and must have seen the murders. He said he called out to her, but she kept running.'

'Did you believe him?'

'At the time, yes I did.'

'Isn't it true that a number of people had it in for Edward Owen?'

'It did seem that way, yes.'

'So any one of those people could have committed the murders.'

'Yes, I suppose so.'

'Rose Owen had been the first to be shot, is that correct?'

'Yes, she had been shot in the chest. The shot had been fired at close range. The force of the shot had ripped the dress off her.'

'So Rose Owen would have seen the murderer and presumably knew them if they had let them into the house.'

'That's right.'

'Did Mr Galbreith have a key to Manstead Manor?'

'Yes, he did. All the staff members had keys.'

'Thank you, no further questions for the moment.'

Fran looked at Ewan Galbreith. His expression was unreadable.

CHAPTER FIFTY-FIVE

PRESENT DAY

Leon closed his laptop and drained his coffee cup. He was about to get up for a refill when he saw his boss, Malcolm, walking towards him. An official-looking woman was with him. He sighed. He had imagined the police visiting him at home, not at his place of work. He gave them his best smile and stood up.

'Leon, this is Inspector Marshall. She'd like a few words.'

'I was just off to get a sandwich.'

'I won't keep you long,' said Fran, smiling.

'It's nothing serious, is it?' asked Malcolm.

Leon kept the smile pasted on his face.

'No, not all, I'm just wondering whether Mr Lapotaire can help with some enquiries. He certainly isn't in any trouble.'

'Oh, that's good then. I'll leave you both to it.'

Leon sat back down at his desk and pointed to another chair.

'Thanks,' said Fran, sitting down.

'What's up?' asked Leon, reaching into a drawer for a packet of crisps.

'You did some time in Belmarsh, didn't you?'

Leon wrinkled his brow.

'So what? I did my time. I'm clean. I've got a good job and...'

'Yes, Malcolm was telling me how good you are with computers. Just how good are you at hacking into someone else's?'

'Do what?' He laughed.

'I think you heard me. You were pretty good at that at one time.'

Fran opened a notepad.

'Twelve years for fraud. Didn't you hack several large bank accounts and syphon off a tidy sum of money?'

'That was a long time ago. I've got a clean record now.'

He offered her the packet of crisps.

'No thanks. I'm watching my weight.'

Leon nodded. Women were always watching their weight, it seemed.

'You were banged up with Ewan Galbreith, weren't you?'

Leon frowned.

'Can't say I recall a dude by that name.'

'You were friends.'

'Like I said, it was a long time ago. I don't think about those days much.'

'I heard you two were very matey.'

Leon pushed the last few crisps into his mouth and wiped his hands on a tissue.

'Like I say, I don't recall the name.'

Fran stood up.

'He was released a few months back.'

'Is that right? Good for him.'

'You haven't seen him by any chance?'

'I just told you, I've got a new life now.'

'That's good to know. Only, Libby Warren had her laptop hacked. It's my job to find out who's behind that.'

Leon held out his hand.

'I don't know that chick. Thanks for coming.'

'I think you do. Ewan was in prison for the murder of her aunt and uncle.'

Leon stood and walked past her.

'I'm going to get my lunch. I'm sorry I can't help you.'

'It would be a shame for you to get into trouble just because you felt you owed someone a favour.'

Leon laughed.

'I don't do no favours.'

'So you won't mind us taking a look at your computers. It would save us getting a warrant.'

He gave a nod and left the room. He could feel Fran's eyes on him. He kept his head held high and walked to the cafeteria. He wouldn't admit to knowing Ewan, not even if they pulled his fingernails out. He was no grass.

CHAPTER FIFTY-SIX

Libby

'I'm afraid,' I admit to Donna. 'I keep thinking he's listening, even now, to everything we're saying.'

Donna's eyes widen and she looks around the room nervously.

'Jesus,' she mutters. 'I can't believe the police won't do anything.'

'What can they do? I can't prove anything.'

'Have you checked for microphones?' she whispers.

'I wouldn't know what to look for. Anyway, the police said there weren't any.'

'This is ridiculous. He can't intimidate you like this. Let's see if we can find anything.'

I watch as she searches behind curtain rails, looks at the plugs and studies the landline phone. I look around the walls for anything suspicious, anything that wasn't there before. We don't find anything unusual.

'Maybe he didn't get into the flat,' she says finally.

I click the kettle on to make more tea.

233

'How did the rat get in?'

'Letterbox?'

'I don't have one. The mailboxes are downstairs.'

Donna bites her lip. 'There must be rats in the flats.'

'He mentioned Merlin in his text. How does he know his name?'

'Did you talk about Merlin in any of your texts or emails?' says Donna.

'Of course not, why would I talk about my cat?'

She sighs. 'Joel said you should come and stay with us for a while, you know, until things settle.'

'What does that mean exactly?' I say, jumping up. 'I need a drink.'

She follows me into the kitchen, concern etched across her face.

'Libby, don't take this the wrong way but don't you think you're becoming a bit obsessed with this Ewan Galbreith guy?'

'What?'

I don't believe I'm hearing this. My closest friend now thinks I'm overreacting. Ewan would love this.

'He killed my aunt and uncle and now he's threatening me, and stalking me, and you're telling me *I'm* obsessed?'

She takes the wine bottle from my hand and uncorks it.

'Look Libby. I'm sure he is harassing you, but I don't know that he got into your flat. Unless he's some kind of amazing magician, I can't see how it could have happened. Joel says people get viruses on their computers all the time. Maybe your virus checker is out of date. Joel said he's happy to have a look at it for you.'

I pour the wine into a glass and throw it back.

'I don't believe this, Donna. I'm always on the ball. Everything was up to date on my laptop. I'm so security conscious it's unbelievable.'

'Libby, I never said...'

'What do you call it then? You doubt my sanity. You doubt what I say is true. Ewan has been in my flat. I don't know how. Maybe he stole the keys from me,' I say.

'But you'd know if...'

'It could have happened anywhere. I'll have to retrace my steps. Try to remember when it was possible. At your party for instance, I think I may have left my bag to get some food. There must have been other times...'

'Ewan Galbreith wasn't at our party, Libby,' she says defensively.

'I know that,' I say, fighting to hide my irritation. 'But there must have been other times like that, where I left my bag for a few moments.'

Donna gives me an odd look.

'But surely if Galbreith had been that close you would have seen him?'

My head spins and I pour more wine into my glass. Donna is right though, I am losing my grip. She never said as much but I know that is what she's thinking. I'm making insane statements. It's a fact that without keys, Ewan couldn't possibly have got into the flat.

'Perhaps he got someone else to do it,' I say.

Donna sighs.

'Please, Libby, come to us for a few days, if only for a break.'

I shake my head.

'No, I won't give into this. Besides, I'm going to Padley at the weekend. Maybe I'll speak to his sister and friends while I'm there. I'll get them to pass on a warning message to him.'

'I don't think you should get involved with him,' says Donna worriedly.

Donna doesn't have a clue what I'm going through.

'Just a break, Libby, it might really help. Have you thought of talking things through with a counsellor?'

That's the final fucking insult. I'd seen my fair share of bloody counsellors and shrinks since the murders. Channel your feelings, they'd said. Put that energy into something positive. So, I'd done just that. I took myself to art school and studied graphic design, night and day until I had erased Ewan Galbreith from my brain.

'Yeah, maybe I will,' I say to shut her up. I just want her to leave me in peace so I can think things through. The locks are being changed tomorrow. I'm not giving anyone a set of keys. Not even the concierge. The only person able to get into my flat will be me.

CHAPTER FIFTY-SEVEN

FIFTEEN YEARS EARLIER

Molly nervously took the stand. Her cheeks were red from the heat in the courtroom. She couldn't look at Ewan. It felt like a bad dream. A terrible nightmare that she wished they could all wake up from. She still couldn't believe that Rose and Edward were dead. Poor Rose, oh, just the thought of what she went through makes Molly want to cry all over again. Who would want to kill lovely Rose Owen? It just didn't make sense. Not Ewan, surely not. Surely he wasn't capable of that.

'Please state your name for the court.'

'Molly Joanne Lane.'

'Miss Lane, you worked at Manstead Manor. Can you please tell the court what your role was there?'

'I was the housekeeper.'

'How long have you been housekeeper at the Manor?'

'Just over five years.'

'So you knew the Owen family very well?'

'Yes,' said Molly, feeling the threat of tears coming over her again. She didn't want to cry in court. It would be in the papers and she couldn't bear that.

'Was this a live-in position?'

'No, it wasn't. I would start at eight and then normally finish about five, unless there was something special happening and Mrs Owen wanted me to stay later. I was always paid overtime. We all were.'

'I imagine you knew the other members of staff very well?'

Molly nodded. 'Yes, I did... I do.'

Her voice had started to tremble. She knew he was going to ask her about Ewan.

'No need to be anxious, Miss Lane,' the barrister said kindly.

Molly smiled weakly.

'How well would you say you know Ewan Galbreith?'

'Quite well, we were friends... are friends.'

'Mr Galbreith lived in, didn't he?'

'In the gamekeeper's cottage, yes.'

'I see. Would you describe him as an easy-going person?'

'Yes, I suppose I would.'

'You suppose?'

She nodded. 'Yes.'

'Would you say that there is an air of arrogance about him?'

Molly shook her head emphatically.

'No. Not arrogance. Confident, I'd say he was confident.'

'Would you describe him as reckless?'

Molly looked puzzled.

'I don't know.'

'Did he take chances?'

'Yes, perhaps sometimes. But everyone takes chances, don't they?'

'So, he could be a bit rash. Would you agree with that?'

'I don't know,' Molly said, looking confused.

'Did you ever see Mr Galbreith take a shotgun from Edward Owen's gun cupboard?'

'Yes, often. It's a country estate and Ewan kept the rabbits and vermin under control.'

'Did you ever see him take a gun when he wasn't supposed to?'

'No, I didn't,' she said firmly.

'But he took liberties, didn't he?'

'No.'

The barrister smiled indulgently.

'You all took liberties, didn't you?'

'No,' she said, her cheeks reddening.

'Isn't it true that you borrowed a Gucci handbag belonging to Rose Owen and that Libby Owen saw you in town with it just before Christmas?'

'I...' She glanced over at Libby who had her head bowed.

'Mrs Owen said I could borrow it. I wasn't taking liberties.'

'Really, it's a shame that Rose Owen isn't here to corroborate that story, isn't it?'

Molly wrung her hands.

'It's true.'

'So Miss Owen is lying?'

'No, she did see me, but I did ask to borrow the bag.'

'I see, and did Ewan Galbreith take liberties too?'

'I... sometimes he took whisky when he shouldn't, but Mr Owen never seemed to mind.'

'On the night of the 31st December did you work late?'

'Yes, I did. Mrs Owen was having people for dinner and she asked if I would help with the preparations.'

'What time did you finish that evening?'

'About 8.30 but I'm not absolutely sure. Mrs Owen said she had a migraine and they wouldn't be entertaining after all. I remember feeling a bit irritated because I had to wrap all the food that had been delivered and put it into the freezers. The dining room had been prepared so that had to be cleared away.'

'Did anyone else stay late to help you?'

'Yes, Kevin stayed to help.'

239

'Did you hear Edward Owen and Ewan Galbreith arguing that evening?'

Molly took a deep breath.

'Yes.'

'Do you remember what time that was?'

'No, I don't but it was just before I left.'

'Do you recall hearing Ewan Galbreith shout, and I quote "I should take a shotgun to you, you heartless bastard, that's all you deserve"?'

Molly bit her lip and glanced at Ewan. He nodded and she gave a weak smile.

'Yes,' she said.

'Thank you, Miss Lane, no more questions for the moment.'

CHAPTER FIFTY-EIGHT

Libby

I close the doors and lock them only to unlock them all over again and re-lock for a third time. He can't possibly get in. They're new locks. No one can get in except me. I drop the keys into my handbag and pick up Merlin's basket.

Ian smiles as I enter the foyer.

'Miss Warren, thank you so much for the get-well card.'

'You're welcome, Ian. I'm so glad to see you back.'

'Thank you, ma'am.'

I look through the doors to see Simon waiting by his car.

'I'll be home on Monday,' I say.

I don't mention the change of locks. He nods. Simon waves and Ian opens the door for me.

'I just need to drop Merlin at Donna's,' I tell Simon.

'No problem,' he says.

He smells of Marc Jacobs' 'Men' aftershave. It's fresh and soft. Ewan never wore aftershave. Neither did Uncle Edward. They were alike in a way. I push the thought of Ewan from my mind and smile at Simon. His blond hair has fallen across his forehead. He looks different without it gelled back. His eyes are covered by sunglasses. I'm nervous about going to Padley. I don't want to face Manstead Manor. There are too many memories and I'm still not sure that I'm strong enough to face them. After dropping Merlin off at Donna's, I make an effort to relax but I still find myself looking out of the back window to see if a car is following us.

'You need to chill,' Simon says, putting on some music.

The car is clean and looks fresh.

'I like your car. Is it new?' I ask.

He smiles apologetically.

'It's a rental. My car broke down a few days ago. Clutch problems. It wouldn't have been ready in time.'

The thought of breaking down on an isolated road with the possibility of Ewan tailing us sends a shiver down my spine. I feel vulnerable outside of my flat. I'd been feeling pretty vulnerable in it the past few days but now the locks have been changed I'm feeling a bit more relaxed. It's the not knowing when Ewan will make his move, if he intends to make a move at all. Perhaps he wants to keep me in a constant state of fear. Yes, that would be Ewan's style. I try to picture the Ewan I had seen at the nightclub. Does he have a girlfriend? There were always women in his life. Fifteen years without a woman must have driven him mad. The last time I had seen his face was in the courtroom all those years ago. The hatred in his eyes had been frightening. Now, I'm going back again. Back to the town that had once been my home. Back to Manstead Manor and my hands tremble at the thought.

'Thank you for coming with me,' I say, turning to Simon.

'I'm only glad I can help.' He smiles.

I look out of the window. Maybe Ewan is in Padley already. He always seems to be one step ahead of me. Is that where he will confront me? If only I could stop thinking about him. Was it fair to bring Simon?

I am brought out of my reverie by the trilling of my phone. My heart starts to beat that little bit faster. It's Fran.

'Have you arrived?' she asks without preamble.

'No, we're on our way.'

'We?' she questions.

'I'm with a friend, Simon Wane.'

'Let me know when you arrive. Where are you staying?'

'At William and Caroline's beach house.'

'Alone?'

I glance sideways at Simon.

'I'm not sure yet.'

'Let me know if you're going to be alone and I'll come over.'

'Do you think he might...?'

'No, but I know that you think he might.'

'Thanks Fran.'

I click off the phone and turn to Simon.

'I'll be staying at William's beach house. William was my guardian after the murders. You're welcome to stay there too. It has two bedrooms.'

He smiles.

'Sounds great,' he says.

I try not to show my surprise. It was not the response I had been expecting. He's always shied away from staying too long at my flat so the last thing I expected was him to agree so readily to stay a whole weekend in a house with me.

'Great. I'll let Fran know. She was going to come over otherwise.'

'No need,' he said.

I send Fran a quick text.

Simon is staying over with me. No need to come.

If Ewan is able to hack my phone then he'll read the messages. He'll know I'm not alone. He'll know the police are suspicious of him. I've no need to be afraid. But nevertheless I am.

CHAPTER FIFTY-NINE

PRESENT DAY

Fran read Libby's text before strolling into Mike's office. He looked up and she felt sure his eyes lit up with pleasure.

'I'm going for lunch,' she said. 'I don't know if you...'

'Yeah,' he said, standing up. 'Let's visit Ben Mitchell while we're at it.'

'Ben Mitchell?' said Fran, surprised.

'If Libby Warren is coming here for the weekend I don't want any trouble. Padley's a small place.'

'She's staying at William Stephen's beach house. Some guy named Simon is coming with her. She must have a boyfriend. She kept that quiet.'

Mike whistled.

'Brave bloke to take that one on.'

'What do you mean?'

'You think we've got baggage. I wouldn't like to see the size of her suitcases.'

Fran smiled. No one could have more baggage than Mike.

'Nice top,' he said flippantly but Fran blushed with pleasure all the same.

———

Mike wrinkled his nose in disgust at the smell of fish from Ben's truck. Rumour had it that Ben Mitchell spent more time in his truck than he needed to. People in Padley felt sorry for him. His wife was a lush, they said. Patti had become a dedicated drunk since the Owen trial. She'd drink until she passed out, sometimes with the bottle still in her hand. Everyone in Padley knew. Some said she drank to forget the baby that Ben had knocked out of her. Patti was seldom sober these days. Fran had never understood Patti standing by her man like she had. It was common knowledge that he knocked her about but she'd never reported it. During the murder trial Fran had tried to talk her into pressing charges, but she wouldn't. A baby may have been their saving grace, but Ben just couldn't keep his hands off her, not even then. That had been ten years ago. Patti had declined more with each year. There was a violent side to Ben Mitchell and Fran had always been suspicious of him. But after Libby had accused Ewan of the murders, Fran had to drop her enquiries into Ben, but she'd always been suspicious of him. Had Libby made a mistake? Was it possible?

Ben was sitting by his boat eating a sandwich. The smell of fish and Ben's angry features threw Fran's mind back to fifteen years earlier.

———

Ben Mitchell sauntered to the witness stand, his hands loosely pushed into the pockets of his jeans. He took the oath and looked up to face the barrister.

'Please state your full name for the court.'

'Benjamin Mitchell.'

'Mr Mitchell, would you please tell the court what you do for a living?'

'I'm a fisherman,' Ben said flatly.

'Do you know the accused, Ewan Galbreith?'

Ben's face twitched.

'Yes I do.'

'Is it true that on the 4th December you went to Manstead Manor with Adam Price and Matt Broughton?'

'I might have done.'

'Yes or no, Mr Mitchell.'

'Yes.'

'Is it also true that you went with the intention of "giving Ewan Galbreith a good seeing to"?'

Ben frowned and looked around the courtroom before replying.

'Yeah, I might have said something like that.'

'And this "seeing to" was revenge for the accused's affair with your wife. Is that correct?'

'They weren't having an affair,' snapped Ben.

'They were having sex though, weren't they?'

'Yeah,' muttered Ben.

'So, on the afternoon of the 4th December according to Miss Owen's testimony, you broke Mr Galbreith's arm and caused some other minor injuries. Is that true, Mr Mitchell?'

Ben sighed.

'Yes.'

'Isn't it true that Mr Owen stopped this "seeing to" and removed your balaclava, revealing your identity?'

'He shouldn't have interfered.'

'You must have been very angry with Mr Owen. I imagine you wanted to give him a good seeing to as well...'

'Objection.'

'Mr Fosh, please don't make me warn you again. Please rephrase the question.'

'Were you angry with Mr Owen?'

'No, I gave Ewan a warning, that's all I wanted to do.'

'Did you though? Didn't you tell Adam Price that if it hadn't have been for Mr Owen, Ewan Galbreith would have been on life support?'

'I don't remember saying that.'

The barrister picked up a sheet of paper.

'I have Mr Price's testimony here, Mr Mitchell. During his testimony he was quite emphatic that you said those words.'

'Like I say, I don't remember.'

'Is it also true that you went back to Manstead Manor a week later?'

Ben chewed his lip.

'Yeah I did. Galbreith shot at my boat. That was my fucking livelihood. The bugger knew what he was doing. Only Galbreith can shoot like that. He shouldn't be allowed a gun.'

'Are you sure it was the accused? Wouldn't it have been quite difficult for him to shoot with a broken arm?'

Ben laughed. 'That wouldn't stop Galbreith.'

'The housekeeper at Manstead Manor recalls you visiting on the 23rd December. Why did you visit the house on that day?'

'It was his rifle that wrecked my boat. I figured he could pay for the repairs.'

'Why didn't you report the incident to the police?'

'I...'

'Wouldn't that have been easier?'

'I didn't want everyone knowing about him and Patti.'

'And you thought you could get some money from Mr Owen? Is that also true, Mr Mitchell?'

'I suppose so.'

'Did you get what you wanted?'

'Yeah, I did.'

'Molly, the housekeeper, has stated that she overheard the conversation and, in her words, said that it didn't sound like you were happy. You've got a temper haven't you, Mr Mitchell?'

'Not really.'

'Isn't it true you sometimes lose your temper with your wife?'

'No!'

'Did you go back and shoot Edward and Rose Owen on New Year's Eve?'

'No, I did not.'

'No more questions.'

———

Present day

Ben looked up as Fran and Mike approached. He gave a cynical smile.

'So Libby Owen comes home and everyone crawls out of the woodwork.'

'How are you doing, Ben?' Mike smiled.

'Not so great but thanks for asking.'

'Who said Libby Owen has come home?' asked Fran.

'Rumours, you know how they travel.'

'She's been having a bit of trouble with someone,' said Fran. 'Is that right?'

'Have you seen Ewan Galbreith since he was released?'

'Yeah, I saw him being greeted like some celebrity in the pub,' Ben sneered.

Nothing but fucking trouble was Libby Owen and Ewan Galbreith. Between them they'd ruined his life.

'That truck stinks,' said Mike, putting a tissue to his nose.

'Yeah, well I'm a fisherman.' Ben grinned.

'Just don't cause any trouble,' said Mike, walking away.

Ben laughed.

'Yeah, right.'

'Bloody fish,' grumbled Mike.

Fran laughed but she couldn't shake the uneasiness she always felt when around Ben Mitchell.

CHAPTER SIXTY

FIFTEEN YEARS EARLIER

It was two days before New Year's Eve and Libby had plans. The first thing she wanted to do was to take a trip into Exeter and buy herself the perfect dress for the celebrations. She wanted to look irresistible for Patrick. She was seeing him later and she wanted them to make plans. In April she would be eighteen. He only had to wait a few months and then he wouldn't have to worry about her age or what people said. She'd been invited to a New Year's Eve party and she wanted to take Patrick. It was going to be a wonderful start to the millennium.

She changed into her riding gear and made her way to the stables. She saw Ewan go in with a worried expression on his face. He hadn't used the wallet she'd bought him for Christmas. She knew that because she saw him put money into his old wallet when he was in the kitchen the other day. Maybe he would also be different with her when she was eighteen. He'd probably be really interested if he knew the things she could do. The things Patrick had shown her. She felt her legs turn weak at the thought of doing them with Ewan and quickly pushed the images from her mind.

Ewan was looking at Princess as she lay in the stable.

'Hi,' Libby said.

He turned and she thought she saw a flicker of irritation cross his face.

'How is Princess today?' she asked.

Ewan turned back to the horse.

'She's not good. The vet's on his way.'

'What are you doing New Year's Eve?' she asked.

'I don't know,' he said dismissively.

'I'll be eighteen in April.' She smiled, unzipping her jacket.

'Yeah.' He smiled.

'I never thanked you for rescuing me from Peter that night.'

Ewan turned and stared at her. 'What?'

'When Peter tried it on.'

She'd unbuttoned the top of her blouse. There was a throbbing in her loins that was aching for release.

'Peter didn't mean any harm.'

'No,' she said, squatting beside him.

She leant her hand on Ewan's knee and looked at the horse. She could smell the fragrance of the soap Ewan used.

'Did you like the wallet?' she asked softly.

She knew her bra was clear for him to see. Ewan stood up so quickly that Libby tumbled over into the hay.

'Yeah thanks,' he said abruptly.

'Ewan...' she began but Ewan was getting a blanket for Princess.

'Shouldn't you get going?' he said. 'The weather's going to change. The wind is building up.'

She wanted to tell him how good she could make him feel. They could do it in the hay. No one would know.

'You could come out with me and my friends on New Year's Eve,' she said.

Ewan glanced at her.

'Thanks, but I'm meeting mates down the pub.'

'Oh, I...'

His mobile rang and she never got to finish. It's probably that slut Patti, she thought. She saddled up Georgie while he went out with his phone and then she waited until he had finished.

'Why don't you use my wallet?' she asked bluntly when he came back into the barn.

'I will when my other one is worn out,' he said with a smile.

'Great,' she said, leading Georgie out.

She felt like crying. Why didn't he like her? He liked all the other women. She climbed onto Georgie and waved at the vet as he walked towards the barn. Sometimes she thought Ewan preferred the horses to her. To hell with him, she decided. She'd see Patrick later. The thought of Patrick and his hands on her made her suddenly hot. She'd find a quiet spot and relieve herself in a bit.

CHAPTER SIXTY-ONE

PRESENT DAY

Libby

My hands tremble and my breathing quickens as we drive into Padley. I've not been back for ten years and everything looks different. I hadn't expected this. Things have changed so much. The front is busy. It's holiday season. The pub is still there and I push the memories from my mind before they overwhelm me. The sea is shimmering in the summer sun. I used to love coming down to the front in the summer. After swimming and sunbathing we'd get fish and chips from the chippy.

'It's gone,' I say aloud.

Simon turns.

'What has?'

'The chippy,' I say, feeling a sense of loss wash over me.

It was by the chippy that they'd said Ewan fucked Patti Mitchell. He'd no doubt fucked her in lots of other places too but for some reason that had always stuck in my mind. I wonder what she's doing now? Does she look different? Is she still with Ben? A shiver runs down my back at the thought of Ben

Mitchell. What am I doing? I should never have come back. What is the point? It'll just bring back memories and going to the house will be even worse.

'Do you want to go to the house first?' Simon says, as though reading my mind.

'No,' I say forcefully.

I'm not ready. I need to prepare.

'Let's go to the beach house. William and Caroline will be expecting us.'

'Okay,' he says but I sense his disappointment.

I see the pub. At least that hasn't changed, and then I see her.

'Stop,' I say.

Simon brakes suddenly and I'm jolted forward.

'Is everything all right?' he asks, concerned.

It's Molly. She looks exactly the same. Maybe a little older but still the same Molly with her rosy red cheeks. She glances at our car before crossing the road in front of us.

'I know that woman,' I say.

He nods.

'Do you want to get out?' he asks. 'It's awkward to park here.'

'No,' I say. 'Let's carry on.'

I text William to let him know we are close. We climb the hill to the cove and pass the field where Patrick had his caravan. The field is full of holiday chalets. I try to picture Patrick in my mind as I have numerous other times. But I can't see him clearly.

'You can park over there,' I tell Simon, pointing to a space.

I climb from the car and inhale the acrid smell of seaweed. A cool breeze blows in from the sea and I close my eyes, lifting my face to the sun. If only things had been different.

'I'll bring the bags,' says Simon.

I see Caroline waving from the beach and I wave back. Simon carries our bags and we make our way along until we reach the steps that lead down to the narrow path that will take us to the beach house. William meets us halfway and hugs me.

'It's good to see you in Padley,' he says, taking the bags from Simon.

'This is Simon,' I say.

'Nice to meet you,' says Simon, extending his arm. William looks at him curiously before shaking his hand.

'Welcome to Padley or have you visited before?'

'I haven't.'

'It's perfect this time of year.'

I look out to the calm sea and listen for a moment to the calling of seagulls. Caroline waits for us at the beach house. I've never understood why it's called a beach house. It's more a white timber bungalow. It sits alone, its front weathered from the cold winds and sea spray. It's homely though and you can step outside straight onto the beach and that's what I love about it.

Caroline is waiting at the door. I feel a surge of warmth for her.

'I'm so glad to be home,' I say, and I mean it.

It's good to be back in the place that is so familiar. If only the bad memories weren't there. If only I could enjoy Padley without thinking of Ewan.

'It's lovely to see you,' she says, kissing me. 'Come in. I've made everything nice for you. But we insist you come to us this evening for dinner. I'm making a pot roast. You always liked pot roast.'

She glances past me to Simon.

'Hello.' She smiles. 'Thanks for coming with Libby.'

'It's a pleasure.'

'Libby said you're interested in seeing the house,' said William, ushering us in.

The beach house is exactly as I remembered it from the last time I was here. Full of light and covered in bright cheery fabrics. The fragrance of Caroline's favourite Jo Malone candles reaches my nostrils.

'I've made a bit of lunch,' says Caroline.

'Simon's a chartered surveyor,' I say.

'Really, who do you work for?' asks William.

'Myself, I have my own company.'

'I'll look you up.'

'I'll give you my card.' Simon smiles. 'What a wonderful view.'

He walks to the window.

'Have you seen Ewan?' I say softly to Caroline.

'No, I know a few people who have.'

'Where's he living?'

'I don't know, Libby. Don't think about him.'

'No, I won't,' I lie.

I'm in Padley, how can I not think of Ewan Galbreith? Have I ever not thought about Ewan?

'He wouldn't dare bother you,' she says.

If she only knew what he'd been putting me through.

'Here are the keys to the manor house,' William says.

I stare at the heavy bunch of keys and then allow him to drop them into my hand.

'I have some letters for you, I don't know if you want them.'

'I'll take them when I leave.'

'Great. It's good to see you. You're looking well,' says William.

'A bit tired,' says Caroline. 'Are you overworking?'

'I'm fine,' I say.

Don't make a fuss I want to scream.

I'm tired, I'm so very tired. I'm tired of thinking of Ewan Galbreith. Maybe he'll come. Maybe he has been waiting for me to come to Padley. Maybe this is where he wants it to happen.

CHAPTER SIXTY-TWO

PRESENT DAY

'Libby Owen is in town,' said Fran.

'Huh,' said Dianne, 'I'm sure she is not using the name Libby Owen anymore.'

'We don't want any trouble. Is your brother in town?' Fran asked.

'I haven't seen him, if that's what you mean? As far as I know he's in London.'

'Where does he stay when he comes to Padley?'

Dianne sighed.

'I'm bloody sick of you hassling Ewan. Just leave him the fuck alone. Leave all of us the fuck alone. It's over, well and truly bloody over. Now let me close my door.'

Fran put her hand on the door.

'It isn't over for Libby.'

Dianne's face darkened.

'Fuck Libby Owen. Fuck all of you. That bitch has caused nothing but trouble for our family.'

The door slammed in Fran's face. She stood there for a while and then wiped the perspiration from her forehead. She looked at Mike sitting in the cool interior of the car. Lucky bugger, she thought. He raised his eyebrows as she approached.

'Not cooperating then?'

'I don't blame her. Maybe we should keep a check on Libby while she's here.'

Mike snorted.

'Give over, Fran. If she wanted security she should have brought it with her. Let's get back. There are more important cases for us to be dealing with.'

Fran sighed and climbed gratefully into the car.

———

Rumours were rife in the pub. Someone said a woman from London was in town to look at the Manstead estate. It wasn't long before the name Libby Owen was mentioned.

'Why would she come back now?' asked one.

'Nah, it isn't her. This woman is blonde, so George said. He saw them at the beach house.'

'Maybe Manstead is going to be sold,' said another.

'No one said it's being sold,' corrected Luke. 'Christ, the way people talk around here. Someone has come up from London, a couple as I understand it, to visit William and Caroline. No one has said they're buying Manstead.'

'They seemed pretty friendly according to George.'

'I reckon it's her,' said another.

Luke thumped his fist on the bar.

'Look, I don't want trouble; if Libby Owen has come back to sell the house then that's her business. Now let's forget it.'

Ben sat quietly at the back of the pub. He'd had a bellyful of the Owen's. They'd been nothing but trouble for him. Things had never been the same since the court case. It had finished him and Patti off. Owen had deserved everything he'd got. Why hadn't Libby stayed in London? Didn't she ever learn? What did it need to keep her away? Her and her fucking family rolling shit deep in money while the rest of them fucking struggled. Now she'd come to rub their noses in it. Libby Owen would get what was coming to her if she hung around Padley.

'We've had enough of the Owen family,' he said.

Molly spun around.

'The Owens were very good to some of us.'

'While they treated others like shit,' he spat.

'No need to drag up the past,' said Luke firmly.

'Arse lickers,' muttered Ben before leaving the pub.

CHAPTER SIXTY-THREE

FIFTEEN YEARS EARLIER

E wan watched as Libby climbed onto Georgie and trotted away. This was getting out of hand. He ought to speak with Edward about it. She fancied the pants off him, that was clear. Christ, of all the things. He'd been aware of it but had thought she would grow out of it, but clearly her time with Patrick had awakened something within her. He'd not known what to do about the wallet. He'd thought about giving it back but hadn't wanted to cause offence. Now things were getting too hot. Christ, she'd practically shoved her tits in his face. He smiled at the memory of how blatant she'd been. He could have had her there and then in the hay if he'd wanted. Had it been anyone else he wouldn't have thought twice, but Libby, no way. That was out of bounds for sure. Not that he fancied her anyway. She was far too young. But his respect for Edward would stop him ever doing anything like that. He'd speak to Edward about it. He'd wait until the New Year was over. Patrick would be moving on, now he'd got some money, and then Libby could be more trouble than ever with him gone. He had to put a halt to it.

The sound of a car pulling onto the drive broke into his

thoughts. Moments later, Neil, the vet popped his head around the barn door.

'How is she?' he asked, venturing closer.

'I'm not happy with her,' said Ewan, stroking Princess gently.

'Let's have a look.'

Ewan stepped aside for Neil to examine the horse.

'We'll try another course of antibiotics but quite honestly, if these don't work we will have to consider letting her go.'

Ewan nodded.

'Are you on call over the New Year?'

'I'm not but don't hesitate to phone me. Paul Ledder is on call, but I know you're not comfortable with him. Just give me a bell, okay?'

'Thanks Neil.'

Ewan took a deep breath, pushed his hands into his pockets and walked from the barn. He needed a drink.

———

Patrick shoved the last of his belongings into a tatty suitcase and checked the time. He was meeting Libby and he was dreading it. Lil had been clingy all afternoon. The kids had been a fucking nightmare. Lil wanted to do something special on New Year's Eve. It was all getting too much. Bloody women, they were more trouble than they were worth.

They'd been kicked off the field by the bloody farmer. He'd come at them with a shotgun.

'Jesus Christ,' Lil had screamed. 'Don't shoot my kids.'

As if the bastard would shoot the kids. All the same, it had scared her shitless and she wanted to get off the land right away. They'd have to leave the caravan. It was a pile of shit anyway, and it would cost more to move it than he would have got for it.

Best to torch the thing, he'd reasoned. Burn it to the ground and then go to the council. They'd have to put them up somewhere, they'd got kids. Meanwhile, he'd got them fixed up in a hostel just outside Padley.

The money old man Owen had given him was going fast. He'd had to pay some of his debts. It was either that or lose his kneecaps. He needed more. Easy come, easy go, he thought. He'd go back to Owen. Ask for a bit more. He'd show him the air tickets. They'd be out of his hair in a week, he'd tell him. Out of Libby's clutches too. He'd miss her. She was a good little fuck. Did whatever he asked. Christ, he couldn't believe some of things she agreed to do. She loved it. Sometimes he thought she was thinking of someone else when he fucked her but what the hell. He didn't care.

Owen would give him more money, he was sure of it. They wanted to see the back of him. He knew what he was going to tell Owen if he refused. He'd leave a little going away gift with Libby. She'd like that. *Wouldn't you like to be a grandfather?* he'd ask Owen. He laughed at the thought. He'd ask for another grand. That would be nothing to him with all his millions. He could ask for more but best not to push things too far. He didn't know what the fuck he was going to do for dosh if Owen said no. He owed money left, right and centre.

'Let's go,' he said to Lil.

He'd be glad to get off this stinking farm and out of Lil's clinging clutches. Hopefully she'd calm down once they got to the other place. He wouldn't have time to see Owen tonight. Maybe he'd go tomorrow or even New Year's Eve but then again, that might piss him off. Still, the more pissed off he was, the more likely he'd be to pay the money. He'd get Lil settled and then go to the pub. Tank up a bit before telling Libby he was going to Australia sooner than he had admitted.

CHAPTER SIXTY-FOUR

FIFTEEN YEARS EARLIER

E wan held the bible in his hand and swore to tell the truth, the whole truth and nothing but the truth. He handed the bible back and lifted his head.

'Would you please state your name for the court?'

'Ewan Michael Galbreith.'

'Mr Galbreith, what was your job on the Manstead estate?'

'I was gamekeeper for Edward and Rose Owen.'

His voice faltered over Rose Owen's name and there was a murmur from the jury.

'Can you tell us exactly what being a gamekeeper involves?'

'I take care of the land, I'm in charge of the gardeners and I make sure the wildlife doesn't get out of control. I organise shooting events and hunting parties. I also did other jobs for Mr Owen.'

'How long had you been gamekeeper for the Owens?'

'Six years. I began working on the estate when I was eighteen.'

'We've heard evidence during this trial of your skill as a marksman. Would you agree with that? Are you an excellent shot with a gun?'

'Yes, I would agree with that,' said Ewan without hesitation. 'I am a certified marksman.'

'Some say you never miss your target. Would you agree with that?'

'Yes, I guess I would. It's better for the animals if it is a clean kill.'

'Do you like killing things, Mr Galbreith?'

'Objection.'

'The witness may answer the question.'

'No I don't. I love animals. It's sometimes necessary though.'

'So you worked six years on the estate. Did you always see eye to eye with Edward Owen?'

'No, not always. I respected him though.'

'Mr Galbreith, did you take rifles from Mr Owen's gun room for uses other than hunting?'

'A couple of times.'

'Did Mr Owen give his permission for this?'

'Not always.'

'Did you use one of Edward Owen's rifles to shoot at Ben Mitchell's boat?'

'Yes I did.'

'Did it ever occur to you that you could have hit one or more of the men on the boat?'

'No, my intention was to shoot the boat.'

'So you took guns from the gun room when you shouldn't have?'

Ewan hesitated.

'Yes.'

'Did you threaten Patrick O'Leary with a rifle?'

Ewan's jaw twitched.

'It wasn't loaded.'

'How many other times have you taken rifles without Mr Owen's consent?'

'A few times, he would turn a blind eye to it.'

'Was Edward Owen a bit soft with you, Mr Galbreith?'

Ewan cracked his knuckles.

'We had a mutual respect for each other. I liked him.'

'Not many people did, did they?'

'He had his fair share of enemies.'

'But you weren't one of them?'

'No, I wasn't. He was harsh and thoughtless sometimes, but he would listen.'

'But on the evening of the 31st December you were overheard telling Edward Owen that you'd like to take a shotgun to him.'

'It wasn't how it sounds.'

'How was it then, Mr Galbreith?'

CHAPTER SIXTY-FIVE

PRESENT DAY

Libby

'We'll see you in a couple of hours,' says Caroline, hugging me.

I watch them walk up the steps and then close the door. Simon is standing by the French doors looking out to the beach.

'It's beautiful here, isn't it?' I say.

'Yes it is.' He smiles.

He looks into my eyes and for a second I feel lost in his.

'Which is my room?' he says, jolting me out of the dream.

'Oh yes, of course, let me show you.'

I lead him to the second bedroom. It's bright and cheerful like the rest of the house.

'It's got its own bathroom,' I say shyly.

'Great, I think I'll take a shower.'

'Right,' I say uncertainly, stepping out of the room.

I hear the lock click behind me. I look at the French doors and debate whether to lock them too. I decide to play safe, at least until Simon comes back. A few minutes later I hear the shower running and walk into my room to unpack my case. I stupidly can't stop my hands from shaking. Just the smell of the seaweed has evoked so many memories. It all seems so long ago now. We were young then. Invincible, I'd thought. I ought to visit Uncle Edward and Aunty Rose's grave. But what if someone sees me? They'll know I am Libby Owen. Who else would visit their grave? I can't risk it. I'll be too vulnerable. I'd be a perfect target for Ewan.

My phone bleeps. My heart races and my hand shakes even more. It's most likely harmless. Just another email or a text from Donna checking I have arrived okay. I can't have a panic attack every time it bleeps. I look at the screen. It's a text from Fran.

Have you arrived?

I send a reply letting her know that I'm at the beach house.

Keep in touch she replies.

Has Ewan now read those messages? If so, then I have just told him where to find me. Maybe now he'll come. I'm ready for him. I'm almost hoping he will come. I want it over. I want my life back once and for all.

CHAPTER SIXTY-SIX

FIFTEEN YEARS EARLIER

Libby was shivering on the bench. He was late. Lil had been a fucking pain. Kept saying she'd top herself if he left her.

'What if the farmer comes?' she kept repeating.

'We're off his land. He won't come after us now,' he had assured her.

'But the caravan, Pat, it's a fucking burnt-out mess. He's going to be pissed when he sees it.'

He pulled her hand from his arm.

'I've got to go out, Lil. There's this guy who owes me money. It's the only night he can meet up. We need the money, you know that. I'm as sick as fuck about the caravan too but what could I do? The bugger won't come. He's got us off his land, that's all he wanted. They don't fucking shoot people, you stupid bitch.'

He'd got a slap across the face for that.

'Fuck off,' she'd screamed.

It had worked anyway. But he was nearly an hour late and Libby was almost blue with cold when he got to her. She was wearing a skimpy little dress with a cropped cardigan over the top. It must be minus three. He pulled his coat off and threw it around her shoulders. She jumped and turned to face him.

'Pat,' she said through chattering teeth.

'I'm sorry, baby. I got held up. I had a bit of trouble with the farmer on that field with the caravan.'

She pulled the coat around her and pushed her icy hands into the pockets.

'Come on. I'll get a bottle of something to warm us up.'

Libby grabbed his hand and said, 'I brought some whisky.'

'You're a star, do you know that?' He smiled.

'Pat,' she said, hesitantly. 'Why don't we get a room at one of those B&Bs? It will be much warmer.'

Patrick hesitated. He couldn't afford a room for a start, but he knew if they did get one he'd have trouble getting away. Libby would want him to stay the night and he couldn't do that.

'I don't know, babe,' he said. 'It's an expense and...'

'I'll pay,' said Libby eagerly.

'I can't stay the night, babe, you know that.'

'I know.'

It would be warmer. This fucking weather was doing him in. He'd be glad to get back to Australia. At least the weather was bloody decent.

'All right, let's do it.' He smiled.

But it was difficult to find a B&B where the owners didn't know Libby. They ended up in a dive just outside Padley, but it was warm and the bed was soft, and Libby was more than willing to do anything he asked in a warm cosy bed. He was beginning to find her a bit much. She was insatiable. He couldn't always get it up for her. Even her warm lips couldn't arouse his tired cock.

'I can't, baby,' he said.

Libby smiled and sat up to pour whisky into their glasses.

'Your breath will smell when you go home,' he said.

'I don't care. I told them I was out with my mates tonight.'

He took a long slug of whisky and lay back.

'Pat,' Libby said hesitantly. 'When I'm eighteen I get my inheritance from my parents.'

Pat's ears pricked up.

'I didn't know you had an inheritance.'

Libby nodded.

'My parents were rich. I don't remember much about them. I was only seven when they were killed in a car accident. The car caught fire. I only know what my aunt tells me. That my dad was in property like his brother Uncle Edward and that everything they owned I'll inherit when I'm eighteen. I was thinking. I could come to Australia. I'll have the air fare then easily and...'

Patrick sat up. Christ, she had to be joking? He didn't want her on his heels when he got back home.

'Look babe, that's horrible about your parents and that but...'

'You could leave Lil and we could go together...'

'Libby,' he interrupted. 'I'm leaving for Oz in a week. I...'

'What?' she said, surprised. 'I didn't think you were going yet. I thought when your visa ran out. That's another month yet.'

'Look Libby, it's been great and everything but... the thing is your uncle has threatened to tell the police about us and...'

Libby's eyes widened.

'When?'

'A few days back. It was your uncle or that Scottish bastard that told the farmer. I like you, Libby and we've had some laughs, haven't we?'

'I love you,' said Libby, tears pricking her eyelids.

'Come on, babe, you knew I was married. I've got kids. I've got responsibilities.'

'What about me?' She pouted.

'You're going to be eighteen soon. Like you said, you'll get your inheritance. There will be tons of men coming after you.'

'I want you,' she said.

He sighed.

'It's not going to happen, Libby. It's not...'

'You can just fuck off then,' she said, her fists pummelling his chest.

'Jesus, Libby, calm down.'

'Get out. I hate you.'

'Libby.'

'I'll tell Uncle Edward you raped me.'

He grabbed her by the throat, careful not to squeeze too tight.

'No, you won't. I'm leaving here and you won't do anything. Do you hear me?'

'I'm only seventeen. You could get into trouble for what you've been doing to me.'

Patrick's heart pounded. Christ, what had he got himself into?

He released Libby and climbed from the bed.

'I'll think about Australia,' he lied.

'Really?' Libby said, calming down. 'You will? I'll have my inheritance. We'll be able to buy a nice house and everything.'

'Great, let me think about it. I ought to get back.'

'I love you,' she said. 'Can we spend New Year together?'

'I'm not sure, babe. I promised the kids... you know how it is.'

She pulled a face.

'But New Year's Day,' he said to console her.

He wouldn't be here on New Year's Day. The sooner he got on a flight to Australia the better. He'd need money. He'd tell Owen that Libby was getting demanding and that she wouldn't leave him alone. Christ, he couldn't stay here. It was getting out

273

of control. Stupid bastard, that's what he was; thinking with his cock instead of his brain. Jesus, he could lose his kids.

'I've got to go,' he said bluntly.

'I'll see you New Year's Day,' Libby said.

He felt trapped. If Owen didn't give him the money then he was fucked. He needed to get away from Libby Owen as soon as possible.

CHAPTER SIXTY-SEVEN

Fran pulled off her thin cardigan and stood under the fan in the probation office. It was stifling and the water dispenser was empty.

'Hello, Inspector Marshall?'

Fran turned to a fresh-faced lad who couldn't be more than twenty.

'Hi, I'm waiting for Rob Jackson.'

He smiled and held out his hand.

'I'm Rob.'

Fran tried to hide her surprise.

'You're Rob Jackson? Ewan Galbreith's probation officer?'

'That's me. Can I get you some water? I'm sorry about the fan. The air con isn't working and this was the best I could get.'

'Water would be great.'

Christ, thought Fran, either they're getting younger or I'm getting older. He returned with two bottles of Perrier, handed her one and then pulled out a chair for her. She sat down.

'How can I help?'

'Ewan Galbreith. I can't seem to get hold of him.'

'I don't really know how I can help you. He reports when he should.'

'He phoned in sick at work...'

'That's not a crime.'

'I'm aware of that,' she said impatiently, standing up. The weather was making her irritable.

'You know he's working in London?'

'Yes, he told me.'

'Do you have any idea where I could find him?'

Rob looked thoughtful.

'He could be at one of his theatre workshops,' he said thoughtfully.

'Theatre workshops?' said Fran. 'I wouldn't have thought Ewan was the theatre type.'

Rob smiled.

'You'd be surprised what type people become when they are in prison. He became very interested. He completed a diploma course in stage make-up. Prison can open up new worlds for people.'

Fran's eyes widened.

'You're telling me. Thanks a lot.'

Fran left the stifling office and walked out into the fresh air. Who'd have thought it? Ewan Galbreith into stage make-up. Now that was a first.

———

Libby

Simon strolls out of the bathroom. His hair is damp from the shower and his glasses slightly steamed up. He looks at the French doors and then to me.

'Are you happy to have them open if I'm here?'

I nod, although I'm not happy about having them open at all. Simon is nice. I like him but he's no match for Ewan. I watch as he fumbles with the doors and steps out. The cool air drifts in and I'm grateful.

'I'm making tea,' I say, 'would you like some?'

'Great.' He smiles. 'I'm just going to wander down to the beach.'

'Oh,' I say.

It seems a bit thoughtless to open the doors and then leave me alone. I'm being paranoid again. I know I am. He hasn't come here to be my bodyguard. I should have brought Jimmy if I wanted that.

'It's fine,' I say.

'Be back in a bit.'

I pop teabags into the mugs and wait for the kettle to boil. My eyes travel around the beach house and land on Simon's open bedroom door. I clench my fists and turn back to the kettle. It would be wrong of me to go into his room. The kettle clicks, and I pour the hot water onto the teabags. I can see Simon from the window. He's strolling towards the sea. He's relaxed and carefree. It's how I'd like to be. I sigh and pick up my mug. My eyes again drift to Simon's room and I walk slowly towards it, one eye on him as he looks out to sea. I peek around the door. His suitcase is empty. Everything has been neatly packed away it seems. The dressing table has his phone charger and toiletries bag on it. A wallet sits by the charger. I feel myself pulled into the room. It smells of his aftershave. The blue shirt he was wearing earlier has been neatly folded over a chair. I have an overwhelming urge to smell it, to hold it close to me. I step into the room just as my phone bleeps. I turn to go back to the kitchen and freeze as a shadow passes by the window.

CHAPTER SIXTY-EIGHT

FIFTEEN YEARS EARLIER

'Mr Cook, you're the landlord of The Crown public house, is that correct?'

Luke nodded. 'Yes I am.'

'I imagine on the evening of the 31st December last year you were very busy?'

'We're always busy on a New Year's Eve, but yes, that was busier than other years.'

'And yet you can recall Mr Galbreith's words that night?'

'Yes I can. He was upset and Ewan didn't often get upset.'

'What was he upset about?'

'One of the horses at Manstead Manor, it had been sick for a few days.'

'This was Princess?'

'Yes.'

'What was the time when Mr Galbreith came to the pub that evening?'

Luke frowned.

'I can't be sure of the time. It was sometime around ten, maybe a bit before. He'd been in earlier for a pint. He was a bit upset then. The medication for the horse wasn't working and he'd called the vet.'

'So he left earlier in the evening to go back to Manstead Manor?'

'Yes.'

'Tell us what happened when he returned.'

Luke glanced at Ewan who sat stony-faced.

'He was distraught, couldn't get anything out of him at first.'

'Was Mr Galbreith distraught or angry, Mr Cook?'

'Both. He was angry and upset.'

'And you had time to notice this with the pub being really busy.'

Luke jutted out his chin.

'Yes, I have time for my regular patrons and Ewan wasn't just a regular, he was a friend.'

'Had you often seen Mr Galbreith angry?'

'No more than any other man.'

'We're not talking about other men, are we? We're talking about Ewan Galbreith. Did you know about the shooting of Ben Mitchell's boat?'

'Yes, but I never knew who did it until later.'

'Did you ever see Mr Galbreith take risks?'

'I don't know. I don't think so.'

'You knew he was playing around with Patti Mitchell, didn't you?'

'Maybe.'

'That was a risk wasn't it? Doing it like that under everyone's nose. Making a fool of her husband?'

'I suppose so.'

'So, who paid the vet's bills at Manstead Manor?'

'Edward Owen, I imagine.'

'Not Mr Galbreith?'

Luke laughed.

'I doubt Ewan could have afforded those kind of vet bills. There were horses, dogs and other animals kept on the farm. I reckon the vet did all right out of Edward Owen.'

'Thank you for your expertise.'

Luke smiled.

CHAPTER SIXTY-NINE

PRESENT DAY

Libby

I stand with my hand on the door handle of Simon's room. I strain my ears for any sound, but I can only hear the beating of my heart. A chill runs through me and I shiver despite the heat. I should have closed and locked the French doors. A loud banging on the door makes me jump. Surely Ewan wouldn't knock, would he? I breathe again. Something sitting on the dressing table catches my eye. Something's familiar but I'm too preoccupied with the person outside. I move cautiously from the bedroom and towards the door. I look around for a weapon to protect myself and snatch a knife from the kitchen counter. My phone bleeps again but I ignore it.

Through the frosted glass of the front door I see a tall slim figure. It's a man. Ewan was muscular. I hide the knife behind my back.

'Who is it?' I call.

'Libby Warren?' questions a voice.

No one here knows my surname, no one except Ewan Galbreith.

'Who is it?' I call again.

'Chief Inspector Mike Magregor.'

I slide the safety chain across and open the door.

'Libby?' he says.

I recognise him. His face is lined and weather-beaten. He's changed a lot. I wonder how I look to him. He's staring at me and I shift uncomfortably on my feet.

'You scared the shit out of me,' I say, relaxing my arm from behind my back. His eyes widen at the sight of the knife.

'That's not sensible,' he says. 'Sorry, I didn't mean to scare you. I thought you had someone with you, so I figured it would be okay to drop by.'

'I thought you were Galbreith,' I say.

'That's why I'm here. Can I come in?'

I open the door and allow him to enter. From the window I see Simon walking back from the beach. Inspector Magregor follows my gaze and then looks back at the knife in my hand.

'Perhaps you'd like to put that away,' he says.

'Has something happened?' I ask.

'Inspector Marshall is concerned about you,' he says, looking around. 'Nice place you've got here.'

From his expression I get the impression that it is only Inspector Marshall who is concerned about me.

'It isn't mine,' I say. 'Why would Fran be concerned?'

'Ewan didn't turn up for work last night and he phoned in sick today. It's probably nothing but Fran thought you should be made aware of it.'

'You think he's here in Padley?'

'I don't know. Why didn't you bring your bodyguard with you?'

He doesn't disguise his irritation.

'I shouldn't even have to have a bodyguard,' I snap. 'If the legal system in this country worked properly, Ewan would still be in prison.'

'He was released because of good behaviour.'

I let out a little scoff.

'Anyway, it might be best to keep all doors locked,' he says, looking at the open French doors. 'Obviously phone the police if at any time you feel threatened in any way. I wouldn't recommend taking a knife to someone.'

'I've felt threatened ever since he was released.'

'Unfortunately, there isn't much I can do about that.'

'How do you know he doesn't have a gun?'

'We have no evidence to indicate that Ewan Galbreith has a gun.'

'He could have bought one from the criminals he got to know in prison,' I say.

'Yes, he could have,' says Mike. 'But I don't think he's that big a fool. Someone is trying to scare you, but I don't think it's him.'

'There's no one else.'

He shrugs.

'Thank you for coming,' I say, opening the door.

'Enjoy your visit.' He smiles.

I close the front door behind him and curse. My phone bleeps and I pick it up. My mouth turns dry at the messages. They're all texts from an unknown number.

Welcome home. How do you find it?

You're looking good.

Perfect weather for a visit.

There's a photo attachment. I click into it with shaking hands. It's a grainy photo of the beach house.

Ewan knows where I am. It's just a matter of time before he comes.

CHAPTER SEVENTY

FIFTEEN YEARS EARLIER

New Year's Eve

'What are you doing tonight, Ewan?' Peter asked.
'I'll probably go to the pub.'

'There's a big party at Diamonds in Exeter. Why don't you come with us? Molly and Kev are coming. Kicks off around ten, it'll be a fabulous night.'

Ewan smiled.

'Thanks for the offer, mate, but I want to keep an eye on Princess.'

'Fair enough,' said Peter, wandering outside. Ewan went to the gun room and prepared the table. Edward had a big shoot tomorrow.

'Clean the shotguns will you, Ewan?' he'd asked. 'I've a couple of friends coming tomorrow. You don't have to be there. It's New Year's Day after all. You'll be able to sleep off the hangover.'

Molly hurried in all flustered.

'Ewan, the delivery van with the poultry for the dinner

tonight has broken down. Could you pop into Padley and fetch them for me? I'm already behind with getting the food ready.'

Her cheeks were bright pink from the heat in the kitchen.

'Sure, don't panic. It won't take me long.'

'Thank you, Ewan.'

He grabbed his jacket from the back of the chair and headed out. He thought about seeing Princess before going but decided against it. An hour wasn't going to make much difference to her now. He sighed and started the engine.

———

Patrick looked at the aeroplane tickets in his hand and sighed with relief. He, Lil and the kids would be on a flight home this time tomorrow. He'd wrapped everything up. They had to be at the airport at 2am. Lil wasn't happy about that, but it was the best they could offer when he'd asked to change the tickets. He wasn't going to argue. He just wanted to go home. Get away from Libby Owen before the shit hit the fan. He figured he'd go and see Edward Owen at about eight. Libby would be at her party by then. He'd text her afterwards to see if she'd meet him for a drink. After all, he ought to say goodbye. If she got arsy he'd get in his car, pick up Lil from the hostel and drive to the airport. He'd keep Libby sweet. After all, she might come to Oz, who knows. He wouldn't say no to a sugar mummy. This made him laugh and Lil demanded to know what was so funny. He'd be a fool to cut all ties. Once she's eighteen no one would care, and he might do all right out of it. It might as well be him as anyone else. He wouldn't give her an address. He'd got her number. He'd stay in touch. Yeah, that's the best way. Stay in control.

He checked the time. It would be good to see Libby one last time. Although she did wear him out. At least Lil had never demanded anything. She was too bloody knackered no doubt. It was no fun with Lil anymore. Jesus, her pussy was so fucking large he got lost inside there. Why they'd had three kids he'd never know.

'What are you thinking about?' Lil asked. 'There are a hundred and one things to do and you're bloody daydreaming.'

'I'm dreaming about our life when we get home.'

'Huh, you tosser. You'd be better off thinking about the job you're going to get.'

He picked up his coat. He was sick to death of Lil's moaning.

'Where are you going?' she demanded.

'I'm going to see a man about a dog. I'm fucking sick of your moaning. I'll be back in a few hours.'

'You think I don't know what you're up to,' she said, her voice rising. 'Everyone knows you're fucking half of Padley. You think I give a shit?'

'Oh shut up,' he snarled and slammed the door behind him.

———

Ben checked the rear of the boat. There was no doubt about it, the bastard was leaking.

'Fuck.'

The bloody thing hadn't been right since Galbreith shot at it. He couldn't keep repairing the damn thing.

'You weren't going out tonight anyway were you?' said Adam.

'Just as bloody well, ain't it?' retorted Ben.

'That boat hasn't been the same since...'

'I know that. Bloody Owen should have compensated me.'

'He's got plenty,' agreed Adam. 'There's a big shoot up there tomorrow, and a dinner party tonight, so I heard.'

Ben's jaw twitched. It wasn't bastard fair the way Edward Owen had covered for Galbreith. It wasn't bastard fair at all.

'Fucking bourgeois,' he snarled.

Adam looked puzzled. He had no idea what bourgeois meant, and he didn't think Ben did either.

CHAPTER SEVENTY-ONE

PRESENT DAY

Libby

I ask Simon to stop as we reach the gates of Manstead Manor. 'I'm sorry,' I say. 'I just don't feel ready.'

'Not a problem,' he says.

The drive to the house has been nerve-wracking. The closer we get the more nauseous I feel. Now here we are at the gate and it looks exactly the same as it did all those years ago. There's a bit of rust, but not much. There's a padlock and chain on the gate. I fumble for the keys in my handbag and Simon takes them from me without speaking and opens the gate. I can see the drive is overgrown. Where once it had been immaculate, it now has an untamed weedy track leading to the house. I look at the gravel and can almost feel the stones digging into my bare feet as they had that night.

'Do you want to drive around for a while?' Simon asks. 'Or shall I go up to the house.'

I shake my head.

'It's okay. Can we take it slowly though?'

'Sure.'

My heart skips. Ewan used to say 'sure'. It was more flippant when he used it though. Simon starts the engine and slowly we make our way along the overgrown driveway. We turn the corner and the house comes into view. The sun is shining on its grey stone and it looks uncannily inviting. Maybe everything was just a dream. Any minute now, Uncle Edward will come out to greet us and Aunty Rose will have a pitcher of home-made lemonade to cool us down. I'm feeling calmer now. I glance at the stables, almost expecting Ewan to stroll around from the side of them, but of course he doesn't. I can't resurrect the past. Aunty Rose won't be sitting under the chestnut tree drinking Earl Grey tea and enjoying the hot weather. The sun disappears behind a black cloud and suddenly the house seems cold, grey and imposing. Simon stops the car and I stare up at the house. It's tatty from the outside. The windows are dark and dirty. The shrubs at the front are overgrown, covering some of the windows. Simon is silent. He stares at the house as though in wonder.

'It looks neglected,' I say.

'Yes.'

'Maybe no one will want to buy it.'

'There's always someone,' he says without taking his eyes off the house.

I can't shake off the feeling that Ewan is here somewhere, just waiting for me. I curse myself again for not bringing Jimmy.

'I'm very anxious,' I admit. 'I think I ought to phone the security company and see if they have anyone in this part of the country that can come to the beach house.'

'He won't do anything while I'm with you,' he says confidently.

I almost laugh. Ewan would eat Simon for breakfast. He has no idea what we're dealing with. Simon opens his door. *I'm not ready yet,* I want to shout but I don't. Instead, I climb from the car too.

I watch Simon go up the steps and fiddle with the keys. It seems to take forever before he finds the right one. The door finally squeaks open. I follow him up the steps and stand on the threshold. The hall smells damp. Simon clicks the light switch, but of course, the power is off. He shines a torch around the hall and I gasp at the sight. Time seems to stand still. It feels like only yesterday that I stood in this hall as a seventeen-year-old.

'What do you think?' I ask, feeling suddenly proud.

'It's beautiful,' he breathes.

'Nothing has changed,' I say.

'Nothing?'

'No, things look exactly the same as fifteen years ago.'

Simon walks through the hallway and to the corridors beyond.

'I can't,' I say.

'Do you mind if I take a look?' he asks.

I don't want to be left alone. I don't want to go to the other rooms and I don't want to stay here.

'Can we come back another time?' I ask childishly.

He smiles.

'It will be the same whenever you do it.'

He's right, I know, but it's too hard. The memories hit me like a sledgehammer. He walks ahead of me and I hurry to keep up with him.

'We should lock the main door,' I say, speaking my thoughts aloud.

'It's fine, Libby,' he says.

It's the tone you'd use for a child and I suddenly feel stupid. I follow him along the corridor. He stops at the library and glances inside.

'They were avid readers,' he says, looking at all the books. It's a statement not a question.

'Uncle Edward was.'

'It's much brighter in here,' he says.

My eyes are locked on the door to the morning room.

'Do you mind if I use my Dictaphone?' asks Simon.

'Dictaphone?' I repeat.

'So I can note down what needs doing.'

'Oh yes, of course.'

My heart is hammering. Just being in the house again makes me edgy. Could Ewan be hiding somewhere in the house? Will he appear at any moment? My hands shake at the thought of facing Ewan with a shotgun in his hand. No, I'm being stupid. The gates and the main door were locked.

'Water stain in ceiling of main hall,' says Simon.

'What?' I say, coming out of my reverie.

He doesn't turn around and I realise he is talking into his Dictaphone.

'I'm just going to look outside.'

'I'll come with you,' I say, quickly following him. I don't want to be alone in the house.

I watch as he struggles with the kitchen door. After a heavy shove it opens.

'It always used to get stuck,' I say, remembering how Molly used to complain. It's bright in the kitchen and I see a mouse scuttle into a corner. Simon unlocks the back door and strolls outside. I look at the stables. I can picture Ewan as clear as anything. His dark hair brushed back, the frown lines on his forehead. That sensuous mouth that I had so much wanted to kiss and the warm brown eyes that had looked at me with such hatred in court. I push his image away with a shake of my head. The lawn at the back of the house is overgrown. Aunty Rose's beloved cornflowers are buried beneath a mountain of weeds.

'Five missing slates on roof,' Simon says into his Dictaphone.

I wish he'd speak to me rather than into that stupid machine. He wanders back inside giving me a smile as he does so.

'Beautiful house,' he says.

'It's been so neglected,' I say sadly.

It's my fault. I should have paid someone to keep the grounds nice. I'll ask William to get a gardener. I find myself wondering what happened to Kevin and Molly. I always liked Molly.

I'm relieved that we seem to be avoiding the morning room. Maybe I won't have to go in and relive those horrific last moments of Uncle Edward and Aunty Rose's life.

'Evidence of woodworm on the stairs,' Simon says climbing them. I feel nauseous and so shaky on my feet that the stairs become a massive effort. Simon leaps up them, leaving me way behind. It seems he has forgotten all about me now he's seen the house.

'Simon,' I say, giving him a gentle reminder that I'm still here.

'Okay?' he asks, turning to me.

'Yes, I think it's the stress,' I say, forcing a laugh.

Our voices echo in the empty space. I don't want to go into my old bedroom. I don't want to be here anymore. I want to be back in London where the memories weren't this close. In London it somehow felt like those things happened to someone else. It was so distant. Here at Manstead everything is so real. We pass Aunty Rose's dressing room and I see her hairbrush sitting on the dressing table.

'Oh,' I gasp, feeling myself sway.

Simon's arm steadies me, and I cling to it.

'It's as if she is still here,' I mutter.

Don't think about it. Don't think about the ripped dress. Don't think about the screams. Simon waits a moment while I compose myself and then continues on. They're just memories I tell myself. I have difficulty keeping up with him. He goes back down and waits for me at the bottom of the stairs.

'Do you still plan on selling it?' he asks.

'I... I don't know. I can't think...'

'It needs some work,' he says walking through the hall.

I follow until we're outside the morning room. He stops, and I hold my breath.

'This is where it happened,' I say, my breathing now shallow.

He flings open the door and I let out a small gasp.

CHAPTER SEVENTY-TWO

New Year's Eve

'Princess is not doing well,' said Ewan.

Edward didn't look up. He was studying some papers on the desk.

'I called the vet.'

'What?' barked Edward, his head snapping up.

'She'll need to be put down.'

'For Christ's sake, can't you do it? Isn't that what you're good at?'

'I'd rather not. Not with Princess.'

'Jesus,' muttered Edward. 'He's going to charge us an arm and a leg.'

'You can afford it.'

Edward dropped his pen and walked around the desk.

'Don't you tell me what I can and can't afford. I pay you to do this kind of stuff.'

'I'm a gamekeeper. I'm not a vet.'

'It's New Year's Eve. He'll charge double, and what do I get back from a dead horse?'

Ewan turned to the door.

'Don't worry, I'll pay.'

'I don't know why I put up with this crap from you, boy, I really don't.'

Ewan didn't answer but opened the door and walked out of the room. He closed it quietly behind him.

———

Libby examined herself in the mirror and frowned. The dress she had bought especially for New Year didn't look so good now. She picked up her phone and smiled at the text message.

> I can get away for a short time at around ten. Can you meet me? I can't stay long. Let me know, Patrick.

It was a surprise. She hadn't expected to see Patrick, so this was an added bonus. Maybe he would go back to Laura's party with her. She could show him off. After all, she'd be eighteen soon and it wouldn't matter then who knew. She pulled the clothes along the rail until she found the thin cotton dress that she'd bought last year with Aunty Rose. It would be a bit cold, but that didn't matter. No one cared about the cold, especially not on New Year's Eve. She pulled the dress over her head and studied herself in the mirror. The dress was flimsy and she could see her breasts through it. Patrick would love that. She'd freeze without a bra though. Her hair hung loose and she pulled it back into a bun. It made her look older. She thought of Aunty Rose's pearl drop earrings and hurried from her room to find her aunt. She was probably in the kitchen, organising the food for their dinner party. She skipped down the stairs to the grand hall and collided with Ewan. His arms came out to steady her and she felt his hand accidentally brush her breast. The nipple hardened immediately and her breath caught in her throat.

'Oh,' she gasped.

'Sorry,' he said, pulling back quickly. 'I didn't see you.'

She wanted to pull his hand back onto her breast, it had felt so good.

'This is my dress for the party,' she said, twirling.

He looked angry and she wondered what she had done.

'It's nice,' he said without any feeling in his voice.

'How's Princess?' she asked, wondering if that was why he didn't seem himself.

'She's not great. I'd better go.'

'I'll come and see her,' she said.

But he had gone through the hall and out the front door. *Why don't you like me?* she wanted to scream.

Molly came from the kitchen and smiled.

'Lovely dress,' she said.

'Thank you, Molly. Is Aunty Rose in the kitchen with you?'

'Don't you know?' Molly said.

'Know what?'

'Mrs Owen has got a migraine. The dinner has been cancelled. There's an awful lot of clearing up to do and so much food to be wrapped for the freezer.'

'Oh no. Is she in bed?'

'I think so.'

Libby felt a small flutter of panic in her stomach. Hopefully Uncle Edward wouldn't make a fuss about her going out. After all, she had told Aunty Rose, but they'd been so focused on their own dinner party and hadn't been that interested in her plans. She decided not to bother Aunty Rose about the earrings. She had plenty of her own. It was best not to draw any attention to her plans. She glanced out of the window to see Ewan walking into the barn and followed him. It was cold in her flimsy dress and she was shivering when she reached the stables. Ewan was bent over Princess and didn't hear her come in.

'How is she doing?'

He turned, and she thought she heard him sigh.

'I've just given her a sedative. Neil will be out later. He's going to put her down.'

'Oh, Ewan,' she said, laying a hand on his shoulder.

He shrugged it off gently.

'It's for the best,' he said.

If only she knew why he didn't like her, after all, Patrick couldn't get enough of her so it wasn't like she was undesirable. Every time she made it clear to Ewan that she liked him, he rejected her. Not even in a sensitive way. Libby felt the anger mount up inside her. How dare he make her feel inadequate? She was ten times better than that Patti Mitchell, who was nothing but a slut. Everyone said so. She bet he'd change his mind when she was eighteen and had her inheritance. He'd want her then. Well, she'd tell him to go stuff it. She'd look forward to that day.

'Have a good evening,' she said, her voice flat before hurrying back to the house.

CHAPTER SEVENTY-THREE

Libby

I don't know what I'm expecting to see as I look into the room where Aunty Rose and Uncle Edward died. The desk is how it always was. The room is tidy and clean, no one would ever guess what had happened here. My skin tingles and I rub at my arm.

'I need a drink,' I say, pointing to a cabinet on the opposite wall. 'Uncle Edward kept whisky in there. Do you think it's still there?'

'It'll be good vintage if it is.' Simon smiles. He steps towards the cabinet and then hesitates.

'It's okay,' I say.

He opens the cabinet door. It's just how it used to be. Simon takes two glasses and pours a large measure. The whisky calms my shaking body and Simon nods in approval.

'It's good stuff.'

'Ewan used to say that.'

He smiles and looks around the room.

'You should sell the paintings,' he says, stepping closer to study them.

I manage to get my shaky legs to the couch by the desk and ease my body onto it.

'I suppose I should.'

He studies the painting closely and then moves on to another one.

'Do you know about art?' I ask, leaning my head back.

'A bit,' he mumbles, looking closely at another painting.

'Uncle Edward liked his paintings,' I say. 'Although how he got some of them is a bit dubious, so William said.'

'Really.' He smiles.

I nurse my whisky while he studies the paintings. I'd decided that after this room we will leave. It's all too much. I can auction the paintings. I'll speak to William this evening.

'It looks like there is something behind this one,' Simon says suddenly, lifting a painting from its mounting.

'What are you doing?'

He doesn't reply. He's too absorbed with studying what is behind the painting.

'What's that?' I say, looking at a mark on the wall.

Simon reaches up. His hands are shaking.

'Simon...' I begin.

'It's a camera,' he says.

I sit up, my body suddenly alert.

'A camera, what kind of camera?'

He turns to face me.

'A video camera.'

It feels like my heart stops. Everything stands still.

'Didn't you know about this?' he asks.

I let out a long breath and shake my head. He turns from the wall and opens the drawers in the desk.

'What are you looking for?'

'The video recorder,' he says, rummaging in the drawers. 'It will be interesting to know if the camera was used or not.'

'Simon... I...'

He opens a cupboard next to the drinks cabinet.

'Bingo,' he says triumphantly as he pulls a tape from the machine.

I'm confused. Why did Uncle Edward have a camera in the morning room?

'You know what this means?'

I shake my head in confusion.

'If this is the last tape, then that means the murder will be on it. It could well have recorded the whole thing.'

He holds up the tape.

The room suddenly spins around me and then everything turns black.

———

Fifteen years earlier

Ewan didn't watch Libby leave the stables. He was too preoccupied with Princess. She was sleeping calmly now. In an hour or so Neil would come, and it would all be over. What a way to start the millennium, he thought.

He stood, took one last look at Princess and wrapped a scarf around his neck. He'd get a few pints into him; that would help.

He hadn't expected the pub to be so busy, later perhaps but not yet. People were starting early it seemed. He made his way to the heaving bar and waved to Luke.

'Evening Ewan, starting the celebrations early?'

'I wouldn't call it celebrating.'

'You all right, Ewan?'

'Yeah, Princess is being put down later.'

'I'm sorry, mate.'

Ewan shrugged.

'That's how it goes.'

He spotted Dianne with her mates and made his way over to her.

'It's going to be a good night,' said Greg. 'Have that as a chaser. Let me get some more beers in.'

Ewan nodded. The more he drank the less he'd have to think about Princess.

'How's the horse?' said one of Dianne's friends, fluttering her eyelashes at him.

Ewan gave her a smile. Any other time he'd be up for a bit of fun, especially tonight of all nights.

'She's not so good, thanks.'

'Well, if you need company tonight just let me know,' she said huskily.

He thought back to Libby in the stable and frowned. He needed to talk to Edward. He didn't want to leave Manstead, but he didn't want that kind of hassle every day at work. He didn't know what to do with the wallet. He didn't like to throw it away but using it might encourage her even more.

'I'm really sorry about Princess,' said Dianne. 'I know how fond you are of her.'

He took the beer offered by Greg and drank half in one go.

'Yeah,' he muttered, checking the time on his phone.

He had time for a couple more.

'Things will liven up here later,' said Greg. 'Luke has a band coming in. Pop back if you feel up to it. There's not much else you can do.'

'Yeah, maybe I will. Thanks.'

'I saw Libby the other day,' said Dianne, leaning closer to him. 'She had loads of make-up on.'

He shrugged.

'She's going to get into trouble one day,' said Dianne.

'It's not my problem,' he said, finishing the beer.

'I'll get the next,' he said, getting up.

Soon he would have to go back and be with Princess. He wanted to be there. He didn't want her to face it alone.

CHAPTER SEVENTY-FOUR

PRESENT DAY

Libby

I open my eyes to the sound of my phone vibrating on Uncle Edward's desk. I turn to look at it and then realise I can't move. Panic rises within me. My wrists and ankles are tied to Uncle Edward's chair with duct tape. There's no one else in the room. I open my mouth to shout and then stop myself. I try to breathe steadily but fear has now overwhelmed me, and my breathing comes out in sharp pants.

What's happened? Is Ewan here? Where is Simon? Is he tied up somewhere too? I try to look behind me.

'Simon?' I whisper.

My phone stops vibrating and then there's silence. The only sound is the occasional rumble of thunder. My bag, where's my bag? I groan when I spot it on the table, way out of my reach. The car keys and Simon's wallet are next to it. I look at the wallet. I can't take my eyes off it. I turn to the door as it opens and Simon walks in.

'You've come round,' he says nonchalantly.

'Simon, I...'

'You had a shock.'

I watch in horror as he pulls at his hair. I am shaking so much that the chair rocks on the marble floor beneath me. He's tugging so hard I feel sure blood will soon run from his head, but it doesn't. Instead, the hair comes away in his hands. He pulls off the wig to reveal gelled-back brown hair. I gasp. My eyes roam back to the wallet and then I realise. It's the wallet I bought Ewan all those years ago. I'd seen it in the bedroom at the beach house, but it hadn't registered. The leather is still new and the antlers can be seen as clear as anything.

'Good disguise don't you think?' he says, peeling away his blond eyebrows.

The Scottish accent is as pronounced as ever. The shock is too much and I feel my head swim again. He smiles and puts a glass of whisky to my lips. I turn away angrily, but he forces my head back.

'Don't be a fool. Drink it. It'll help with the shock.'

I take a gulp and feel the liquid burn my stomach. I watch mesmerised as he removes fake teeth from his mouth and takes off his glasses. Above his left eye I can now see a faint scar. I close my eyes and when I open them again I see he has removed the blue contact lenses and in front of me now stands Ewan Galbreith.

———

Fran tried Libby's number again, and again it went to voicemail. She'd tried her at the beach house but there had been no reply there either. It was stupid to worry but it wasn't like Libby not to answer her phone. Fran felt somehow responsible for her now she was in Padley. She looked out of the window thoughtfully and then grabbed her jacket and hurried to Mike's office.

'I can't get hold of Libby,' she said without preamble.

Mike didn't look up.

'Mike, did you hear me?'

'Yeah,' he muttered. 'I'm just finishing this report.'

She sighed.

'Do you think just once you could give me your attention? God knows, I've waited for it the past sixteen years,' she snapped.

He lifted his head.

'You threw me,' he said. 'I was about to come to your office and ask if you wanted to come out for dinner tonight. Then you come in here and I'm totally thrown.'

'Dinner?' she repeated.

'You do eat dinner?'

'Of course I eat dinner.'

'Great, I'll book us a table.'

'Mike, about Libby Warren.'

Mike fought back a sigh.

'Perhaps she doesn't want to talk to you. She's brought a bloke with her, don't forget. Maybe they don't want to be disturbed.'

Fran bit her lip.

'It just isn't like her. If we could get hold of Galbreith I'd feel happier.'

But Ewan Galbreith was nowhere to be found.

CHAPTER SEVENTY-FIVE

New Year's Eve

Patrick watched as the taxi drove out of Manstead Manor with Libby in the back. He checked his watch. Eight fifteen. This gave him plenty of time. Hopefully there wouldn't be too much trouble getting in to see the old man. As luck would have it he saw Edward Owen walking to the stables. Patrick smiled. At least he wouldn't have to knock on the main doors. This made things a whole lot easier. His luck was finally in. He rehearsed in his head the words he was going to say to Edward Owen. He needed this money. It was not like Owen couldn't afford it. He had plenty. It didn't seem right some people having so much while others had fucking sod all.

He reached the stables, ran his hand through his hair and was about to walk in when he heard a gunshot from inside. Patrick froze.

'What the fuck?' he muttered, looking around. What the fuck was going on? He wasn't going to stick around and get shot. He needed to get out and fast. Christ, he was only a few hours away from a plane ride home. He turned on his heel only to be stopped by Edward Owen.

'What the hell are you doing on my land?'

Patrick stopped. His legs felt suddenly weak beneath him. He turned to face Edward who stood in front of him, a shotgun held loosely in his hand. Jesus, thought Patrick frantically. The man's mad. Who the fuck did he just shoot?

'I...'

'Speak up, man,' growled Edward.

'I came to...'

'Came to what? I thought you'd gone. What do you think you're playing at?'

Patrick's eyes were fixed on the shotgun. He couldn't stop shaking, damn it. Edward looked down at the gun in his hand and smiled.

'I'm not going to shoot you, you moron.'

'I... I came to ask for money,' Patrick blurted out. 'I'm flying to Australia tonight but Libby...'

'Libby what?'

'She said she's coming out to Australia. I've tried to get her off my back. I really have but she's insistent, says she in love with me. That she wants us to have a baby together.'

Edward's lip curled.

'Why on earth would I want to give you more money?'

'Because, maybe I'd like to give her a baby,' said Patrick with a grin.

The butt of the gun whacked him in the face and sent him reeling backwards. He clutched his jaw and groaned in pain.

'Jesus,' he moaned, tasting blood in his mouth.

'You're getting no more money from me, you dirty-smelling gypo. Get off my property before I really lose my temper and blow your head off.'

Patrick spat out the blood and felt his front tooth wobble.

'Fuck,' he groaned. 'I'll get the police onto you.'

'Do that,' said Edward giving him a shove. 'If you get my niece pregnant, I promise I will find you and castrate you.'

'When she gets her inheritance at eighteen there is nothing you can do, and if she decides to share that with me, then that's her choice.'

'You won't get her inheritance. My God, I'll kill you first.'

Patrick moved away slowly, his jaw throbbing.

'Fuck you,' he mumbled. 'Fuck you to hell.'

Edward had started walking back to the house and didn't hear him. Patrick watched him disappear from sight and then made his way back down the drive. Christ, he'd never expected that. He stopped and leant against the wall. For a moment he thought he might faint. A drink was what he needed. The bastard never gave him a penny either. Calling him a dirty gypo too. Who the fuck did he think he was? *You let everyone walk over you,* Lil was always saying. Maybe she was right. Maybe it was time to stop.

'Fucker,' he groaned, feeling another tooth wobble. 'Rich stinking fucker.'

CHAPTER SEVENTY-SIX

PRESENT DAY

Libby

'Fifteen years.' Ewan smiles. 'They've treated you well. The hair is an improvement, it suits you.'

I stare at his face. At his brown hair now flecked with grey, and into his brown eyes which are hard and angry. I'd wanted to see what he looked like and now here he is. I've never been more terrified in my life.

'They said I had a flair for acting when I was in prison. I think I got quite good at it. The stage make-up was what I enjoyed the most. I spent hours trying to decide who I would be when I came out. What do you think? God knows I had enough practice,' he says. 'I think playing the part of Simon Wane was my best work. Did you like the accent?'

'Oh God,' I mutter.

What was it Fran had said; something about stage make-up and the theatre? How could I have been so stupid?

'But Donna and Joel,' I say, unable to comprehend what is happening.

'Ah, yes,' he says, pouring whisky for himself. 'That dog was useful. I cut its lead just enough so that one tug and it would break. That was easy. You know how they love that dog. So I became their friend and it was only a matter of time before they introduced me to you. It worked like clockwork.' He smiles again.

'How did you find me?'

'You make friends in the nick. They all have their skills. A favour owed. It wasn't hard.'

I quiver as he pulls a chair forward and sits in front of me, placing a hand on my knee.

'Are you still up for it, Libby?'

I shiver. He licks his lips and reaches behind him for the whisky bottle.

'That's what you always wanted wasn't it?'

'You bastard.'

He slides his hand up my thigh and smiles.

'You were never my type, darling. You were too young, too selfish, too privileged, but I felt sorry for you. Sorry I wasn't more forthcoming as Simon. I could tell you were gagging for it.'

'You make me sick.'

It's all starting to make sense. It was Ewan who copied my keys. That night he rushed to the loo. He had them in his hand. How could I have been so stupid, so trusting? Damn it, he even watched me enter the alarm code.

'Idiot,' I mutter, struggling in the chair.

'You were so trusting, Libby. You let me into the flat. You kept giving me your phone number. Lovely cat is Merlin by the way. I felt sure at any moment you'd realise it was me. I thought you were smarter.'

'There were times,' I say.

'Yeah, I realised I slipped up occasionally.'

'Ewan... listen...'

'Fifteen years I've been inside. Fifteen. Fucking. Years. Do you have any idea what I've been through?'

'Ewan...'

Caroline will raise the alarm. Once we don't turn up for dinner, she'll phone the police. They'll contact Fran and they'll be here. I just have to stall him.

He waves the video tape in front of my eyes.

'I'd forgotten about this. That's where I was the idiot. I remembered it ten years ago. I didn't know if your uncle had gone ahead with it. He didn't really want to discover that a member of staff was stealing from the desk drawer. He was fond of us, all of us. I told him not to be so sentimental and install a surveillance camera. He must have done it. I imagine this is the only tape there is.'

I try to work out what time it could be. It must be about five, perhaps later. Caroline is expecting us for drinks at six. A whole hour before she'll start worrying where we are. How can I stall Ewan for that long?

———

Fifteen years earlier

'Please state your name for the court.'

'Patrick O'Leary.'

'Mr O'Leary, do you know the defendant?'

'I had a run-in with him, if that's what you mean.'

'A run-in? Would you explain to the court what that means?'

'I had an unpleasant experience with him. He threatened me with a shotgun.'

'When was this, Mr O'Leary?'

'I don't remember the actual date. It was just before Christmas.'

'You're from Australia aren't you, Mr O'Leary.'

'Yeah, can't you tell?' Patrick laughed.

'You were here on a visa, is that correct?'

'Yes I was.'

'And you didn't pay rent to the farmer where you kept your caravan and you didn't pay your bar bill at the pub, The Crown. You also owed money at the betting shop in Padley. Is that correct?'

'Yes, but...'

'And according to Mr Galbreith you asked for money to stop seeing Libby Owen?'

Patrick looked at Libby.

'Yeah, I asked for money.'

'Edward Owen didn't much like your friendship with his niece, did he?'

'No, I guess not.'

'Were you sleeping with Libby Owen?'

Libby bowed her head. Patrick glanced at Lil.

'No, she was too young. We were mates.'

'Are you sure Mr Galbreith threatened you with a gun?'

'Oh yeah, I saw it all right. It scared the shit out of me.'

The barrister nodded.

'So you were afraid?'

'Yeah, I was.'

'Even though the defendant had one arm in plaster?'

'He had the gun in the other hand.'

'I see. You're absolutely sure you saw a gun?'

'He aimed it at my fucking balls. I saw it.'

'Why would Mr Galbreith threaten you?'

'Libby's uncle sent him. He didn't want Libby being mates with a gypsy.'

313

'Did Mr Galbreith seem in control of himself?'

'Oh yeah, cool as a cucumber.'

'So, he didn't seem like someone who would lose it easily?'

'Objection, the witness is not a psychologist.'

'Sorry, Your Honour, I phrased that rather badly. Mr O'Leary, are you saying that Mr Galbreith was calm and didn't do you any harm with the gun?'

'Yes, but...'

'No more questions, Your Honour.'

Patrick let out a sigh of relief. He glanced at Libby, but she still had her head bowed.

CHAPTER SEVENTY-SEVEN

Libby

The room is getting dark. Heavy black clouds cover the sun and rain beats against the window. I can't take my eyes off Ewan. He pulls a jumper over his muscular torso. He's still attractive in that same confident and easy way he always had.

'Weather's changed,' he says.

It's cold in the house and I shiver.

'You never liked me,' I say miserably.

He pushes his hair from his forehead and throws kindling onto the fire.

'You were a kid, Libby.'

'I was nearly eighteen.'

'You were still a kid. You were spoilt. Edward and Rose spoilt you.'

'Edward was too soft on you,' I say angrily. 'Sometimes I think he thought more of you than he did of me.'

Ewan laughs.

'Ridiculous,' he says, throwing a match to the wood. The glow lights up the room.

'I'm going to untie you now and I don't want you to try anything stupid. Do you understand?'

I nod. I've a better chance of escaping if I'm not tied to a chair. I just need to get to the gun room. I have no idea if the guns are still there, or if the cartridges are in the cupboard but it's the only chance I've got. I must not be too eager. He'll be expecting me to try and escape. He would have thought about the guns. He's not stupid. He's probably taken the cartridges, but I have to try.

'We're going to look at that video together,' he says.

He's untying my wrists. He's very close to me and that familiar smell that is uniquely Ewan's, washes over me and almost takes my breath away. Even now he can get me aroused simply by being close. He looks into my eyes and I swallow nervously.

'I can't watch the video, Ewan, don't make me.'

I can't relive that terrible night.

'Memories are always worse than the reality,' he says with a smile.

'I can't,' I whisper.

'You can, and we will.'

There is no warmth in his eyes.

'Ewan...'

He steps back from me. My feet are still tied so any plans I had of making a run for it are hopelessly dashed. He has no intention of untying them.

'Lean forward and put your hands behind your back,' he says firmly.

I consider clawing at his face but what would be the point? I can't go anywhere and it will just make him angrier. I glance at my phone. If I can just hit button two to speed-dial Fran, she'll be able to hear everything. Maybe it is worth the risk. I lift my arms and lash out at his chest with all my strength. I take him by surprise and he loses his balance. In that second I reach for my phone. But Ewan is fast. He always was. His hand slams into my cheek sending me reeling back in pain. The phone slips from my fingers. The pain shoots down my neck and into my shoulder. Ewan had shown me no mercy. He grabs me by the throat and I gasp in shock.

'Don't play games with me, Libby,' he growls. 'I've lost fifteen years of my life so don't expect me to be soft on you.'

Tears rain down my cheeks. Has Caroline raised the alarm yet? It must be six o'clock by now.

'Ewan, please, I can give you money.'

The moment I say it I realise what a mistake I've made. He glares at me.

'I don't want your fucking money, Libby. Maybe everyone else did but not me.'

'Ewan, you don't understand...'

He pulls my arms roughly behind my back and I cry out.

'We're going to watch this video together,' he says. 'I'm sorry I didn't think to bring popcorn.'

I fight to control my sobbing. I realise there is no use pleading with him and when he unties my ankles I make no attempt to escape. There's nowhere to go and with my hands tied I'm helpless. Ewan has me exactly where he wants me, and I hate him for it.

CHAPTER SEVENTY-EIGHT

FIFTEEN YEARS EARLIER

Libby clapped her hand over her mouth when she saw Patrick's face.

'It's all right, babe,' he said. 'It was a little accident. I'm okay.'

'Your face is all swollen,' she said, tears springing to her eyes.

Patrick had wanted to meet in The Crown, but Libby knew that Ewan and that lot would be there and that was all she needed.

'Meet me at The Wine Bar,' she'd said.

The Wine Bar was too expensive and upmarket for Patrick but he met her there anyway. He was still fucked that Owen hadn't given him the money. His thoughts were on the inheritance that Libby had talked about. He could keep her sweet. Once he got the dosh out of her, he, Lil and the kids could up sticks, leave Sydney and move to a nice place in the country. Lil always wanted to go out to the country. Libby wouldn't find them and if she did, so what? He'd just tell her to get lost. But if they kept a low profile there was little chance that Libby would find them.

'What happened?' Libby asked, stroking his face.

'Have you got money?' he asked. 'Only I'm skint. I could do with some rum.'

'Yes,' she said, pushing her hand into her sparkly clutch bag.

She looked appealing, thought Patrick. He liked it when she wore revealing dresses like this one. She had a bra on, but he could see the outline of her nipples, and Patrick felt himself growing erect. He took the money from her and went to the bar. He ordered a rum and coke for himself and a white wine for her. He didn't bother giving her the change.

'Your uncle hit me,' he said.

Libby gasped.

'What? Why? I don't understand.'

'I went to ask him for money. I'm fucking skint, Lib. Lil just blows money like I don't know what. I've got some debts and...'

'Oh Patrick, what did you say to him?'

'It don't matter,' he said vaguely. 'But he got really upset when I said you planned to come to Australia when you get your inheritance and...'

'He can't stop me going,' she said quickly.

'No, and he knows that. That's why he got angry I suppose.'

'I wish you weren't going to Australia, Pat.'

'You'll come. As soon as you get your money, you can fly over. I'll get a place for you and we can meet up regularly and...'

'You'll leave Lil?' she said, but there was doubt in her voice.

'Sure, of course. I just have to let her down lightly, you know. There's the kids and everything.'

'We'll give her money,' she said. 'I'm inheriting a lot.'

Patrick smiled. He'd certainly landed on his feet here, just as long as Owen didn't poke his nose in. He'd be set up for life. So would Lil. He'd need to talk to her about this. It was too good an opportunity to let go. Maybe they could sort something out.

Get as much of this inheritance as they could. The thought of the money and the sight of Libby's nipples were making him horny.

'Let's go somewhere,' he said, sliding his hand along her knee and up her thigh. Libby shivered. She loved it. It would be good if he didn't have to give this up. Money and great sex, what more could a man ask for?

'I have to get back to Laura's party. You can come with me if you like.'

'I've got a plane to catch, Libby.'

She pulled back from him.

'When?'

'In a few hours, they changed the flights,' he lied.

Her face darkened and he felt her stiffen against him.

'I don't want you to go.'

'Libby, you're going to come out, remember, as soon as you get your inheritance. I'll be waiting for you.'

'How do I know I will hear from you again?'

He pulled her towards him and kissed her hard on the lips.

'That's how.'

Libby clutched his hand.

'But I thought we were going to spend tomorrow together.'

'Yeah, me too, doll. That's why I've come tonight. It wasn't easy getting away.'

'Oh Patrick,' she said, tears rolling down her cheeks.

Christ, this was all he needed. He'd been hoping for a good fuck not bloody tears and a scene.

'I have to get on that flight, babe. I don't want any trouble from your uncle.'

Libby hugged him tightly and he felt her breasts straining against him.

'I don't want you to go.'

'It's not me, babe, it's him.'

'Let's go somewhere,' she said huskily.

He nodded. He might as well end things on a good note.

CHAPTER SEVENTY-NINE

FIFTEEN YEARS EARLIER

New Year's Eve

Ewan finished his beer and glanced at his phone. It was time to head back to Manstead.

'I'd better go,' he said.

'We'll see you later?' asked Dianne.

'Yeah, I'll pop back.'

Neil should be on his way, he thought. The sooner it was done the better. He walked from the pub with a heavy heart. People were already celebrating down by the promenade. It was freezing. He was glad he'd put the electric blanket over Princess. She'd be calm and warm now. He sighed and walked slowly to Manstead Manor. Neil would wait for him.

A battered old car shot out of the gates of Manstead as he approached. It couldn't be one of Edward's dinner guests in a car like that, and besides, hadn't Rose cancelled the dinner? He shrugged and carried on down the drive. He was disappointed to see that Neil's car was not in the driveway. Surely he hadn't been and gone. That wasn't like Neil. Ewan checked the time on his phone. It was just on eight-thirty. Maybe he was running late. He strolled around to the stables and stopped at the door. Something was wrong, he sensed it. He opened the stable door slowly. Princess was lying as he'd left her, but things weren't right. Her eyes rolled towards him and between her groans she let out a sigh. She'd come out of the sedation early. She hadn't groaned like this before. Damn Neil, where was he?

'I'm back, Princess, you should be sleeping.'

He leant down to pat her, and it was then he saw the blood-soaked blanket. Princess's groans seemed to vibrate through him. He stared in horror at the gunshot wound in her neck. What the...?

'Christ,' he groaned.

He laid his hand on her chest.

'It's all right, my gorgeous, it's all right.'

Her pulse rate was weak. He punched in Neil's number with his bloodied shaking hands.

'What the fuck, Neil? What the fuck happened here?' he yelled.

'Ewan? I haven't been to you. Edward cancelled my visit. What's happened? Ewan... Is Princess...'

'What the...?'

He threw the phone to the ground and hurried to the house. His anger was so intense that he had to fight the urge to barge straight into Edward's study. He pulled a rifle from the rack in the gun room and forced himself to take a deep breath. He couldn't miss. He daren't miss. He couldn't put Princess through any more. That bastard, that tight-fisted bastard, so help him God he'd murder the slaughterer. He ran back to the stable. How long had it been? Jesus, how long had she been suffering like this? He should have come back earlier. Damn him to hell.

Princess looked at him, her eyes pleading.

'All right my lovely, all right,' Ewan said, his voice thick with emotion. He couldn't do it. Not to his Princess.

He lifted the gun, struggled to steady his aim and when he finally felt sure he could do it, he fired. He knew he'd hit his target by the way Princess relaxed. He threw the gun outside and fell beside the horse. He cradled Princess in his arms.

'I'm sorry, I'm so sorry, my beautiful girl.'

He had no idea how long he stayed with his arms around the horse but when he finally stood his jeans and top were soaked with blood and his bad arm throbbed. He walked slowly from the stable and picked up the shotgun. There was one cartridge left. He thought he should take it out before he did something stupid. But he didn't. Molly spoke to him as he passed through the kitchen. He ignored her. She was busy wrapping chicken for the freezer and didn't notice the blood on his clothes. He went to the morning room, but Edward wasn't there. He helped himself to a large glass of whisky and downed it in one. It helped a bit but not enough, so he poured himself another and took it with him to the library. The gun hung loosely in his other hand. He didn't bother knocking. Edward turned as the door opened.

'Oh it's you,' he said on seeing Ewan and then his eyes travelled down Ewan's blood-soaked clothes.

'You bastard,' Ewan said.

Edward's eyes moved to the gun.

'How much would it have cost? I said I'd pay.'

'What are you on about, boy? What's happened?'

Ewan laid his glass onto a side table.

'You know what I'm on about. I should take a shotgun to you, you heartless bastard, that's all you deserve.'

Edward shook his head.

'Ah, the horse. I can't waste money on an old horse.'

Ewan leapt forward, his hands grasping Edward by the throat.

'You fucking lowlife,' he shouted.

Edward struggled to get out of Ewan's grasp, but he was young and strong. Edward was no match for Ewan and he knew it.

'Let me go, Ewan,' he gasped.

Ewan released his grip and stepped back, pointing the shotgun at Edward's chest.

'You didn't even do it properly. You just left her.'

Edward stared at the shotgun with fear in his eyes.

'Don't be a fool, Ewan. It was only a horse.'

Ewan's eyes narrowed and he aimed the gun, his finger moving onto the trigger. Edward began to shake. Their eyes met and Edward nodded.

'I'm sorry,' he said.

Ewan slowly lowered the shotgun and took a step back.

'I'm finished here. You need to get yourself a new gamekeeper. I'll clear my stuff out tomorrow.'

He turned and made for the door.

'Ewan, don't be...'

The door slammed shut and Edward fell into a chair.

CHAPTER EIGHTY

PRESENT DAY

It was a fancy restaurant and Fran was surprised. Mike's style was normally cheap and cheerful.

'This is very nice,' she said, smiling.

'Yeah,' said Mike, clearly embarrassed. 'I thought if we're going to dinner, we should do it properly.'

Fran nodded, impressed. The waiter showed them to their table and Fran began to worry that maybe she was underdressed.

'I'd have worn a dress if I'd known,' she said.

Mike scoffed. 'You in a dress?'

'What's wrong with that?'

'I just can't imagine it, that's all.'

'You've seen me in a dress.'

'Have I?' he said, looking thoughtful.

'At the Christmas party.'

'Oh yeah.'

He probably hadn't noticed, thought Fran, looking down at the menu. She'd been expecting her phone to bleep. It was worrying her that Libby hadn't texted back. She would surely know that Fran was concerned. She slipped her hand into her bag and pulled the phone from it. There were no new messages. She didn't like to voice her concern to Mike yet again. It would be a shame to spoil this dinner. She'd pictured this dinner for the past sixteen years, never imagining that it would really happen.

'What are you having?' asked Mike.

Fran glanced at the menu. Maybe she should phone William. Everything's probably fine. Libby is no doubt enjoying her time with her new beau, Simon.

'Erm...' said Fran.

'Do you want a beer?'

'Great.'

'I'm having the poached salmon,' said Mike. 'Do you want a starter?'

'They're expensive,' said Fran.

Mike laughed.

'I knew I could rely on you to watch the expenses.'

She smiled.

'Thanks for inviting me, Mike.'

He looked uncomfortable.

'Yeah, well... I'm not good with this stuff. There's no need for us to advertise it at work is there?'

'No.' She smiled.

'Maybe we could go to the cinema one night, or the theatre.'

'The theatre? I never had you as the theatre type.'

'You like it though.'

She smiled.

'I'll have the salmon too,' she said.

The waiter took their order and she relaxed back in her chair and sipped her beer. Mike clinked his glass against hers.

'To new beginnings,' he said. 'Isn't that what they say?'

She was about to answer when her phone rang. It wasn't Libby and her heart sank.

'Hello.'

'Inspector Marshall?'

'Yes, who is this?'

'I wasn't sure if you were still on this number. It's William, Libby's...'

'Yes, I know who you are.'

'I hope I'm not disturbing anything.'

Fran hid her irritation. 'No, it's fine. How can I help?'

'It's probably nothing but Libby was due to come over for dinner. They're staying at our beach house. They were due here about forty minutes ago. I've tried her mobile but she's not answering. We tried the beach house too but they're not answering that phone either. It's probably nothing but...'

'We're on our way.'

CHAPTER EIGHTY-ONE

PRESENT DAY

Libby

Ewan unties my ankles and I fight the urge to kick him. I don't relish another slap. He lifts me to my feet and pushes me forward.

'We'll have our own little video night.' He smiles.

I watch with a sinking heart as he grabs my phone from the table. I now see a video player has been set up by the flat-screen television. He pushes me into a chair and ties my feet again.

'Won't be a sec,' he says.

He leaves the room. Is it worth screaming? No, not here at Manstead. Only someone on the estate would hear me and who is going to be on the estate now? My eyes search the room. I've got to get help but how? Ewan comes back into the room carrying a shotgun and I freeze.

'Right,' he says purposefully.

I squirm in my seat as he unties my hands.

'You need to call William,' he says, thrusting my phone at me. 'You're not feeling well. We can't make dinner.'

'I...'

'Do it, Libby,' he says, pointing the shotgun at me.

I take the phone and fumble with the buttons.

'Speaker phone,' he instructs. 'Don't do anything stupid.'

William answers on the first ring.

'Libby, we were getting anxious.'

'I'm sorry. I'm really not feeling well. I've got this terrible migraine. Do you mind if we leave dinner tonight? I'm so sorry. I was hoping it would go but...'

'Oh right. No, of course, it's fine. Erm... the thing is I phoned Fran and...'

Ewan stares at me. The shotgun is steady in his hand.

'Oh, okay, I'll call her.'

'We'll see you tomorrow?'

'Yes, we'll come first thing.'

I hang up and look at Ewan.

He grabs the phone from me.

'We'll send Inspector Marshall a text,' he says.

I feel deflated. He throws the phone onto a chair and places the shotgun onto the floor before retying my hands.

'Nice and cosy,' he says, putting more logs onto the fire.

'Ewan...'

'Showtime.' He grins.

'Ewan, please don't make me... You don't understand.'

'You owe me, Libby Owen. You owe me big time. You fucking lied in court. You put me away for fifteen years. Why did you do that? I was twenty-four. I had my whole life ahead of me. Was it revenge? Was my rejection of you that hard to take that you'd want to destroy the best years of my life?'

Tears run down my cheeks.

'Ewan, you know I didn't...'

'Stop it,' he yells. 'Did you actually see anything that night?'

'You're insane,' I cry. 'You killed them and you're going to go back inside for what you're doing to me.'

'I'm never going back inside, Libby.'

'You ruined my life,' I spit at him. 'You took everything from me. I have no one.'

'You lied.' He lifts my chin and looks into my eyes. 'You underestimated me.'

I avoid his gaze.

'You had the perfect life. How the hell did I ruin that?'

'Patrick,' I say.

He laughs.

'That Aussie idiot? He had three kids, Libby. He was only interested in money.'

I meet his eyes.

'He loved me. He wouldn't even have thought about going back to Australia if you hadn't told Uncle Edward about him. You scared him off. Why couldn't you have kept out of my life?'

'Bollocks. Your uncle paid him off. He wasn't going to stay here. He didn't want you. He wanted money and a nice virginal bit of stuff on the side. You were able to provide both.'

'That's not true,' I shout. 'He loved me.'

'You needed someone to love you, but he played you for a fool, Libby.'

'Shut up,' I yell.

'He lied too, didn't he?'

'To protect me.'

'To protect himself you mean. Did you think of me when I was banged up? Did you think of me and feel yourself?'

I blush.

'I thought as much. I feel sorry for you, Libby. I always did. That makes me a bigger fool I suppose.'

He moves away from me.

'I'm wasting time. Let's have our video night, shall we? I'm looking forward to this.'

I close my eyes and feel the tears run down my cheeks. My

eyes are sore and gritty from crying and my head aches. I can no longer feel my hands where Ewan has tied them too tightly. My heart begins to hammer in my chest as I watch him slide the cassette into the video player. Oh God, please let it not work. Don't make me watch that horror all over again. Fran, please come, please rescue me.

CHAPTER EIGHTY-TWO

FIFTEEN YEARS EARLIER

'*Mr Galbreith, on the night of the 31st December 1999 did you shoot Edward and Rose Owen?*'

'*No, I did not.*'

'*Libby Owen said she saw you.*'

Ewan looked over at Libby, his lips tight.

'*She didn't see me shoot anyone. She was upset. She made a mistake.*'

'*But you did threaten Edward Owen that evening?*'

'*I was upset. I didn't mean it. The words came out in anger.*'

'*Would you say you have a short temper, Mr Galbreith?*'

'*No.*'

'*But you can be impulsive?*'

'*No, I'm not impulsive. I give everything careful thought.*'

'*When was the last time that you saw Edward Owen alive?*'

'*I'm not sure. Sometime after eight-thirty. Neil gave Princess a sedative at around seven-thirty. He said he would come at eight-thirty to put her down.*'

'*Why didn't you put her down? You're an excellent marksman?*'

Ewan swallowed.

'I was too fond of her. I didn't want to do it.'

'I see. Edward Owen didn't want you to call the vet, is that correct?'

'Yes, he said it would cost too much and was a ridiculous waste of money. He thought Neil would charge double as it was New Year's Eve.'

'So, what did you do during that time before the vet came?'

'I went to The Crown.'

'People have testified seeing you there and confirmed you were upset.'

Ewan nodded.

'So, later that evening you went back to Manstead?'

'Yes.'

'Did you go to the stables first?'

'Yes.'

'What did you find?'

Ewan looked down at his feet. He clenched his jaw before looking up.

'Princess had been shot.'

There was a gasp from the jury.

'Who'd shot her?'

'Edward Owen.'

'Why would he do that?'

'He didn't want to pay for the vet.'

'So, what was the problem with that? Princess was going to be put down anyway, wasn't she?'

'Edward had cancelled the visit and shot Princess himself.'

'Go on, Mr Galbreith.'

'He botched it. She was still alive and in pain. The bastard hadn't finished the job, so I had to.'

'This was a horse you were extremely fond of.'

Ewan nodded, his jaw twitching.

'So you must have been very angry.'

'Yes. But not angry enough to kill him.'

'But angry enough to threaten him?'

'It wasn't a threat.'

The barrister looked down at his paperwork.

'"I should take a shotgun to you, you heartless bastard. That's all you deserve". Are those your words?'

'Yes but...'

'I put it to you, Mr Galbreith, that on the night of the 31st December you were overcome with rage and grief after what had happened to your horse and that under the influence of alcohol consumed at The Crown, you returned to Manstead Manor in a murderous rage...'

'That's not true,' said Ewan.

'...and that Rose Owen, seeing the shotgun in your hands, screamed in fear and so you shot her.'

'No,' said Ewan firmly. 'That didn't happen.'

'Miss Owen said she saw you shoot her uncle.'

'She didn't see me.'

'Are you saying you didn't see Miss Owen that night?'

'Yes I did but...'

'So you admit that you were at the house after midnight on the 31st December?'

'Yes, but...'

'No more questions, Your Honour.'

Ewan cracked his knuckles in frustration.

CHAPTER EIGHTY-THREE

PRESENT DAY

Libby

There's no warmth in Ewan's smile.

'Are you sitting comfortably? Anything you need before we start? It could be a long one, if it even works of course. We might be disappointed if it runs out before the murder scene.'

He grins at me.

'There's nothing you want, like a pee or...'

I shake my head.

'I've got some beers in the car. Don't go anywhere will you?'

I can feel beads of sweat on my forehead, but I'll be damned if I'll ask him to wipe them away like I'm some fucking child. My phone bleeps and I stare at it longingly. Ewan returns, cracks open a can of beer and then picks up my mobile.

'There's a message from Inspector Marshall. *"Thanks for letting me know, Libby. Have a good evening. Don't hesitate to call if you're worried"*. That's nice isn't it?'

I have to escape. There has to be a way. He thinks he's in control. I have to make sure he isn't. He clicks the video recorder button and a fuzzy picture appears on the screen. Ewan leans forward to study it.

'It worked,' he says.

The monitor flashes and a jerky frame pops up onto the screen. It's Molly entering the room. Ewan turns and smiles at me.

'Shall we fast forward?'

He pushes a button on the remote and my head thumps as I watch the frames. Then I see myself. Ewan hits the play button and there I am. Seventeen years old.

'You've changed.' Ewan smiles.

Memories rush through my brain and it's as though it was only yesterday that I lived here at Manstead Manor. I watch mesmerised as my other self opens the desk drawer. I'm looking around furtively. I'm wearing my blue chiffon dress. I remember this. I'd wanted some extra money for New Year's Eve.

'I did wonder if it was you who was taking the money,' Ewan says. 'Patrick liked a good time with you, didn't he? Was that why you took it?'

I don't reply. I wriggle my hands behind me in an effort to squeeze them out of the tape. They're hot and swollen. I fight back tears. I don't want Ewan to know how scared I am. The rifle lies at his side. Is it loaded or is he bluffing?

'How much did you steal?'

He's goading me.

'It wasn't much.'

'But you bargained on the blame falling on Molly or Peter...'

'That's not true.'

The video is forwarded and I struggle again to pull my hands through the tape.

'Ah,' he says, 'what's this?'

The frame is paused. Aunty Rose is lying on the couch. It looks like Uncle Edward is putting a log on the fire. Nausea rises up in me. It begins as a small crampy pain in my abdomen and then builds up until no number of deep breaths help.

'I'm going to throw up,' I say.

———

'Who is this new bloke Libby Owen's seeing then?' Mike asked. He'd had a couple of brandies and was feeling relaxed. He'd ask Fran back to his new flat maybe. He couldn't imagine her saying no.

'Simon Wane, he's in property, so Libby said.'

'Is that why he's interested in Manstead Manor?'

'I guess so.'

Fran finished her brandy and sat back with a sigh of contentment.

'That's a good one.' Mike smiled.

Fran wrinkled her brow.

'What are you talking about?'

'It's my passion for anagrams.'

'What is?'

'Seeing words within words.'

'I think you've had too much brandy, Mike.' She laughed.

'Think about it. Wane. W - A - N - E, what do you see?'

She shrugged.

'I'm not sure what we're talking about.'

'Wane, it's an anagram for Ewan.'

Fran's eyes widened. Her alcohol-fuelled brain took a while to make complete sense of what Mike was saying.

'Jesus,' she said, jumping up.

'Fran, what's...?'

'Why didn't we realise? Of course, he practically lived at the dramatics society while inside. He got a sodding diploma in stage make-up.'

'Now I'm confused.'

'Simon Wane is Ewan Galbreith.'

———

Ewan holds a glass of water to my lips. It helps slightly and the nausea passes over.

'I wish you weren't so dramatic,' he snaps. He pulls his chair next to mine and clicks the video back on. He scrolls through the frames and stops. I can see the clock on the mantelpiece in the frame. It says 12.30am. Uncle Edward walks to the bar. He pours a drink. The next frame shows Aunty Rose drinking from a tea cup. I turn from the screen and my eyes land on the glass paperweight that sits on the side table. It's within reach. If I could grab it with both hands, I could hit Ewan on the head with it. The clock in the frame now says 12.35am. My heart is hammering in my chest. I can't watch this. I need to get help. The next frame shows the morning-room door opening. Ewan sits forward, the muscles in his jaw twitch.

'This is it,' he says and there's a tremble to his voice.

'I can't feel my hands,' I say.

He drags his eyes from the screen and walks around to study my hands. He loosens the tape. He then looks around the room and removes the paperweight. Damn him.

The video restarts and I stare mesmerised as the next frame hits the screen. Aunty Rose and Uncle Edward turn to the door. Ewan stares intently, his body tense.

'Oh my God,' he exclaims.

I close my eyes.

CHAPTER EIGHTY-FOUR

FIFTEEN YEARS EARLIER

Ewan

I looked at Dianne. She didn't want me to leave. It was the kind of atmosphere I liked best. I strangely wished Patti was here. She'd most likely have said *'Poor sodding horse. I know what will take your mind off it.'* That's what I needed, something meaningless and fleeting.

'Things have only just started,' said Dianne.

'I'm going to get back,' I said.

I'd check the horses and wrap Princess in a blanket ready for Neil to collect her in the morning.

'It's New Year's Eve,' she said.

'I need to pack up my stuff.'

'Give yourself a day to think things through. Wait until your head is clearer,' Dianne said, squeezing my arm.

'I'm moving out.'

'Where will you go?'

'There are plenty of places.'

'We'll come round tomorrow and help,' said Greg, slapping me on the back.

I gave Luke the thumbs up and walked to the door. The icy cold air hit me in the face and I realised I'd drunk too much. The weather didn't seem to be bothering anyone and the sea front was heaving with revellers watching the fireworks on the beach. Padley was usually pretty lonesome in the winter. New Year was never this busy. Everyone had high hopes for the new decade. I felt a twinge of unease as I approached Manstead. There was no reason for it but nevertheless I couldn't shake it off. I cursed myself for not lighting the log burner earlier. The cottage was going to be freezing. The first gunshot surprised me and at first I thought it was fireworks. I was almost at the cottage when I heard another. It was definitely a gun being fired and it came from Manstead Manor. Nobody would be out shooting at that time of night. I hurried to the house. The unease I had felt earlier returned and when I saw the front door ajar I knew that something was wrong. I pushed the door and called out.

———

'How many shots did you hear, Mr Galbreith?'

'Two.'

'You're quite certain about that?'

'Yes.'

'Did you see Miss Owen when you entered the house?'

'No, at least not right away.'

'What did you see, Mr Galbreith?'

'There was music coming from the morning room, so I made my way there. I could smell where the gun had been fired.'

He paused and took a long breath.

'Carry on, Mr Galbreith.'

'I opened the door of the morning room and found the bodies of Edward and Rose. The shotgun was on the floor.'

His voice broke and he struggled to compose himself.

341

'Are you all right to continue, Mr Galbreith?'

'Yes.'

'Did you pick the gun up from the floor?'

'Yes, I picked it up and checked the cartridges.'

'What kind of rifle was it?'

'It was a double-barrelled shotgun. A 512 Gold Wing.'

'Why did you check it?'

'I don't know. Habit, I suppose.'

'What did you do after you found the bodies?'

'I checked to see if they were alive and then I heard a noise, like a sob, and I rushed out into the hallway to see Libby Owen running out of the front door.'

'Why would she run from you?'

'I imagine she thought I had killed them.'

'In her statement Miss Owen claimed to have seen you shoot her uncle.'

'That's not true. She didn't see me shoot anyone. I called out to her, but she ran down the drive. She was obviously afraid and I was in shock. I went back into the house and waited for the police and ambulance.'

'Mr Galbreith, do you know anyone who would want to kill Edward Owen and his wife?'

'I know people who say they would like to, but I can't think of anyone who actually would.'

'Thank you. No more questions, Your Honour.'

CHAPTER EIGHTY-FIVE

FIFTEEN YEARS EARLIER

Libby clung tightly to Patrick. She didn't ever want to let him go. Her breasts ached from where he had squeezed them earlier. She felt raw both inside and out. The music ended and he pulled away from her.

'I have to get going, babe.'

'Can't you stay at the party for just a bit longer? It'll be midnight soon.'

'I really have to go, doll.'

Libby thought her heart would break.

'You'll be in Australia before you know it.' He smiled, kissing her on the nose. 'I've got things to see to before I go. Debts to settle and all that, you know.'

'When I get my inheritance, I can pay your debts.'

'Sounds super-good, babe.' He smiled. 'I guess you'll be really rich one day.'

'Really rich?' she repeated.

'When your aunt and uncle die, you're the only dependant aren't you?'

Libby laughed.

'They're not going to die anytime soon.'

He nodded and pulled her back into an embrace.

'All the same,' he said thoughtfully.

The loud music started up and Patrick tried not to sigh. They were all so bloody young here.

'Stay just five minutes more,' she said.

A giggling couple bumped into them.

'I can't. There are things I need to take care of before the flight. We'll stay in touch though, babe, don't you worry about that. You let me know when you're coming. I'll get a really nice place for us.'

He remembered those new houses they were building on the beach. He'd love one of those. With Libby's money he could get two; one for him and Lil and another for him and Libby. He smiled at the thought. How the other half live.

_____

It had been a great night. It was a shame that Patrick wasn't able to stay to see in the millennium with her. She supposed he was on his way to the airport now. She felt her sore breasts and remembered their lovemaking from earlier. It was exactly thirteen weeks before her birthday. It wasn't long.

'Happy New Year,' Laura said, hugging her as the clock chimed. 'Isn't it so exciting?'

Libby nodded.

'I'm so happy,' said Libby. 'This year is going to be the best ever.'

'I really liked your bloke,' said Laura, feeling all grown up. She had been going to say *boyfriend,* but Patrick was a man, not a boy. Lucky Libby, she thought. She imagined Patrick knew all sorts of tricks.

'I'm going to Australia to live with him.'

It was the happiest Libby had ever been. Party poppers

exploded around them and Libby danced with joy. The boys gave her admiring looks. One asked if she'd like to walk along the beach with him. They were young, like her but she was experienced now, and she felt confident and worldly. She didn't want to be with boys her own age.

'You lucky thing,' said Laura.

'Hey girls, you up for some fun,' said one of the boys, holding out some blue pills. 'Have a Molly.'

'What's that?' said Laura nervously.

Libby took a pill.

'I've always wanted to try Ecstasy,' she said.

Laura gasped.

'I don't think...'

Libby swallowed the pill with the beer the boy gave her. She couldn't remember how many beers she'd drunk. She felt all light and airy and not afraid of anything. She'd walk home along the beach, that would be exhilarating and when she got to Manstead she'd talk to Uncle Edward about having her inheritance earlier in the form of a loan from him and Aunty Rose. After all, it was only a few months before her birthday. That way she could travel to Australia earlier. Maybe she could study there instead of going to that stupid college Aunty Rose had signed her up for. It was stupid someone like her studying anyway. She'd have loads of money. It's not like she'd need to work.

People were dancing on the beach and Libby joined in with them for a short time. Everything began to look fantastic. She felt a sense of euphoria like she'd never known before. The boy kissed her and it was heaven. Even Patrick's kisses hadn't felt as wonderful as this. She watched in awe at the fireworks, the festival of colours seemed to take her breath away. It didn't even feel cold anymore.

'I love you,' she told Laura, hugging her tightly. 'You've always made me feel special.'

'Don't talk daft,' said Laura, pulling away.

Libby danced along the beach. Her whole life was ahead of her and she could do what she wanted. Anything and everything was within her reach. Once she had money there would be nothing she couldn't accomplish. She'd go home and ask Uncle Edward now.

'I'll see you tomorrow,' she called to Laura.

She was shivering when she arrived at Manstead and her head had started to ache. The lights were on and the thought of a roaring fire cheered her. She felt happy and positive. The year 2000 was going to be wonderful.

CHAPTER EIGHTY-SIX

PRESENT DAY

Libby

Ewan stares at the screen. His hands are shaking. He turns around and looks at me. His eyes are hard and menacing. His hand grips the rifle until his knuckles turn white.

'Fifteen years, Libby,' he says, his eyes narrowing. 'You weren't the only one with dreams.'

He lifts the rifle. I go to cover my face and realise I can't.

'Ewan,' I whisper. 'Please.'

'You fucking bitch.'

'Ewan...'

'I'm going to fucking kill you,' he roars. 'I've got two cartridges. So help me God I'll pump them both into you.'

He glances back at the screen.

'For fuck's sake, Libby, what the hell happened? Why did *you* kill them?'

Fifteen years earlier

Libby pushed her hand into her sparkly clutch bag and admired it all over again. Maybe she'd buy another one in red. Libby liked red. She'd buy Laura one too. She pulled her keys from the bag and opened the door. She stepped into the hall and then remembered that she had sand in her shoes, so quickly pulled them off before making her way to the morning room.

'Hello, it's me,' she called.

She opened the door. The heat from the fire hit her and she felt suddenly dizzy. Her head was fuzzy and strange, and she had to blink several times to see clearly.

'It's freezing out,' she said.

Aunty Rose was lying on the couch, her legs covered with a blanket.

'How are you feeling?' asked Libby, warming her hands by the fire.

'You're late,' snapped Uncle Edward.

'It's New Year's Eve,' Aunty Rose said softly.

'I left as soon as it was midnight,' said Libby, feeling herself sway on her feet. Uncle Edward poured himself a brandy and looked at Rose.

'Do you fancy a nightcap?'

'Not with this headache.'

'How is it?' asked Libby.

'It's much better than it was. Did you have a nice time tonight?'

'It was wonderful,' breathed Libby.

She sat on the rug in front of the fire and crossed her legs.

'How's Princess?'

Rose looked to Edward and then bowed her head.

'Did the vet put him to sleep?' Libby persisted.

'I shot him,' said Edward.

'Does Ewan know?' she said, shocked.

Edward didn't speak.

'Yes, he knows. He's very upset,' said Rose.

'I should go and see him,' Libby said, turning to go.

'I think we'd be best to leave him in peace,' said Rose.

Libby thought of Princess and had to stop herself from crying. Uncle Edward didn't like tears. He said they were a weakness and she wanted him to see her as strong and adult.

'I'm going to be eighteen in a few weeks,' she said, smiling at Aunty Rose.

'Yes dear, is there anything special you would like? We'll go for dinner, obviously, but is there a show you'd like to see? Maybe there's a ballet on.'

Fireworks boomed outside and Edward sighed. Libby stared, fascinated at the flames leaping up from the fire. The colours were amazing.

'We're not going to get much sleep tonight,' Edward said, banking down the fire.

'Oh,' said Libby as the dancing flames slowly disappeared.

Aunty Rose sat up.

'Well, you think about it, dear, and let us know,' she said to Libby.

'What I'd like,' Libby said breathlessly, 'is an advance on my inheritance.'

Edward stopped banking the fire and looked at her.

'Your inheritance?' repeated Rose.

'It was left in trust for me. As my birthday is only a few weeks away I thought it would be all right to have some of it early. I want to go to Australia.'

Edward shook his head at Libby.

'Australia,' exclaimed Aunty Rose. 'You've never mentioned this before.'

'You inherit at eighteen if we, your guardians, think you're responsible enough to handle your inheritance and quite honestly I don't think you are anywhere near adult enough. Your parents didn't leave you their hard-earned money for some lazy layabout Australian to enjoy,' Edward barked.

Libby blushed.

'What are you talking about, Edward?' asked Rose.

Suddenly the room felt too hot for Libby.

'Ewan told me that Libby has been seeing some Australian gypsy. He's twenty-seven, married with three kids, no money. He doesn't work and sponges off anyone he can.'

'Oh Libby, tell me this isn't true,' pleaded Rose.

Libby rubbed her eyes. Aunty Rose seemed to be fading in and out of her vision. Why didn't she keep still?

'Ewan's a liar,' Libby cried. 'Why do you always believe what Ewan says?'

'That's enough, Libby,' said Rose.

'Ewan threatened him with a rifle. That's against the law,' Libby said, pouting.

'You need to grow up Libby,' Edward said firmly. 'This is not how a mature eighteen-year-old would behave. I don't think you're grown up enough to receive your inheritance. I'll increase your allowance, but that's it. We will review the situation at the end of the year and I don't think flying to Australia to be with a married man is very sensible. I won't give you money for that. The sooner he goes back the better. You need to think about your studies or get yourself a job.'

'But that's not fair, and I don't need a job with my inheritance.' Libby snivelled.

'You'll work, damn it, like everyone else.'

Libby clenched her fists with anger. Patrick would be waiting for her. She had to go to Australia. Her whole life was there. Patrick might find someone else and then what would she do?

'I hate you!' she screamed. 'I hate you and I hate Ewan. You've always preferred him to me.'

'Don't be so ridiculous,' said Edward.

'Libby...' called Rose but Libby had already run from the room.

She was glad Princess was dead. It served Ewan right. If he hadn't told her uncle about Patrick she would be getting her inheritance as she deserved. How dare they hold back what was rightfully hers. It was her right. She couldn't wait a year before seeing Patrick again. What if her uncle took her passport? She'd promised Patrick. This was going to be the best year ever and now it was all ruined. She would have her inheritance. She wouldn't let them take everything from her. Not Patrick. He was the only person who loved her. She'd force them to give it to her. Her parents had left the money to her, not to Uncle Edward and Aunty Rose. They had plenty of their own money. She fidgeted on her feet. Her cheek twitched and she put her hand to her face to try and stop it. Her head was throbbing now and she began to regret taking the Ecstasy pill. She was feeling so dizzy. It was going to be okay. They would give her the money. It was all going to be all right. She would see Patrick again soon. She walked slowly to the gun room. Patrick would be at the airport now. Maybe if she got her money tonight she could be on a flight by tomorrow. It would only be a few days and she'd see him again. They could choose a house together.

The black gloves that her uncle always wore when he went hunting slipped easily onto her hands. They were too big. She'd only loaded a gun once. Uncle Edward had taken her shooting. She'd hated it. He'd shown her how to load the gun and allowed her one shot. It had been horrible, and she never wanted to go on a hunt again. She'd make them give her the money. There was nothing wrong in her forcing them. It was hers after all and they were in the wrong for keeping it from her.

CHAPTER EIGHTY-SEVEN

FIFTEEN YEARS EARLIER

Edward was livid. He hated being ripped off and that bloody vet ripped him off all the time. But he should have waited. He felt sure he'd finished the horse off. Bugger it. He didn't want to lose Ewan. He'd speak with him tomorrow. Ewan reminded him of himself thirty years ago. He was a good bloke to have around. He'd sort it out. Probably best to leave him alone tonight to cool off, like Rose suggested.

Now this ridiculous business with Libby and that bloody Australian. He thought he'd seen the back of him. He never imagined Libby would ask for her inheritance. He couldn't let her throw her life away on some lowlife gypsy.

'You need to go and speak to her,' he said to Rose after Libby had stormed out.

'What is all this about exactly?'

Edward sighed.

'She thinks she is in love with this bloke. He's been here asking for money. I paid him off to get rid of him. He's been having sex with her, Rose. She thinks she's in love with him. I can't give her money. It will go straight to him.'

Rose clapped a hand to her head.

'Oh no, Edward, why didn't you tell me?'

'I didn't want to worry you.'

'Poor Libby, I'll talk to her.'

Rose stood up and was about to go to the door when it was flung open and Libby stood there on the threshold. The shotgun shook in her trembling hands. Her eyes were wide and her hair wild where she had tugged at it in her agitation. Rose stared in horror at the shotgun. Saliva dribbled from the side of Libby's mouth and she fought to stop her cheeks twitching.

'You can't stop me being with Patrick,' she sobbed, tears running down her cheeks. 'I won't let you.'

'Oh my God, Libby, what are you doing?' Rose said, her voice breaking.

Libby ripped a sheet of paper from a pad on the desk. She threw a pen at Uncle Edward and then stepped backwards with the gun aimed at him.

'I want in writing that I can have half of my inheritance now and the other half on my birthday.'

Edward stared at the rifle. He couldn't be sure it wasn't loaded but he felt pretty certain it wouldn't be. Ewan didn't leave loaded rifles around and Libby would have no idea how to load it herself. He felt sure she was bluffing and by God, she'd pay for this later.

'Libby, you're angry and upset and you've had too much to drink. It's an exciting night and I can understand you've got plans for the future. We can talk about it in the morning when we're all calmer.'

'Sign the paper now!' Libby screamed.

'Edward, do as she asks,' begged Rose.

Edward moved towards the desk.

'There'll be other men, Libby,' said Rose. 'I'm sure your chap is lovely but what future is there with a married man?'

'If I have my money we can have a future.' Libby sighed. 'Why won't you understand?'

'You think this is right, pointing a shotgun at the people who have given you everything? You'd threaten us like this for a man you barely know?' said Edward.

'I love him and he loves me. He's going to leave his wife and...'

Libby faltered. It was too hot in the morning room, she felt dizzy. Her hands were slipping off the rifle butt. She lowered the shotgun slightly so she could wipe her forehead. Edward saw his chance and, feeling sure that the gun wasn't loaded, leapt towards her and grappled with the rifle.

'Oh Edward, no!' screamed Rose.

He took Libby by surprise. The recoil from the shot sent Edward reeling back. Libby stumbled with the force and pain shot down her arm. For a moment neither of them could hear anything except the ringing in their ears. Libby thought she'd heard Aunty Rose scream but she couldn't be sure. Now she stared in horror at the limp body where it had been thrown against the wall. It looked like one of Libby's old rag dolls. They used to fall with their legs askew and their heads on one side in exactly the same way, except this wasn't a rag doll, this was Aunty Rose.

'Rose, Rose,' cried Edward.

'I didn't mean to,' said Libby. 'It wasn't my fault.' Edward sobbed into Rose's blood-soaked chest, his hands clutching at her hair. His whole body shook with shock.

'Edward,' moaned Rose. 'It's going to be all right isn't it...? Edw...' Her voice trailed off.

Libby's hands clenched and unclenched around the rifle. Aunty Rose would be all right. Of course she would. Edward looked up, his face full of pain. His sobs echoed throughout the house. Libby wanted to block out the sound. She stared in horror at Aunty Rose's breasts, at the blue veins that stood out. A rivulet of blood dribbled across the nipple and Libby had to fight down the acid in her stomach that threatened to pour forth.

'Jesus. Oh Rose, Rose,' Edward cried.

Libby looked away. She hadn't meant to shoot her. It was his fault. All she wanted was for him to sign the piece of paper. Edward cradled Rose in his arms, her blood soaking through his white starched shirt.

'Sign the fucking paper!' Libby screamed.

Edward turned puffy red eyes towards her.

'You bloody psychopath. You won't get anything now except a prison sentence. Get out of my way. We need to call an ambulance.'

'Don't make me shoot you.' She trembled.

'I'm calling an ambulance and if that means you shoot me then go ahead.'

His words paralysed her. She couldn't go to prison. She had to get to Australia to be with Pat. He was waiting for her. Aunty Rose would be all right once they got her to hospital. It was an accident. She wouldn't go to prison. Surely they wouldn't put her in prison; she was only seventeen years old.

Libby's finger hovered over the trigger as Edward lifted the phone receiver. He was the only one who saw her shoot Aunty Rose. No one else was here. The staff had all gone home. She couldn't go to prison. What would happen to her?

'Don't,' she yelled, her hands shaking. If only she didn't have to keep looking at Aunty Rose's bloodstained breast.

Edward ignored her.

Do it, said a voice in her head. *Shoot him now.*

'No,' she whispered. 'Don't.'

Her finger pressed onto the trigger.

You have to.

'No, don't, please,' she pleaded.

But it was too late. She'd done it and Uncle Edward slammed against the wall. His eyes were wide and accusing. She felt sure the room shook under the force. She watched, fascinated as he slowly slid down the wall. The shotgun slipped from her hand and fell with a thud onto the floor. The room was silent. Perspiration mixed with her tears and for a moment she just rocked back and forth.

'Everything is going to be all right,' she whispered. 'It's all going to be all right.'

She stepped closer to Aunty Rose. Her feet slid on the blood and she stared at them in surprise. She went to cover Aunty Rose's breast but, somehow, she couldn't do it. She touched her face and stepped back, wiping her eyes with her bloodied hands.

There was the sound of someone running into the hall and she froze.

'Edward?'

It was Ewan. She hurried from the morning room and kicked open the kitchen door. Damn it, why hadn't she locked the main door behind her? She tiptoed from the kitchen and out into the cold. The freezing air took her breath away. She began to run. She'd only got partway down the drive when Ewan called to her. She turned and her eyes met his. Keep running, she thought. Everything is going to be all right.

CHAPTER EIGHTY-EIGHT

PRESENT DAY

Libby

I can't stand the hate in Ewan's eyes. The rifle is so close. His finger is firm on the trigger. I can barely breathe.

'They were good people, Libby,' he says finally.

'I only wanted what was rightfully mine,' I say defensively.

'That's what the fucking courts are for. If you weren't happy with Edward's decision you could have got a solicitor. You don't fucking kill people.'

'Patrick was waiting for me and...'

'Bollocks,' he yells, jumping up. The coffee table crashes to the floor. I try to stand up.

'Don't move, Libby,' he snarls, 'don't fucking move.'

He picks up the broken glass from the floor and leaves the room. I look around. It's growing dim. I fight to release my hands but it's hopeless. Ewan returns with a whisky bottle. He takes a long swig.

'Ewan...'

'You knew all along that I didn't do it and yet you let them crucify me. You put me away to save yourself and for revenge.

Revenge because I wouldn't fuck you and because I told Edward about Patrick. That loser didn't give a shit about you.'

'I was seventeen, I couldn't go to prison.'

'I was twenty-four, you evil bitch.' He spat in my face. I feel his saliva run down my cheek. 'I was an innocent man and you let me go to prison.'

'You ruined my life.'

'How can you live with yourself? I was sure that Patrick had killed them. I never for one minute imagined that you were capable of such horror, Libby.'

Tears prick at my eyelids.

'I didn't mean to kill Aunty Rose,' I sob. 'If Uncle Edward hadn't tried to get the gun then it wouldn't have gone off. I didn't know what to do. I couldn't go to prison and I knew Uncle Edward would tell them it had been me. What choice did I have, Ewan? There was no other way out. I had to shoot him.'

He switches off the video machine and pulls out the tape.

'I'm handing this over to the police, Libby.'

'Ewan, think about this. What will it achieve now?'

'It will clear my name, Libby, that's what it will achieve.'

My body trembles at the thought of prison. I can't go to prison, I can't. They'd never believe it was an accident. I feel nausea rise up and gag.

'Jesus,' says Ewan, pulling me to the loo.

I try to breathe normally but the panic is overwhelming me. He unbinds my wrists and opens the bathroom door. I realise this is my only chance. It's him or me. I pretend to gag again and bend forward. I turn sharply and swing my arm, punching him hard in the groin. Ewan groans and doubles over, the shotgun falling to the floor. He tries to reach for it, but I stamp on his foot. I grab the gun and point it at his chest.

'Kick the tape to me,' I say, my eyes not leaving him.

His face creases in pain but he's smiling and it unnerves me.

'I can't go to prison, Ewan.'

'So you're going to kill me too?'

'It will be self-defence. Everyone knows you've been tormenting me.'

'I don't believe you can do it,' he goads.

I lift the rifle. What if he'd been bluffing all along? What if the gun isn't loaded? I look into his eyes and then I know. It's loaded and Ewan is just hoping I don't have the guts to go through with it.

I look down at the video tape and then throw it on the fire.

'No,' he pleads as the plastic writhes and twists in the heat of the fire before bursting into flames, giving up its secrets and erasing the evidence that would have destroyed me.

———

Fran knocked on the door of the beach house. The house was in darkness.

'Break the door down,' Fran instructed the police officer with them.

'Look, Fran, come on. It's just an anagram,' said Mike.

'It's him, I know it.'

'You'd better be right.' Mike sighed.

He nodded at the officers. He fully expected Libby or her boyfriend to come running from the bedroom but Fran was quite right, the place was empty.

'He's got her at Manstead,' said Fran.

'Let's go,' yelled Mike.

Fran hurried to their car and cursed.

'I should have listened to her.'

'Don't start blaming yourself,' said Mike, placing a hand on her knee. 'You weren't to know.'

'I only hope we get there in time,' said Fran.

———

'You're a fool, Ewan. You could have had money. Life could have been comfortable for you. Now you'll go back to prison.'

There's the sound of sirens and I smile.

'Sorry, Ewan.'

The sirens grow louder and the room flickers with blue lights.

I turn to call out. It's a mistake and Ewan uses it to his advantage. The rifle is knocked from my hand and my attempt to stop him sends me falling to the floor. There are shouts from outside. I look back at the fire. The video tape is now ashes.

———

Fran turned to Mike. 'Let's go,' she said.

Armed police followed behind them.

'We're coming in,' Fran yelled.

'In the morning room,' called Libby.

Mike aimed his gun, beckoned to the officers behind him and then flung open the door. At the sight of Fran, Libby burst into tears.

'Oh God, Fran, I thought he was going to kill me. He's held me prisoner here. I managed to overpower him somehow, but he got away.'

'Search the house and grounds,' yelled Mike.

'It's okay, Libby,' said Fran, putting her arm around Libby's shaking body.

'He disguised himself. He said if I didn't give him money he would kill me and...'

She stopped at the ringing of her phone. Fran glanced at the screen.

'It's Simon Wane,' she said, reaching out for it.

Libby leapt forward.

'No!' she screamed.

Her hands clawed at Fran's.

'Libby,' said Fran, surprised.

'Give it to me!' Libby screamed.

Fran looked down at her hand where Libby had drawn blood. She nodded to a policewoman who roughly pulled Libby off her. Tears rained down Libby's face. Fran clicked the phone onto speaker.

'Hello Ewan,' she said.

'Hello, Inspector. I thought you might like to hear this.'

Libby's jaw tightened. Her voice clear and strong rang out.

'I didn't mean to kill Aunty Rose. If Uncle Edward hadn't tried to get the gun then it wouldn't have gone off. I didn't know what to do. I couldn't go to prison and I knew Uncle Edward would tell them it had been me. What choice did I have, Ewan? There was no other way out. I had to shoot him.'

Fran gave Libby a sad look.

'It's all over, Libby,' said Ewan.

'The Dictaphone,' she said wearily. 'You had it running all the time.'

'You underestimated me, Libby. You always did.'

CHAPTER EIGHTY-NINE

SIX MONTHS LATER

Fran watched as Libby entered the room. She looked around and her face softened when she saw Fran.

Fran nodded. Libby sat opposite and smiled shyly.

'Thanks for coming.'

'I just thought I'd see how you were doing.'

'Not great.'

There were dark circles under her eyes, but she'd made the effort of putting on make-up and Fran wondered if Libby had hoped it was Ewan who'd come to visit her. Poor Libby, Fran found herself thinking, convicted by her own words on a Dictaphone and the evidence from a video hidden in the morning room of Manstead Manor. It had been a shock to Libby to discover that Ewan had swapped the tapes. The original had been in the video player all the time. He was right when he said she had underestimated him. Fran had found the video difficult to watch during the trial and Libby had broken down several times. It had all seemed overwhelming for her. A psychiatrist testified that Libby had truly convinced herself that Ewan had killed her family.

'It was a coping mechanism,' he'd said. 'It was too difficult to face the horror that she had done it.'

The jury found her guilty of one count of murder and one of manslaughter. She'd also faced a charge of perverting the course of justice. Fran had thought that Libby was going to have a heart attack when the sentence was read out. She was let off lightly on account of her age at the time of the murders and was given fifteen years, but she'd collapsed with the shock all the same.

'It's good of you to come,' said Libby.

'I always thought it wasn't Ewan, you know, but I never for one minute guessed it was you.'

'I'm sorry I deceived you.'

Fran nodded.

'William hasn't been,' said Libby.

'No.'

'Is that why you're here?'

'No, I just figured you might appreciate a visit.'

'Thank you.'

Mike had thought she was mad coming here.

'*Why the hell do you want to go and see her?*'

'*Because she's got no one, she's never had anyone.*'

'*You're soft, that's your problem.*'

Libby reached her hand across the table.

'I appreciate it.'

Fran moved her hand back.

'Don't milk it.'

Libby smiled. It may only be one friend. But an inspector for a friend could be worth having.

———

Richard Mullard saddled the mare and walked her out of the stables. He waved to Ewan as he strolled from the house.

'Just the man,' Richard said, smiling at Ewan. 'Jasmine could do with a trot if you have time.'

'Sure,' said Ewan.

'Settling in at the gamekeeper's cottage okay?' Richard asked.

'Yeah, it's perfect.' Ewan smiled.

'Perfect for us too,' said Richard. 'We hadn't bargained on getting a gamekeeper so soon after moving in to Manstead.'

'It was good of William to recommend me.'

Ewan stroked Jasmine's flank.

'She's a beautiful horse.'

'She sure is. By the way, you don't know anyone local who'd be interested in a housekeeping position, do you? William said you might know of someone.'

Ewan smiled.

'As it happens I do. Molly, who works in the teashop, is looking for a more permanent position. There's no work for her there in the winter.'

'Wonderful, tell her to pop along one day this week and we can chat about it.'

Ewan nodded. They both turned at the sound of the Mercedes travelling up the driveway.

'Ah,' said Richard. 'That will be Miranda, my daughter.'

A slim blonde girl climbed from the car. Richard waved.

'Come and meet Miranda,' he said.

She hugged Richard and then turned to Ewan.

'Oh hello,' she said.

Her bright blue eyes flashed his way and she deliberately thrust her breasts forward.

'I'm Miranda.'

'Miranda is a keen rider,' said Richard. 'I'm sure you'll both get on very well.'

Miranda smiled warmly at Ewan.

'Call in tonight for a drink,' said Richard.

Ewan turned his eyes from Miranda.

'Thanks, but I can't. I have a dress rehearsal with the Padley Players.'

'Brilliant, I didn't know you were into the theatre stuff. What part are you playing?'

'I'm playing Dr Jekyll in a production of *Jekyll and Hyde*.' Ewan grinned.

Miranda wrinkled her nose.

'I've not heard of that.'

'It's before your time,' Ewan said as he walked away.

THE END

A NOTE FROM THE PUBLISHER

Thank you for reading this book. If you enjoyed it please do consider leaving a review on Amazon to help others find it too.

We hate typos. All of our books have been rigorously edited and proofread, but sometimes mistakes do slip through. If you have spotted a typo, please do let us know and we can get it amended within hours.

info@bloodhoundbooks.com

ABOUT THE AUTHOR

Lynda Renham's novels are popular, fast-paced and with a strong theme. She lives in Oxford, UK and when not writing Lynda can usually be found wasting her time on Facebook.

Lynda is author of best-selling thriller novels including *Remember Me* and *Secrets and Lies*. Her romantic comedy novels include *Croissants and Jam, Coconuts and Wonderbras, Phoebe Smith's Private Blog, Pink Wellies and Flat Caps, It Had to Be You, Rory's Proposal, Fudge Berries and Frogs' Knickers, Fifty Shades of Roxie Brown, Perfect Weddings* and *The Dog's Bollocks*.